MORTIMER, J.

The sound of trumpets

Charges are payable on books overdue at public libraries. This book is
due for return by the last date shown but if not required by another
reader may be renewed - ask at the library, telephone or write quoting
the last date and the details shown above.

*Charade*
*Rumming Park*
*Answer Yes or No*
*Like Men Betrayed*
*Three Winters*
*The Narrowing Stream*
*Will Shakespeare (An Entertainment)*
*Paradise Postponed*
*Summer's Lease*
*Titmuss Regained*
*Dunster*
*Felix in the Underworld*

*Rumpole of the Bailey*
*The Trials of Rumpole*
*Rumpole for the Defence*
*Rumpole's Return*
*Rumpole and Golden Thread*
*Rumpole's Last Case*
*Rumpole and the Age of Miracles*
*Rumpole à la Carte*
*Rumpole on Trial*
*The Best of Rumpole*
*Rumpole and the Angel of Death*

*Under the Hammer*

*With Love and Lizards* (with Penelope Mortimer)

*Clinging to the Wreckage*
*Murderers and Other Friends*

*In Character*
*Character Parts*

*A Voyage Round My Father*
*The Dock Brief*
*What Shall We Tell Caroline?*
*The Wrong Side of the Park*
*Two Stars for Comfort*
*The Judge*
*Collaborators*
*Edwin, Bermondsey, Marble Arch, Fear of Heaven*
*The Prince of Darkness*

*The Captain of Köpenik* (trans.)
*Three Boulevard Farces* (trans.)
*Cat among the Pigeons* (trans.)
*Die Fledermaus* (trans.)

*Famous Trials* (ed.)
*The Oxford Book of Villains* (ed.)

JOHN MORTIMER

# THE SOUND OF TRUMPETS

VIKING

VIKING

Published by the Penguin Group
Penguin Books Ltd, 27 Wrights Lane, London w8 5TZ, England
Penguin Putnam Inc., 375 Hudson Street, New York, New York 10014, USA
Penguin Books Australia Ltd, Ringwood, Victoria, Australia
Penguin Books Canada Ltd, 10 Alcorn Avenue, Toronto, Ontario, Canada M4V 3B2
Penguin Books (NZ) Ltd, Private Bag 102902, NSMC, Auckland, New Zealand

Penguin Books Ltd, Registered Offices: Harmondsworth, Middlesex, England

First published in Great Britain by Viking 1998
1  3  5  7  9  10  8  6  4  2
First edition

Typeset in 12/14.4 pt Monotype Ehrhardt
Typeset by Intype London Ltd
Printed in Great Britain by Clays Ltd, St Ives plc

A CIP catalogue record for this book is available from the British Library

ISBN 0-670-87861-8

*For Sinéad Cusack*

. . . So he passed over, and the trumpets sounded for him on the other side.

Bunyan, *The Pilgrim's Progress*
(Mr Valiant-for-Truth)

'Of course government in general, any government anywhere, is a thing of exquisite comicality to a discerning mind.'

Joseph Conrad, *Nostromo*

# Part One

# Chapter One

A bird, one of the Red Kites restored to our skies as a result of careful breeding in the Nature Area, drifting among the grey and pink clouds of a September dawn, had the best view of the impact of recent history on the Rapstone Valley.

The most serious blot on the landscape was Fallowfield Country Town which, from the bird's eye view, looked like a pile of bricks which a giant's child had failed to tidy up. There lay the towering Computers-R-Us, the monster Magic Carpet store, the multistorey car park, the grim pedestrian walkways and the glass roof of the shopping mall, opened, somewhat grumpily, by the former Minister for Housing, Ecological Affairs and Planning (H.E.A.P.) and local M.P., the Right Honourable Leslie Titmuss.

Away from Fallowfield the Red Kite swooped low over pockets of rural resistance, where woods enclosed an uncultivated grassland in which unusual orchids and butterflies flourished. A few nervous deer, descendants of the herd once paddocked at Rapstone Manor, pricked their way across a road and bolted into the shadows, where an awakened badger lumbered and snorted.

Pale sunlight glittered on the river at Hartscombe, a town in which the shops, hard hit by the Fallowfield supermarkets, had sunk to selling little but greetings cards and pine furniture and frequently changed hands for reasons of bankruptcy. In a house by the bridge Agnes Simcox, née Salter, awoke from an uncomfortable dream which featured death. She felt for a cigarette, lit it and blew a perfect smoke-ring at the ceiling, coughing comfortably. The house, still known as 'The Surgery', had belonged to two doctors, both of whom she had loved. One of them, her father, had often said that a visit to the Surgery was the first step on the road to the cemetery. She thought, not for the first time, that she must clear out the medical equipment, the trusses, crutches, stethoscopes, vaporizers, bandages, swabs and numerous boxes of free samples from drug companies which filled her cupboard under the stairs.

She stubbed out her cigarette in the saucer of last night's cup of tea and went to the window wearing nothing but a man's blue shirt, frayed round the cuffs. A woman just fifty, beautiful, with lines bought with laughter and trouble at the corners of her eyes, she pulled at her hair, shaping and reshaping it as she looked up at the brightening sky and saw a Kite hovering.

Paul Fogarty, grey-haired, sleep ironing out the furrows on his daily troubled face, lay naked in his bed in the Skurfield Young Offenders' Institution of which he was the governor. He saw a line of youths, pinch-faced, matchstick-armed, with huge, sad eyes, chained together at the ankle, straining to lift huge hammers and break stones, the quarry dust turning them grey as statues. The guards were bulky men with cowboy boots and walrus moustaches, carrying bull-whips and shotguns. A boy fell and his dropping hammer cracked his skull, the blood clearing a red channel in the dust. The Home Secretary, it seemed to him dreaming, had passed new laws to crack down on juvenile crime. He awoke to the sound of the telephone and was relieved to find himself back in his bedroom, among the primitive paintings, the curiously suggestive plaster casts and wood carvings, the framed poems descriptive of life in custody, created by the young offenders.

'Fogarty! Didn't wake you up, I hope. Just called to remind you about the lad Johnson.' The voice in the governor's ear was brisk, determined, used to command.

'What about Johnson?' Was it bad news? The governor felt a

moment of dread, a longing to put back the telephone and, returning to bed, pull the covers over his ears.

'You remember you promised I could have him on day release. Give the lad a spot of work experience. Teach him a trade. Weeding. You'll remember we discussed that?'

'I think so.' Paul the governor remembered a visit from a senior politician, interested in young offenders.

'Then you've no objection to making it today? I want to get my money's worth, you know. Give him an early start.'

Day releases were a scheme the governor encouraged. 'I'm sure that will be all right,' he said. 'I'll alert the staff.'

'Good. Norman, my driver, will be with you in half an hour. When will you want him back?'

'No later than six.'

'No problem at all. I'll make sure he's mugged and murdered all the weeds in the rose garden. Oh, by the way, Fogarty. I've given your nick my seal of approval. Happened to bump into the Home Secretary at Chequers.'

The governor put down the phone without saying thank you. No disaster had been announced, and he was glad that one of his young offenders was getting a day's work in a rose garden. However, he could get along, as he had in the last four years, without the dubious blessing of the Home Secretary. He had a moment of unease when he remembered that the boy to be let out for the day was universally known as 'Slippy' Johnson. But then he relied on the impeccable authority of the voice on the telephone and stopped worrying.

At the top of a hill behind Hartscombe church a white house stood in its impressive spread. There were no surrounding trees, so it lay naked and unashamed with its newly built swimming pool flanked by columns on which the coach lamps still glowed, although the day had now broken.

A green towel, still wet, with a pair of spectacles resting on it, was draped over a plastic poolside chair. A light breeze stirred the water, causing a blue and scarlet ball to bump against the concrete. Something else in the pool moved gently. A man in his late thirties, the black hair already leaving the pale crown of his head, crammed into a leopardskin bikini, with his hands manacled behind his back, floated face downwards. The ping-pong ball in his mouth was held in place by a handkerchief tied as a gag. Although he was undoubtedly dead the Kite showed no particular interest in him but wheeled away towards its home in the Nature Area.

The next day's papers announced that Peter Millichip M.P. had suffered a heart attack during an early-morning swim. At the general election his majority had been seven thousand, and his death would cause a by-election in the constituency of Hartscombe and Worsfield South.

# Chapter Two

Lord Titmuss, since the end of his second marriage, had always slept in a single bed.

His first wife, Charlotte, had died accidentally while taking part, unwisely and, he thought, treacherously, in a Ban the Bomb demonstration. Whatever happened to the bomb, he sometimes wondered. Still around, presumably, although it seemed no longer to frighten anyone and had slipped out of the news. His second wife had, he believed, callously forced him to leave her because he would not accept her forgiveness for exercising what he knew were his matrimonial, indeed, his human rights; that is to say, employing a private detective to unearth the infidelities of her dead first husband. Women he had always found to be elusive and unreliable creatures, so when he parted from Jenny he moved into a long bed, narrow as a coffin, and had slept alone ever since.

He had, however, after the loss of his mother Elsie, who had also let him down by dying, bought back Rapstone Manor, going for a song because it now stood, as awkward and isolated as a grandmother who has strayed into a teenage sleep-over, uncomfortably close to the video shop and the Thai take-away, the Girl Power boutique, Pizza Paradise, the Handy about the House stores and the Superbowl in Fallowfield New Town.

It was a house of memories which Lord Titmuss (the First Baron Skurfield, ennobled with Mrs Thatcher's last gasp of authority) didn't care to recall. Presented by Edward IV to a steward with a sense of humour, the Manor of Rapstone had been in the Fanner family since the middle ages. It was here that the late Sir Nicholas Fanner, Chairman of the local Conservative Party, had allowed the young, ambitious and hardly likeable brewery clerk Leslie Titmuss to rise without trace. Here Leslie captured the party from the Knights of the Shires and claimed it for the High Priestess of the Corner Shop. Here he wooed and married young Charlie Fanner, who shamed him with her premature death on Worsfield Heath. It was here that the malicious old Lady Fanner, a glass of champagne in one hand and a lipstick-smeared Silk Cut in the other, cursed and gossiped her way to the grave in a house where the downstairs rooms, with most of their contents sold, were filled with cobwebs and dusty garden chairs. It was to this house he had brought the beautiful Jenny Sidonia, who had fallen in love with him, to the bewilderment of her friends, and here he had parted from her when he was unable to put up with her unendurable mercy. So now, in his narrow bed, he slept alone and had removed from the house, so far as he could, all traces of its past.

He came down the stairs in a pair of flannel pyjamas, as broadly striped as prison clothing, and a dressing-gown corded at the waist like a monk's habit. Although only in his fifties, the long uphill climb from 'The Spruces', Skurfield, by way of the brewery accountant's office, to the Cabinet and the House of Lords, had left him exhausted and prematurely old. Walking with early-morning stiffness, he pushed open his study door, sat down at his desk, coughed and looked about him. There were no family photographs, as he had banished both his wives. He also had little pride in his son, who was a head librarian in some remote northern town, and not much interest in his son's wife Venetia (a bloody affected name, he thought) or his two grandchildren, whose names eluded him but to whom he sent modest cheques at Christmas with strict instructions that the money should be invested and not spent on computer games, C.D.s, rollerblades or any such unprofitable trifles. So, instead of smiling women and hopeful children, the desk, the mantelpiece, occasional tables and the tops of bookshelves were loaded with heavy silver frames surrounding Titmuss and the late beloved Leader, Titmuss with President Reagan, Titmuss with Chancellor Kohl, Titmuss and the Queen Mother or Titmuss with a black leader whose name and part of Africa drifted in and out of his memory like the names of his own grandchildren. There were no, deliberately no, photographs of Titmuss with the present Prime Minister, the man he regarded as having slithered into power after the unforgivable assassination of the Great Lady.

He had a file open now, at a sheet of paper covered with the spidery handwriting which his typist found so hard to decipher. He unscrewed a fountain pen and wrote a sentence about the Slitherer. 'When he had to kiss hands on his appointment, the Daimler drew up at the entrance to Buckingham Palace and no one in particular got out.' He paused, bit the end of his pen, and then heard a knock at the door. It was Mrs Ragg arriving with the newspapers, which she plumped down on his desk, covering the handwritten abuse of his present Leader.

'That's naughty of you, sir, running about the place without your slippers! You'll either stub your toe or catch your death.' Mrs Ragg was a large, pale woman of uncertain age who apparently applied her lipstick in the dark, much of it smearing her teeth. Hers was the first letter he opened as a result of his advertisement for a housekeeper in the *Hartscombe Sentinel*. He lacked the time or the interest to consider other applications. Mrs Ragg, now staring down at his long, white, naked feet, either mothered him or, in moments of wild embarrassment, tried to flirt with him. He met either of these approaches with a stare of cold hostility.

'Will I just run upstairs,' she said archly, as though it were an offer of love, 'and fetch your nice warm slippers for you?'

'You can do what you like, Mrs Ragg. Provided you go away.'

She sighed heavily and went. He sat staring at a photograph on the front page of the *Sentinel*. NEW LABOUR CANDIDATE the headline read. 'Terry Flitton selected to fight Hartscombe seat.'

The face he sat and gazed at was far younger than his and, he would have to concede, better looking, but the set mouth and deep, determined eyes made him feel that he was looking at someone he knew very well indeed.

In the Magic Magnolia three people manipulated their chopsticks with varying degrees of skill, an older man, a man in his thirties and a woman who had the confidence of youth. The older man was wearing a tweed jacket with leather patches, and an orange, woollen tie. His bald scalp, glistening under the hanging lights, bright enough for a surgical operation, was fringed with greying hair, its skin corrugated like an ill-fitting, tonsured wig handed out to an actor playing Friar Laurence. He used his chopsticks best, disposing of sweet and sour pork and sizzling beef like an old China hand after long years as a patron of the Hartscombe Magnolia. 'From all I've heard of you,' he said to the younger man, who looked, under the overhead glare, even more handsome than his photograph in that morning's *Sentinel*, 'you should do better than last time. You should take a considerable bite out of the Tory majority. I look forward to your coming a very respectable second.'

'Not interested.' Terry Flitton stabbed with his chopsticks, showing a determination which was often successful but sometimes sent a glazed ball of sweet and sour skidding across the plate. 'I'm only interested in coming a respectable first.'

'You should do well.' In the face of this uncomfortable optimism Penry, the Labour agent, tried to lead his candidate gently towards reality. 'We'll try and pinch a few thousand off them.'

'I'm looking for a 7 per cent swing.'

Penry glanced nervously at the mobile phone his candidate had put down beside the prawn crackers. Never before had he seen such a device in the possession of a Labour candidate, and he felt a grim foreboding of three weeks' remorseless work, strategic memos, policy documents and midnight phone calls, all leading to an inevitable defeat. 'Hartscombe's been Conservative for years.' He tried to say it soothingly.

'Not in 1945 it wasn't. I've read the history.'

Penry put down his chopsticks and sat for a moment, misty-eyed. In 1945 he had been ten years old, with a father who worked in Army Education. He remembered 'Roll out the Barrel' and the pubs in Hartscombe full of singing soldiers, heralding the unexpected avalanche of a Labour victory. 'We are the masters now' – his father had told him what they said in Parliament. Those memories had kept him in the local Party for the long years when Hartscombe had consistently shown itself not quite good enough for Labour. 'That was after the war,' he said, smiling.

'Exactly,' Terry told him. 'People wanted a better life.'

'I'm afraid,' Penry gave himself a swig of Chinese beer. 'Quite a lot of people in Hartscombe think they've got it already. We don't get many hunger marches in the Thames Valley.'

'We've got to tell them' – Terry slid easily into his mood of quiet persuasion, the soft tones of someone counselling the bereaved on how to bear the fact of death – 'that they've got some sort of duty to the community. They've got to make sacrifices if we're going to achieve social justice. It's one of the privileges of wealth, to help those who aren't quite so lucky. That's what we've got to make them understand.'

Penry felt an enormous relief. The presence of the mobile phone needn't have worried him. He was back on safe and familiar territory. That was what he was used to, the way all his candidates had talked before they relaxed into comfortable defeat. He knew what was coming next, the bit about the price of a safe society.

'And they'll see that there's a whole lot of sense in paying to end the inequality which produces crime and violence, all the things that keep them shivering in their rose gardens.'

'It's a persuasive argument.'

'It's what I believe. Sincerely.'

Penry assessed the sincere look and found it the best he'd seen on any candidate. They could go down with dignity.

'Terry's going to win.' Kate Flitton spoke quietly, her head lowered. She had clear blue eyes, black hair and skin with the pink flush of youth. The agent, whose wife was carrying on a barely concealed relationship with a bank manager in Worsfield, felt a pang of envy for his candidate. 'That's what we've come here for.'

'Of course, we'll do our best.' Penry wanted to comfort her, but now she had lowered her eyes and was poking at her mixed vegetables and fried rice with growing suspicion. 'But there was a lot of respect for Peter Millichip, he was an excellent constituency M.P. And a good deal of sympathy for his unhappy wife.'

'She didn't look all that unhappy,' Terry told him. 'Not in the photograph in the *Sentinel*. The day he died.'

'Didn't you think so?'

Kate, still investigating her food, answered for her husband. 'She looked angry.'

'It was bad luck.' Penry seemed to share in the general sorrow for Millichip, to whom, after the last three elections, he had had to concede victory. 'The poor chap was only fifty-three. A sudden heart attack in the pool.'

'Luck that brought me to the constituency, do you think?' Terry was smiling.

'Well, I hope that's how it will turn out to be.'

'From now on, forget luck.' The candidate looked disturbingly businesslike. 'We're going to start working now! Start here. These waiters, for instance.' He looked at the young men, two in spectacles, trotting between the white-clothed tables, carrying trays of steaming, sizzling food. 'Have they got votes? They must live in Hartscombe. Have you done any work in the restaurants? Indian, Thai, Chinese? Ethnic groups ought to be with us.'

'I honestly don't know. Charlie!' Penry called to the smiling Lin Yew Po, known to him for years as Charlie. 'You on the electoral register?'

'Ice cream or toffee apples?' Charlie answered confidently. 'You like Chinese tea?' And he was about to dart away when Kate Flitton asked him to assure her that the rice hadn't been fried in anything connected with meat. 'No meat. Rice,' Charlie answered her, and she was on the point of calling him back when she sniffed, coughed and flapped with her hand as though to clear a dense and poisonous fog which, having drifted across the table, was about to asphyxiate her.

She turned towards the source of pollution. The woman had copper-coloured hair and skin that had never objected to the sunshine. She was wearing jeans, the sleeves of a blue sweater dangling over her shoulders. She had just lit a cigarette and was putting her lighter away in the pocket of her shirt. Beside her sat a grey-haired man with a creased face and bright, still hopeful eyes.

'You're smoking!' Kate looked at Agnes Simcox, as concerned as if she were about to burst into flames.

'Oh, yes. It's allowed here. I'm afraid I'm going to go on doing it. Do you want to move? We shan't be offended.'

But Kate's attention had been diverted by the excited buzz of Terry's mobile. She contented herself with a convincing imitation of a person dying of bronchitis and slapped energetically at the air.

'Yes. Yes, this is Terry Flitton. Who . . .?' And then Terry fell silent, listening with an expression of growing surprise. 'Well,' he said finally, 'I've got a tight schedule, naturally. I'll have to discuss it with my agent. I'll call you back. What's the number?'

'Who was it?' Kate asked, and he told her.

'Lord Titmuss!' Penry spoke in an awed whisper, as though, some ancient superstition aroused in him, he was looking around desperately for a clove of garlic or a couple of crossed sticks. 'What's that old crocodile after?'

'Probably scared Terry's going to win the seat.'

Penry looked at Kate, touched by her faith, which could persuade her that her husband had the magical power of alarming Lord

Titmuss. 'Don't go near that monster.' Penry gave his first positive advice. 'The Hartscombe Party would never forgive you.'

'Of course I won't.' Terry's fist crumpled the paper napkin on which he'd written a number. Kate was flapping at the air again with angry disapproval. Her husband breathed in a sweet and heavy smell, once the smell of France when he had been on a distant school trip, and one which had wafted through his early childhood in Jubilee Road, Worsfield. At the next table Agnes blew a smoke-ring and, turning to her companion, the Governor of Skurfield Young Offenders' Institution, said, 'It's a good thing I wasn't smoking dope. She'd probably have made a citizen's arrest.'

# Chapter Three

Driving along the motorway, Terry remembered the smell of Gauloises. The road was wide and smooth, designed for commuters to speed to and from London, but it had been turned, apparently by some omnipotent practical joker, into a series of narrow country lanes along which the traffic crawled between hedgerows of cones. On either side of them no work was taking place; empty stretches of highway were temptingly deserted. Only rarely did he see a solitary lorry or a little knot of men in hard hats and orange jackets looking with amusement at the growing tailback; otherwise, the cones were triumphant.

Clarice. Terry's mother hated her name. It sounded like 'chalice' and reminded her of chasubles and cassocks and other ecclesiastical paraphernalia, and brought back the smell of the vestry, the mixture of furniture polish and gently rotting hassocks, which hung in the cold air as she cut up cubes of bread for the communion service. Afterwards she sat in the pew and looked up at her father, his forehead furrowed with anxiety as he quoted the Sermon on the Mount, informing the poorer members of his dwindling congregation that they were, in fact, singularly blessed. As he talked she knew that his constantly nagging worry was not the condition of the poor but whether he and her mother would get, as they had once in the past, an invitation to lunch at the Manor, or be passed over for yet another year. She was sent away to a cold Cotswold boarding school where the rules insisted that she was forever called

Clarice and not any contraction, such as Clary, Clare or Clar, which she much preferred. At the end of her time at school, when her friends were playing Everly Brothers records, she rechristened herself Susie.

Her father, having spent three tedious and almost friendless years studying theology at Keble, told her she had thrown away the golden experience of Oxford and did his best to ignore the fact that she had settled for the University of Worsfield. He still insisted on calling her Clarice, with a particular emphasis on the hated name, and was undeterred by the fact that she never answered to it or came when he called. Her mother, a flustered woman, whose vain ambition it was to please everybody, called her daughter neither Clarice nor Susie but 'dear', repeating the word with decreasing conviction. At university Susie found a new way of life.

It centred round the Bricklayers Arms, opposite the Worsfield bus station. It was in the Brickie that she met Robert, Rob, sometimes Robo, spoken with heavy sarcasm and a mock posh accent when he did anything pretentious, like, after innumerable pints of Newcastle Brown, switching to a small Cointreau for each of them to 'top off the evening'. Rob Flitton was handsome, making good use of the clear features, deep eyes and close curls he handed on later to his son. His shoulders were wide enough to put some strain on the seams of his jacket, and his voice was unexpectedly soft and high. Susie knew he worked in a Worsfield factory, and in her frequent musings she saw him beating glowing ingots in some foundry or, masked like a diver, raising a storm of sparks as he welded heavy metal. The exact nature of his employment she never asked. It was enough for her that he was one of the workers.

She noticed him first when he smiled at her across the public bar of the Brickie. The next night she was playing darts with him and, after the final, unexpected Cointreau, they ended up in the shadows by the wall of the bus station. Her mouth was on his, the sweet taste of the liqueur mingling, and her hand was burrowing into the opening of his jeans. Never had the cold vestry and the smell of hassocks seemed so far away.

Robert lived with his family in a terraced house in Jubilee Road, where Susie was sometimes asked for tea, a meal which her father and mother, facing each other over cottage pie and glasses of water taken with long periods of silence in the vicarage dining-room, preferred to call 'dinner'. By contrast, Jubilee Road was ear-splittingly noisy, full of Rob's brothers and sisters, who laughed, shouted, quarrelled, competed and made her feel, a lonely child, part of a new, garrulous and exclusive family. It was his still-handsome mother, a tall, commanding presence with red hair going grey, shouting louder than anyone else and plonking great plates of undercooked food (the potatoes especially were hard as bullets) in front of anyone who crossed her threshold, who was the boss in Jubilee Road. Rob's father, who didn't work but drew a pension as a result of some industrial disease, sat silent, smiling and examining his long, slender fingers, and allowed his wife to speak for him. 'Jim'd like some more of that jelly,' Mrs Flitton would shout, or 'Jim doesn't want to hear that sort of talk in his house so will you please shut up!', and Jim would smile and nod and raise his voice to no one.

Mrs Flitton spoke not only for her husband but for her son when she proposed marriage to Susie. 'Robert would like it really,' she shouted when they found themselves, on a rare occasion, alone together. 'It's high time he got himself settled. But he's too shy to ask.' The confidence of Rob's love-making made Susie doubt this statement but she was unable to argue with the matriarch who was yelling at her. It was the happiest day in her life when she stood next to Robert, who had a carnation in a silver-paper stalk pinned to his lapel, in a civil ceremony to which she wore a white mini-skirt and stilettos, with flowers in her hair. He had just been elected a shop steward, and she loved him for the sunlight in his curls, his stiff blue suit bought for the occasion and the fact that he was now a leader in the battle for workers' rights.

They moved into the flat she had taken as a student, dismissing the girlfriend with whom she had shared. She had painted the walls purple and put up posters, Che Guevara, Jack Kennedy, Neil Sedaka and Joan Baez. There were bulrushes in pots, peacocks' feathers, purple cushions and joss sticks, which left brown scars on the mantelpiece. There were burns, too, on other pieces of furniture, where Susie had put down her smouldering Gauloises. Into this room she introduced her husband, large, tidy and clearly bewildered. He slept in his Y-fronts, keeping his clothes neatly folded beside the headless bed. The chest of drawers, covered with a fringed shawl and various candles, was filled to overflowing with the dresses, satin trousers, velvet jackets and feather boas she bought at jumble sales, junk shops and charity stores but seldom wore. Six months after the wedding the newly born Terry Flitton was brought to this home in a pink plastic carry-cot. He was known as a 'good baby' and kept quiet at night. When Susie was feeding him from her breast his father used to retreat to the kitchen, or out to the Brickie, in unforeseen embarrassment.

So Terry spent his childhood in a haze of incense and French cigarettes, hearing Bob Dylan, Buffy Sainte-Marie and 'The Sounds of Silence' among the cushions and scattered clothing or, when Susie started work in a Worsfield boutique, being looked after round his gran's, where he was shouted at, picked up, dropped, kissed, occasionally slapped and then returned to his increasingly silent mother and sullen father.

Things began to change when Rob got promotion and they took the flat upstairs. There was a threatened strike at the factory, which was apparently doing well with whatever it might have produced. Rob the shop steward was negotiating, but also accepting invitations to meet the managing director in a private room in Meadowlands, a country-house hotel outside Hartscombe. The strike was called off and Robert got a senior post in middle management. Terry remembered the first day his father went to work in the suit he hadn't worn since his wedding.

He also remembered the walls turning from purple to cream. The bulrushes and scatter cushions moved upstairs to a room where his mother sat smoking something which no longer smelt of cross-Channel urinals but had the sweet reek of burning carpets. Downstairs a new suite of furniture arrived. He remembered the night the managing director and his wife ('Call me Harry'; 'Call me Joan') came to supper and the long silences round the table as his mother, moving like a sleepwalker, dropped things or produced food that had gone slightly but significantly wrong from the kitchen. At the end of the meal she started to giggle like a child, shaking her head helplessly, the back of her hand to her mouth. Harry and Joan left early and after the front door had closed Terry heard the sound of blows, received with no cry or complaint. That was the night he began to hate his father.

Robert was promoted further, to a post which would come to be known as 'Manager in Charge of Human Resources', where his job was to hire a few people and fire many, as the enterprise was slimmed down. For the task of firing, which apparently called for a special tone of voice, particular 'body language' (sympathetic and understanding) and the knack of ending the interview before the dismissed person got a chance to make a fuss, Robert received training. He often told Susie that the kids who applied for work were hopeless and no good and wanted everything to fall into their laps, and they spent their time smoking and listening to music in clubs, and he blamed it all on the way people behaved in the sixties, which was when they met and fell in love and had Terence. But Rob, so he told his wife, and his son if he was listening, had not been infected by the general lassitude, self-indulgence and loony-left politics of that decade because he'd been too damned busy making something of himself, pulling himself up by his bootstraps and generally bettering his position, and he hoped to God that the nipper (meaning Terry) would learn the lesson and pull himself up by his bootstraps too. Susie would listen to all this, smiling remotely, and every time he heard it Terry, who had no idea where his bootstraps were, became clearer about one thing. He was not going to end up like his father.

He worked hard at school. He knew he was going somewhere; although he was not yet sure where, he knew it was a long way away from Robert. It was on a school trip to France that he smelt his mother's cigarettes, going through Customs and in the zinc-covered bar where he first got drunk. When he got back from the trip and went up to his mother's room with the present he had bought for her (a glass ball containing the Eiffel Tower in a snowstorm) he found it empty.

'She's gone. Not coming back to us. Not ever.'

'She's dead.' Terry knew what had happened; he was sure one of his father's blows had killed her.

'Not dead but deserted. She told me there was no one else. 'Course there's a bloke somewhere. Stands to reason. Some pot-head layabout, so they'll live on government hand-outs. She's a liar, son. Your mother always was a liar. She even lied about her name, can you believe it? You and me, Terry, we'll get on just as well without her. I told her myself. You're not needed here, I said, Susie, or whatever name you think up next.' It was the longest speech he ever had from his father.

So they lived together, after that, like a married couple on whom mutual hostility has descended like a blanket of snow. Rob heated the packaged food he bought in the microwave and did most of the housework. Terry sat in his mother's room working, and he did well enough in his A levels to qualify, as she had, for the University of Worsfield. When he told his gran about this she hoped it wouldn't give him ideas so that he became as silly as his mother.

Robert broke a long silence to tell his son that he had voted Conservative in the election because he was sick and tired of keeping his wife's bloke in beer and funny cigarettes. Terry joined the university Young Socialists and became known for his militant tendencies. Still silent at home, he spoke passionately and at considerable length at meetings and was known, around the halls of residence to which he had moved, as 'Red Tel'. He made a special visit home to tell his father this. Robert counter-attacked by admitting that he had asked his secretary, a girl called Dawn Allbright, home to live with him until their position could be made legal. The divorce between father and son was now final and they hardly met again until events in the Hartscombe by-election brought them together.

It would be unfair to say that Terry's beliefs came into being only as a gesture of hate against his father. Perhaps Rob's adoption of the no-nonsense politics of the corner shop and middle management steered his son towards the Labour Party but, once there, Terry found the faith that Susie's horror of churches had denied him in religion. He visited the insanitary and crumbling bed and breakfasts where the families of men slimmed down in Rob's purges were lodged as they waited at the tail-end of housing lists. He took food to street sleepers round the Worsfield bus station. When he became President of the Students' Union he was the delegate on innumerable marches and demonstrations and was invited to visit Young Socialists in Belgium and Yugoslavia. The government seemed so outrageous to him, the unyielding enemy in Downing Street so clearly merciless, that he was able, speaking in common-room debates, outside the gates of factories on strike or once, even, by special invitation, at a fringe meeting at a party conference, to convince not only his listeners but also himself. Some day, perhaps some day soon, the dark age of materialism and greed would be over. The street sleepers and the millions of jobless would be led into the promised land and Tel would be not only of the Party but among its leaders.

In the mean while he had to earn a living. He saw an advertisement in the *Guardian* for a job at S.C.R.A.P. (The Society for Rural and Arboreal Protection). Although he had been more concerned with the Worsfield homeless than the fate of distant rain forests or tremulous and melting ice floes, he went for an interview. Once in S.C.R.A.P. he was determined to succeed and spent the next decade making himself indispensable to the Chairman of the Board, an amiable biologist who had been made a peer and specialized in frogs, a species which he understood better than human beings. This Chairman was only too happy to leave the running S.C.R.A.P. to Terry, who turned up on the radio and television, however obscure the programme, when trees fell, green belts were threatened or when gasping Third World smokers, choking furnaces and coughing engines caused dark clouds to drift across far-eastern islands.

He was into his thirties before he put his name down in Walworth Road. When the Hartscombe seat became available, the lecturer in sociology, who had lost it twice, decided he had grown too old for yet another public humiliation. Terry told the selection committee that he hadn't a moment's doubt that he would win the seat. He was chosen in a moment of helpless astonishment at such an unusual prediction and had to wait while the last of the summer died and leaves began to fall before the government issued the writ for a by-election. He had a battle on his hands, and the rain forests would have to look after themselves.

He was driving along a rare, unencumbered stretch of road when the mobile phone on the seat beside him buzzed again. A strange female voice spoke without introduction and, he thought, with menace. 'Are you there, Mr Flitton? This is Lord Titmuss's private office. His Lordship has asked me to make an appointment at your mutual convenience, sir.' What was this, Terry wondered. An attempt to compromise him, to make him look ridiculous? The Tories, they had told him in Walworth Road, would stop at nothing. Caution overcame him, and all he said, in a deliberately husky voice tinged with a slight Scottish accent, was, 'Wrong number, I'm afraid,' and he switched off the phone.

The trouble had begun again. He was forced to a snail's pace by the speed limit and huge yellow signs charting the flow and counter-flow, the twisting lanes between tall, red-and-white outsize witches' hats. He thought of what Robert's factory produced, the product his mother had never troubled to ask about, a rapidly increasing number of road signs, crash barriers, and traffic cones by the million.

# Chapter Four

'What've you got against the death penalty, exactly?'

'Well, I've got nothing against it personally.'

'I didn't imagine you'd ever committed a capital offence. So what's your problem?'

Lord Titmuss had visitors – Tim Willock, who, having lost his seat in the previous election, had been adopted for a return to Parliament as Tory M.P. for Hartscombe and Worsfield South, and the Local Party Chairman. Willock was a short, perky man with thinning hair and half-glasses. He had a surprisingly deep and penetrating voice for his size, and his head often leant to one side, like an inquisitive bird's. He had spent his years in the wilderness building up his computer-sales business, and now his hands moved nervously, as though he wished to surf the Internet for an answer to the old dragon's difficult question. Deprived of mechanical aids, he came out with the best he could do for himself.

'I'm just thinking about the Party image. We don't want people to see us as hangers and floggers.'

'Why not?' The Titmuss voice rasped out at him from behind a well-cleared desk. 'That was what they used to rather like about us.'

'It may have been so in your day, if you don't mind me saying so. But times have changed, haven't they? Your years in government were a simply enormous success, of course, but didn't the public find them a little . . .' – Willock, without a word processor, paused with his lips pursed, and came out with – 'Metallic? Perhaps a little merciless? Even inhumane?'

'So you don't like it when the going gets tough?'

'Oh, no, indeed. Tough going's what you expect in politics. It's the name of the game, isn't it?' Willock laughed, a rumbling sound that, again, seemed too big for him.

'You said you had nothing against the death penalty, personally.' There was a lamp fixed on a Chinese pottery base which flooded Titmuss's desk with a pool of white light. Around him the library was despondently dark and cold, with a glass screen in the empty fireplace. He sounded like a dangerously experienced police officer about to nail a tricky suspect. 'So, you think it might be a useful deterrent?'

'I think that's possibly true.'

'Possibly true.' Titmuss savoured the words as though they were a confession. 'But you think killers should get away with their lives for the sake of our party image? I mean, so the public can think we're a lot of bleeding hearts and soft on crime. Is that what you think?' He leant back in his chair then and, his voice coming from the shadows, he added, as though to himself but loud enough for the others to hear, 'If you think about it at all.'

'Of course I'm not soft on crime. Certainly not.' Willock's head was now moving in an agitated fashion, like a bird pecking for crumbs of comfort. 'By no means! I'm all for very long prison sentences. "Life" should mean life. Yes, of course. But when I talk about the party image, I'm just worrying about what we present.'

'What you present to me? Not a cut-glass bowl, for God's sake. Cash in hand would be quite acceptable!' Titmuss rotated his swivel chair and laughed, a dry, clattering sound which Tim Willock found even more disconcerting than his Lordship's questions.

'What I think Tim's getting at is this.' The Chairman bravely interposed himself between his candidate and the fusillade of Titmuss laughter. Sir Gregory Inwood had retired early from the diplomatic service; he had a long experience of dealing with cunning and tyrannical mid-eastern sovereigns as well as bringing on tender cuttings and sheltering them from the nips of frost. 'Tim really means we're all agreed that we want to save Hartscombe from Socialism, but we may have different approaches. Yours, of course, has been extremely successful in the past. Didn't you' – Sir Gregory had iron-grey hair, a small moustache, well-kept teeth and a winning smile – 'get the largest Tory majority this constituency has ever known?'

'And I didn't get it' – Titmuss couldn't resist putting the Chairman right – 'by offering a few years of television and cream teas to convicted murderers.'

'Of course not. But we don't want to lose the punters who don't care for hanging. I think there may be some sense in an approach from a number of angles.'

'There may be some sense in daring to say what you think.' His Lordship was keeping a beady eye on the candidate.

'I'm sure, Leslie, you'll say exactly what you mean.' Sir Gregory turned on the full diplomatic charm.

'I certainly will.'

'And the question is, when will you do it? We want to use you as much as possible during the campaign.'

'Really?' Titmuss leant into the light and stared challengingly at Tim. 'And how, exactly, will you want to *use* me?'

The candidate was as unnerved as he would have been if some daunting elderly lady, once a famous beauty, had offered to open her legs for him. He fell back, unhappily on the sort of language he used in planning P.R. for his computer-sales business. 'What we aim to do with you, with your kind co-operation, of course, is to raise maximum public awareness and achieve optimum media coverage. I can't remember for the moment, have you done "Breakfast" with Kenny Iremonger?'

'I have. I have also done lunch with Gorbachev, dinner with Deng Xiaou-Ping and breakfast with Ronald Reagan. I've given up television, having reached the age when I am no longer required to answer foolish questions.'

'I think Tim means' – Sir Gregory could see that steering this candidate towards a safe seat was going to call for all his negotiating skills – 'that we would like you to do one big event. Just one great, great crowd-puller.'

'Absolutely right!' Even Tim Willock realized that to discuss his plans for the Radio Worsfield 'Breakfast Egg' show would not be met kindly. 'What about a speech from the steps of Hartscombe town hall? Before a huge crowd. The way Gladstone and Disraeli played it.'

'Whatever you may think, those politicians were not my exact contemporaries.' Lord Titmuss rose to his feet and crossed the room, making for a table on which stood one bottle of whisky and a siphon. 'All the same,' he went on, mixing himself a drink, 'a speech in Hartscombe Square might be interesting. I won't detain you for a scotch and soda. I'm sure you chaps have got a lot of work in front of you, raising public awareness.'

'Thank you.' Sir Gregory stood up and did his best to look grateful. 'I'm sure Tim will give his all for the Party.'

'Goodnight.' Tim made for the door as though unexpectedly released from custody. 'It's been terribly interesting to meet you.'

'By the way.' Titmuss lowered his whisky and detained the candidate for an embarrassed moment. 'In the leadership election, did you vote for the present Prime Minister?'

Tim stood still, looked longingly at the door and, at last, came out with, 'It was very difficult. I found it so hard to make up my mind.'

'I can believe that,' Titmuss smiled. 'I'm sure you find it almost impossible. So fortunate you've got Sir Gregory with you. Or should I call him Greg? In the great battle of Tim versus Terry, I suppose you find it rather odd that I've never chosen to call myself Les.' When they'd gone he took his drink over to his desk and made another telephone call.

\*

Terry stood in the Dust Jacket, Hartscombe's sole remaining independent bookshop, and looked up at the shelf of second-hand books over the travel section. A line of hardbacks, their covers stained, the lettering on them faded. Some he'd read in his first year at Worsfield, with titles that had been recited like articles of faith by a wispy economics lecturer, so old that he still spoke of Russia as a heroic ally in the war against Hitler. Terry saw *The Ragged-Trousered Philanthropist*, *The Road to Wigan Pier*, *Religion and the Rise of Capitalism*, *The Making of the English Working Class* and a handful of Left Book Club publications whose red covers had faded to pink. Then he got another whiff of Gauloises.

When he turned to look the woman was industriously, even ostentatiously, grinding out her fag on the lid of a tin, which also contained paper clips, rubber bands and a stamp or two, on a desk in the corner of the shop.

'I'm sorry,' she said. 'I know you don't like them.'

'Books about Socialism?' He was smiling.

'No. Cigarettes. I'm afraid I was smoking in the Magnolia the other night. One of your friends objected.'

'That was my wife.'

'She must have thought I was very rude.'

Knowing that this was true, Terry thought it wiser not to answer. Concentrating on trying to inject a small shot of fighting spirit into his pessimistic agent, he had hardly noticed Agnes, except as a face behind a puff of smoke and a lingering smell of foreign tobacco which Kate had resented. Now he saw the fair hair, untouched by grey, which matched the colour of her skin, cornflower eyes and laughter lines which were there whether she was amused or not. He saw a woman of fifty, still as thin, it seemed to him, as a youth, who wore jeans with a wide leather belt and a thick woollen jacket, because she was always cold in the shop. He said, looking back at the shelves, 'Those were the books I was brought up on.'

'They belonged to my father-in-law,' Agnes said. 'He was a kind of well-heeled left-wing vicar. A surplice Socialist. I suppose you could have called him that. I put them out on the second-hand shelf.'

'Because you don't like them?'

'Because I want to convert a few of the blue rinses and tweed suits of Hartscombe to the Labour Party.'

'Any success?'

'I haven't heard anyone going out singing "The Red Flag". Come to think of it, I haven't noticed anyone buying one at all. Can I sell you something?'

'Maps, guidebooks, the history of this constituency.'

'You're a travel-writer?'

'A candidate.'

'Which one?' She looked at him with suspicion. He was delighted to be able to tell her. 'That's wonderful!' she said. 'And I blew smoke at you. What can I do to make it up?'

'Nothing. It was really nothing. It's just my wife . . .'

'I know what I'll do! I'll give you a window. I was going to make up a window for the new Sandra Tantamount. *Backstroke*. All about bonking in the world of Olympic swimming. Well, you're a great deal more important than she is. You've got a lot of pictures of you, posters of you looking meaningful?'

'I'll get them for you,' he promised, and he wondered if Penry had managed to get in a big store of meaningful posters. He thought, perhaps not.

'And I'll give you something. Something for luck.' She moved back to the second-hand shelf. 'You say you've read these?'

'Most of them.' It wasn't entirely true.

'Even this?' She found a small blue volume, a faded World's Classics edition, and handed it to him. 'Oscar Wilde?' He looked at the spine.

'*Collected Essays*. There's one on Socialism.'

'Oscar Wilde the Socialist? It sounds a bit of a contradiction.'

'I know,' she said. 'Like Mrs Thatcher the Romantic Poet. Or Leslie Titmuss the Prison Reformer. But read it. He says the great advantage of Socialism is that we wouldn't have to waste our time feeling sorry for people.'

'Is that a waste of time?'

'You don't think so?'

'Not exactly.'

'Perhaps you're nicer than Wilde. Have it anyway. A good-luck present. Not that it brought him much luck when you think of it. Now then, what've I got about the neighbourhood?'

'My patch.' He sounded, she thought, amazingly confident.

'Is that what it's going to be?'

'Of course.'

'You've got no doubts?'

'I don't think doubts are particularly useful things to have.'

'I know. Some of us can't help them. Let's have a look.'

In the end he bought *Highways and Byways round Hartscombe* and *Wanderer to Worsfield*, a book of photographs of the surrounding villages, which was unnecessarily expensive, and a second-hand Shell Guide to the county. When he'd paid for them she took him out in the street to show him the window that would be his. It was on a prime site on the high street, to be converted into a shrine to Terry Flitton, visible to all the passers-by. It was near the ending of the year now, there'd been a night frost and the sun glittered on the pavement and on Agnes's face, which stood up well to it. She looked up at the name of the shop and shuddered slightly.

'The Dust Jacket,' she said. 'You think that's a terrible name for a bookshop?'

'Well . . .' – he didn't want to hurt her feelings – 'Unusual.'

'I know. It sounds like a boutique. Jilly Bloxham, my partner, wanted me to call it that, and I've never got round to changing it. Well, then. I do hope you win.'

'I told you. I will.'

She moved a step towards him and he thought, for a moment, that she might be going to kiss him in the way actresses kissed goodbye on the first acquaintance. Instead she held her hand out and looked, for a moment, with her short hair and jeans, like a slender and forthright boy. So he shook her hand, promised to let her have the posters, and they parted.

That night Terry and his young wife Kate lay in parallel lines in the bedroom in Tufnell Park. Their legs were straight and their toes pointing upwards like figures on a medieval tomb. 'It's a fantastic site,' Terry said dreamily, gazing at the ceiling. 'Everyone's going to see it on their way to Sainsbury's.'

Kate said, 'Have you worked out why she wants to help you?'

'She's a Socialist,' Terry told her, as though that explained everything.

'If she's such a Socialist, why's she running a bookshop in a privileged place like Hartscombe? Why isn't she running a bookshop in Stoke Newington?'

'There's no law,' Terry told her, 'against Socialists running bookshops. Even in Hartscombe. Anyway, she's got a special left-wing shelf. She's trying to convert people.'

'You want to watch out you don't get too close to her.'

'Kate! What on earth do you mean?'

'There's a whole lot of new statistics, about the people who die of passive smoking.'

He moved his hand towards the inside of her thigh and rolled towards her. She left her position on the tomb and curled towards him. Men in their thirties, men like him, he thought, deceive their wives with girls of Kate's age. They meet them in doubtful hotels in the lunch-hour or invent business trips in order to take them to Sweden. He had his young mistress without guilt or lies or the invention of alibis, because he was married to her. His love-making was, therefore, as sincere and successful as he intended his election campaign to be.

# Chapter Five

'And what will be your priority, Mr Willock, if you win the Harts-combe seat?'

'You mean, *when* I win the seat.'

'Well, yes. I suppose Hartscombe's always been bright blue, hasn't it?'

'And long may it stay so. Look. The fact of the matter is. At the end of the day. People! And I'm thinking particularly of old people. Senior citizens!'

'Plenty of those in Hartscombe, aren't there?'

'Thank goodness, yes. And what a fine old lot they are. Men and women who've given service to the country, who deserve to cross Hartscombe high street with a bag of shopping and without being mugged for their old-age pensions. They deserve the privilege of going out at night!'

'You ever been mugged in Hartscombe, Mr Willock?' Kenny Iremonger was known as Worsfield's most penetrating radio inter-viewer.

'I won't say I have. But let me make this perfectly clear, Kenny. It'll come. It's bound to come. Unless we stop sending the muggers to five-star holiday camps like Skurfield Y.O.I. What these lads need is a tough regime. Like we had in the army!'

'Were you in the army, Mr Willock?'

'No. But my father was. And I know what a year or two's military discipline did for the lads of his day.'

'You mean, your father never mugged anyone?'

'Well, hardly. He was a Major in catering, and you don't get much mugging among senior officers.' Tim Willock had the good sense to laugh. 'But I know what a structured regime that taught you obedience and respect for authority did for lads who never got that at home. That's what it comes down to. At the end of the day.'

'So you'd want to turn Skurfield Young Offenders' Institution into a boot camp?'

'Boot camp? A rather emotive phrase, don't you think? I'd certainly like it to be a place young offenders won't want to revisit. I think we owe that to the frightened old people of Hartscombe. At the very least. And we want to get these little yobs off the streets at night. The fact of the matter is . . . you and I, Kenny, can remember a period when the words "bedtime" actually meant something. And if I might just say this . . .'

'Terribly sorry. I've got to cut you off there. Thank you for coming in. You're listening to Kenny Iremonger on Radio Worsfield's "Breakfast Egg" show. The good news is that the overturned yoghurt lorry has been removed from the Fallowfield approach road, that's the B7015. The bad news is that extended roadworks on the motorway have caused a long tailback at junction . . .'

Kenny died into silence as Paul Fogarty crossed his office and switched off the radio. In the centre of his fortified domain he felt like the commander of a garrison, surrounded and outnumbered by hostile forces who were planning an early attack.

There was a knock at the door, and his senior prison officer, a spare, energetic man, expert in prison regulations, with a pronounced nose which moved slightly sideways during his frequent sniffs of disapproval, came into the room and strode towards the governor's desk. 'It's started again, Clifford,' Paul Fogarty told him. 'They want to turn us into a bloody boot camp.'

'Who are "they", sir?'

'The politicians, Clifford. Amateurs. Who've never spent a single

*34*

night of their lives banged up in a cell. Unfortunately. Well, what is it now?'

'Something rather disturbing, sir, has come to my notice. Concerning costume jewellery. What the lads make in metalwork, sir.'

'Yes, indeed. Beautiful stuff too, some of it.' The governor had bought large quantities of the lads' costume jewellery for the purposes of encouragement, although there was no Mrs Fogarty to sport it.

'It seems, sir' – Clifford sniffed his disapproval – 'that one of the inmates has been using metalwork for other motives than fancy goods.'

'What're you trying to tell me, Clifford?' A huge weariness, the lassitude of resignation, came over Paul Fogarty. He was tempted to go back to sleep, even if it meant being haunted again by dreams of the short, sharp shock.

'I found this, sir. In the cell of one of the inmates doing so-called "metalwork" classes.'

The governor picked up the object presented on the S.P.O.'s palm. 'A key?'

'That's what it is, sir.' Clifford sniffed in triumph. 'A little more work and it might well be made to open the main door on D wing.'

In the silence that followed the governor remembered the threat to his regime at Skurfield. Clifford's discovery would not be helpful in the fight for reason and reform.

'Who knows about this?'

'So far only you and I, sir. And, of course, the inmate concerned. I thought it right to inform you at once.'

'You did very well.' Paul Fogarty lifted the suspicious ornament from the S.P.O.'s hand and locked it away in his safe. 'This is just the sort of story, Clifford, which the government's candidate is looking for. "Tax-Payers Finance Boy Criminal's Escape." I can hear it now, on the radio. Can't you?'

'Indeed I can, sir.'

'All we've tried to do here could be at risk.'

'We've got to face that possibility.'

'All we've tried to do for these boys. I'm simply asking you not to let this incident become more widely known.'

'Not to cause anxiety among the staff, sir?' Clifford's sniff was deliberately knowing.

'Not to give a present to the Tory candidate. In the mean time, we might have a chat with the boy concerned. In D wing, you say? It isn't . . .'

'I'm afraid it is, sir. It seems he's not called "Slippy" Johnson for nothing. The boy's always been trouble.'

'What do you mean? In general his conduct's pretty good, isn't it?'

'Unhygienic. We can't get him to wash. It seems he hates water.' Clifford's sniff was at its most expressive.

'But we know why that is, don't we? We know the history.'

'To know is not to forgive, in my opinion, sir.'

'Very well, Clifford. I'll talk to the boy. And for the moment . . . no further action. Is that understood?'

'If you say so, sir.' And Clifford sniffed.

Half an hour later a boy, short for his age, wearing a clean sweater and jeans brought in by an attentive auntie, stood in front of Paul's desk. S.P.O. Clifford had jangled off about his business. Slippy and the governor were left entirely alone.

Paul said, 'You've got no complaints then, Johnson?'

'Not really.'

'It's not a bad place, d'you think? As young offenders' institutions go?'

'Quite honestly, we're lucky to be here.'

'I'm glad you think so.'

'"Butlins under Lock and Key." That's what they calls Skurfield.'

'I'd rather you didn't broadcast that description.' Paul remembered the 'Breakfast Egg' show.

'And the food's more than adequate.' Slippy seemed determined to hand out compliments.

'We do our best. No one's bullying you?'

'I don't think they'd take it on.'

'Some of them are bigger than you.'

'But not half so slippy.'

'Prison officers fair to you?'

'Fairer than me uncles.'

'Then why, in the name of all that's reasonable, did you want to escape?'

Slippy Johnson struck the top of his head, on which his hair grew upwards, as though to compensate for the fact that he was short for his age. Having kick-started his brain in this way he came out with the only possible explanation. 'Suppose it gets a bit dull here. All right?'

Paul sighed. Politicians could go on about the causes of villainy, greed, supernatural evil, poverty or the denial of breast-feeding. People took to crime, he'd decided, for the same reasons they took to skiing, hang-gliding, football, hooliganism, stock-car racing or riding on Nemesis in the theme park, to colour their lives with risk. For the same reason they sent the adrenalin flooding in bank raids or entering other people's houses by night. And yet the search for excitement ended too often in years of unendurable boredom, brought on by a broken back or a prison sentence. The governor knew about all these things, having spent almost a lifetime in prisons, longer than most long-term offenders.

His father had been a London prison governor. Paul grew up to the sound of banging doors and clanking keys and thought everyone had to get into their homes with an elaborate system of unlocking, relocking and double locking behind them. He was escorted in and out of doors by huge screws who smelt of thick sandwiches. He patted prowling Alsatians and watched pale men in grey clothes weed his father's grimy patch of garden or scrub the floor in the governor's kitchen. He knew his home was surrounded by even-more-secure accommodation, booming galleries which smelt of cabbage and shit. He knew, from the screws who befriended him, about the shed and the graves inside the walls and could remember the mornings when his father, white-faced and irritable, brought the chaplain to breakfast. They spoke in solemn voices but still had hearty appetites, having witnessed a death. He had, it seemed to him, been a prisoner all his life, in his father's gaol or in boarding schools, and then in the institution in which he finally rose to governor's rank. He escaped, when he could, to the company of people like Agnes Simcox, who had nothing to do with crime and punishment, or sat alone listening to great, crashing Mahler symphonies, reading poetry and sometimes, terrified by the risk he was taking, writing it.

He looked at the file on his desk and pretended to read Slippy's record, although he had consulted it so often that he knew it by heart. Slippy wasn't like the usual youth offender, he was a one-off, in a class of his own, a professional. He hadn't started sniffing glue when he was ten, gone joy-riding and nicked car radios at eleven, taken heroin a year later and relied on profitable house-breaking to finance his addiction. So far as anyone could discover, Slippy had never taken any more habit-forming stimulant than diet Coke; he had neither wounded nor raped anyone and was possibly still a virgin. He had merely, like the governor, followed in his father's footsteps. 'Peters' Johnson was an expert safe-breaker, a picker of locks and inserter of well-judged charges of dynamite, and had, apart from one long period of absence during Slippy's childhood, largely escaped conviction. His Uncle Desmond was a frequenter of fire escapes and shinner-up of drainpipes, who could visit you unnoticed by night. His Aunty Mags was a receiver of stolen property and his gran, Elsie Johnson, had a string of convictions for fraud, deception and illicit fortune-telling. Like Mozart, Slippy had achieved an infant prodigy's talent in a family calling, and his skills with forbidding locks and extemporized keys had, no doubt, earned him high praise in the family circle. If *he* had been born the child of 'Peters' Johnson, the governor speculated, he also would have wished to shine in his father's line of business. No doubt that would have meant he got part of his schooling in a young offenders' institution, but that might have been a great deal more comfortable than his minor public school on the Norfolk coast, ruled over by a sadistic headmaster and a maths teacher fighting a losing battle with paedophilia. For these reasons he felt a kind of kinship with Slippy, against which he had to be constantly on his guard.

'You're not doing yourself any good by this sort of thing.'

'No, sir.' Slippy had to admit that goodness was not what he was after.

'You're a bright lad. People notice you. You stand out from the crowd in Skurfield.'

Slippy looked modest and thought he would try not to be noticed in the future.

'Of course there are complaints. About your not washing yourself regularly. Water's nothing to be frightened of here, you know.'

Slippy gave a shudder, as though he didn't believe that water was safe anywhere.

'Important people find you attractive' – Paul changed the subject – 'Did you enjoy your day release? When you weeded the roses?'

'Roses were they? I don't know much about roses.'

'You were back here on time.'

'Gentleman made sure I was.'

'Johnson.' The governor stood, paced the room, tried not to sound as though he were the prisoner on trial. 'If the story about what you were making in metalwork got out, it might have very serious consequences for both of us. I'd have to report it to the prison service. The Home Secretary would be informed. You'd be put on the block and lose remission. And I . . .'

'You might get the sack, sir?' Slippy, from an early age, had acquired an excellent working knowledge of the penal system.

'As I've said. It might have disastrous results. For both of us. So. No one knows about this except us two and Mr Clifford . . .'

'I didn't tell no one. And her in metalwork thought it was jewellery. Mind you, she doesn't take that much notice.'

'So. I'm prepared to overlook it this once. It's my job to come to a decision.'

'And you do your job so well, sir. The lads all comment on it.'

That was very gratifying, but Paul sat behind his desk now, with a severe and judicial frown, to pass no particular sentence. 'Will you give me your word you won't try anything like this again?'

'By my baby's head. I swear it.'

Paul looked at the undersized youth. 'You haven't got a baby?'

'Not as yet. But by its head when I get one.'

'Don't let's bother about the baby you haven't got. There are to be no more of these silly attempts. Mr Clifford will have you under special observation. And I shall withdraw you from metalwork and put you down for business studies.'

'Business studies? Won't that be a bit, like, dull, sir?'

'Extremely. Dullness is the price we both have to pay for security.' The governor pressed a bell on his desk. 'I'll have you taken back to your cell.'

# Chapter Six

Agnes said, 'I used to knock things.'

'What sort of things?'

'Oh, anything that people went on about. Paris. Ballet-dancing. Sunsets.'

'You used to knock sunsets?'

'Only when people went on about them.'

'Do you still do it?'

'Sometimes. One thing I don't knock.'

'What's that?'

'I suppose . . . what you're standing for. You being brave and telling them. Does that sound ridiculous?'

'Not at all.' He had no hesitation in reassuring her. 'It doesn't sound ridiculous at all.'

Of course he was pleased, as he had been when he stood in the high street and saw his face in the shop window, the sincere and meaningful look, the smile of humane understanding, the gaze into the distance of a man about to lead the way into paradise. He went in to thank her and she said the window had gone down, on the whole, very well; even those blue rinses who called in for Delia's recipes or the latest Sandra Tantamount had admitted he looked handsome. 'It's not a beauty contest,' he had told her, and she said, 'No. But that little squirt Tim Willock. Ugh!' Then he said he wanted to go out and woo the countryside vote and wondered if there was any countryside left in the constituency. It was then that she offered to close the bookshop for half a day and show him.

The arrangement hadn't been achieved without a degree of deception. Terry was now established as the candidate, with an office in Penry's gaunt house in Queen Alexandra Road, Hartscombe. He and Kate moved into Penry's top floor, once occupied by the Penry children, one of whom was now in banking and the other a drop-out in Somerset. Penry the agent, with a wife who spent as little time as possible at home, now had his loneliness interrupted, not only by Terry and Kate, but by a large number of volunteers, students, unemployed arts graduates and enthusiastic middle-aged women who stuffed envelopes, sent out election addresses and formed platoons to spearhead attacks when Terry invaded the streets to knock on doors and surprise voters with sudden demands for their political opinions. A new figure had also arrived in Terry's life, an even more expert dampener of spirits than the agent Penry, whose acceptance of defeat was now lightened by the hum of activity and an almost cheerful determination to go down fighting.

There was nothing cheerful about Desmond Nabbs M.P., the Labour member for the neighbouring constituency, which took in most of Fallowfield Country Town. 'They won't send any of the big boys to help you out,' he told Terry. 'None of the Shadow Cabinet will come. They don't want to have their names associated with a Labour defeat. So you'll have to rely on me. Des Nabbs, a humble back-bencher. At least I can see you stick to the party line and don't make a bloody fool of yourself. I'll be with you knocking on doors, and I'll sit in on your radio interviews. Before you open your big mouth always remember, Des will be hearing this.' He was a tall, skinny man with the monotonous, droning voice of an early Puritan. He had a long, disapproving nose and eyes so deeply shadowed that he looked exhausted. He neither smoked nor drank, his only indulgence being curiously strong mints which he sucked for a while and then cracked audibly between strong jaws. He treated Terry as though he hadn't yet completed his education.

'This isn't bloody student politics now,' he said. 'You've got a party line, and I'm here to see you stick to it.'

Nabbs had great faith in banning things. 'I drove past them water-skiing on Riddlesham reservoir,' he said when he first arrived in the office. 'Totally uncontrolled. All those bloody kids in wetsuits, scaring the wildlife and splashing up the water we've got to put in our mugs of tea, right? I'll get them banned when we're in government. It's a bloody menace to the public.'

Nabbs had a long list of things he'd have banned when Labour won the general election. This was an event he saw as so far off that he would have plenty of time to add more undesirable activities to his list of Private Members' Bills. Selling alcoholic lemonade, catapults, war-like toys and bows and arrows of a certain size would be dealt with by imprisonment, as would holding raves, hang-gliding and disseminating books containing racially biased stories to persons of a tender age. When Terry told him he wanted a morning to himself, Nabbs looked up from the mug of tea he was using to warm his large, shiny hands and said, 'What do you want to do that for?'

'To see the countryside. I just want to wander and collect my thoughts. I'd like to think of a fresh way to put the issues.'

'If you want to know how to put the issues, you consult Des Nabbs. That's what I'm here for.'

'I thought you might be glad of the time to draft the answers I'm going to give when I'm interviewed by the *Hartscombe Sentinel*. Will you do that?'

'I'll draft them, all right. We don't want you putting your foot in it.'

'Of course, we don't know the questions yet.'

'We don't have to bother about the questions. Whatever they ask you, you just give the answers I've written down. Right?'

So, on the morning when Agnes closed her shop, they left Harts-combe, Terry driving and Agnes beside him navigating, smelling of a perfume drier and more pungent than Kate's and ostentatiously not smoking. They turned off the main road and twisted down narrow lanes, where branches scraped the side of the car and they had to huddle into the hedgerows when confronted by a postman, an occasional builder's lorry or a string of children on ponies who raised their whips in unsmiling, lordly acknowledgement of their right to pass. They called at cottages which had belonged to woodmen or farm workers when Agnes was a child and found them equipped with outdoor saunas, granny flats and Range Rovers parked ready for the wives while the husbands left the B.M.W. at Worsfield station to await their return from the city.

So they found wives, left in rustic simplicity, bored as Marie Antoinette might have been in her toy-like farmhouse when all the men were away at the war. And such women were glad of any interruption, particularly one by a handsome couple, a man with a meaningful look and an older woman, still beautiful, whether they were alone or drinking coffee with other stranded wives and hearing gossip which they already knew by heart. At first, when Terry told them he was there on behalf of the Labour Party, they flinched and even giggled nervously, as though he were selling pornography door to door or offering to install overhead bedroom mirrors. But when Agnes had softened them up with some new scandal she had heard in the bookshop, and when Terry had told them that his long service with S.C.R.A.P. proved his passionate devotion to the countryside, of which the Labour Party was now the natural custodian, coffee was handed round with little nips of brandy to correct it and chocolate-covered digestives, and some of the wives even hinted that they might take advantage of the secret ballots. Those who had sat next to Tim Willock at dinner parties agreed that he had either ignored them completely or bored them with a lot of talk about prisons.

So it was with a sense of achievement that Terry sat down to lunch in the Badger at Skurfield. Agnes narrowed her eyes to stare at the blackboard which, in the old days had offered ploughman's or sausages and mash and now flirted with deep-fried goat's cheese, sun-dried tomatoes and grilled monkfish with rocket.

'Look at that,' she said. 'It's the sun-dried-tomato voter you've got to win over.'

'We'll win them.' Terry had ordered pints of bitter, which the young waitress, filling in time before starting at R.A.D.A., found amusing in an establishment which now did its best lunch-time trade in New Zealand Sauvignon. Later Terry said, 'Talking to some of those women this morning, I got the feeling they thought it was time for a change.'

'A change of husband, not necessarily of government.' Agnes looked at him over the pint mug, which seemed heavy for her. 'Simcox bitter. It's still bloody good.'

'The local beer?'

'Mainly owned by that rich old Socialist vicar I was telling you about. The Reverend Simeon Simcox.'

'You knew him well?'

'I should say so. I married one of his sons and loved the other.'

'What's happened to him?'

'Oh, he's been dead for a long time. Quietly decomposing in Rapstone churchyard, which has now almost been taken over by the Fallowfield Tesco's. I mean, it's next door to their car park.'

'No. What happened to the one you married?' Terry asked the question without, for some reason, wanting to know the answer.

'Oh, it didn't work out. He started off as an angry young Socialist and ended up a grumpy old blimp. You won't do that, will you?'

'No.' Terry laughed at the idea. 'Of course I won't.'

'Promise?'

'Of course I promise.'

'That's all right, then.'

'And what happened to the other one?'

'Which one?'

'The one you loved.'

'Oh, he became a doctor. Took over my father's practice. Took over his house, too. And then left it to me.'

'He died?'

'Divorced. Died. Men are very unreliable.'

'And your father?'

'Oh, he's dead too, of course. He found out he had cancer, so he decided to take an impossible fence out hunting.'

'You're against hunting?' For God's sake, they had said to Terry at Walworth Road when they briefed him, try to keep off hunting. They're not all that interested in education, Europe and the National Health, but in these rural spots they get ridiculously excited about killing foxes. Keep quiet about it. Whatever you say's bound to be wrong. But Agnes, he thought, would want it banned, and as they sat together over the monkfish he was anxious to please her.

'Hunting? No. I've nothing against hunting. My father found it very useful.' She dug into her jacket pocket, produced a battered packet and then had second thoughts. 'Oh, I forgot,' she said. 'You don't like it.'

'No, I don't mind,' Terry was anxious to reassure her. 'I really don't mind at all.'

A sharp wind sent the golden leaves swirling, and their feet rustled and crushed the brittle beech mast as they walked. Most of the remaining woodland in the Hartscombe constituency had been felled and replanted with fir trees and pine. Here the tall, elephant-grey trunks of the beeches still stood.

'Hanging Wood,' Agnes told him. 'It belonged to a poacher called Tom Nowt. His father was a mean old farmer who left it to him. But Tom kept it well. Actually he did nothing except shoot in it.'

'Is that what he lived on?'

'So far as anyone knew. He had a calling pheasant.'

'What's that?'

'A lady pheasant in a cage. She'd cry out in the night, and all the lecherous cock pheasants from other people's woods would rush over here to date her. Tom put out fish hooks baited with raisins soaked in brandy and caught most of them. Apart from pheasant he seemed to live mainly on deers' brains.'

'Deers' brains?' Not normally squeamish, Terry was beginning to feel that woodland life was even tougher than politics.

'He shot deer with a rifle and hung them up in an old barn he had. Then he'd slit them up and butcher them. He said the brains were a great start to the day and kept him alive.'

So the brain-eating Nowt wouldn't arise, bearded and dirty, from the undergrowth, with twigs and moss sticking to his clothing, to raise his rifle – an uncomfortable vision Terry had feared as they walked under the long shadows of the trees. 'Who owns the wood now?'

'Tom's son, who went to work in South Africa. This wood's been lucky. It's been going for a long time without a change. That's why I wanted to show it to you.'

'So you're really a Conservative?' he laughed at her.

'Of course! That's why I vote Labour. Who said that? Look, there they are!'

Three deer, one very young, trotted, light and soundless on the dry leaves, into a beam of sunlight and then vanished into the shadows, their brains still in their heads. 'There's someone I want you to meet,' Agnes said.

'Who's that?'

'His name's Paul Fogarty.'

'Votes Labour?'

'Oh, I'm sure. He's a good man. Truly good.'

'Not another vicar?'

'No.' She kicked up leaves, smiling. 'As a matter of fact he's a prison governor. A boys' prison.'

'Skurfield Y.O.I.?'

'That's the one. He's trying hard to treat those boys as human beings. To give them some sort of hope, self-esteem. That's what he talks about. He's worried about the Tories and boot camps. I'm sure he'd like to meet you.'

'I'd like to meet him.'

'We'll have a dinner party. I'll cook for you. Proper food. Not rocket and singed fish, I promise you.'

They were going downhill now, into the darkness of the wood, and the leaves were slippery, so Terry was afraid of falling. It was very quiet and they seemed to have run out of conversation. She was looking at some sort of shack, a building green with age, lop-sided as a boat that has run aground, surrounded by brambles and grown over with ivy, its cobwebbed windows blind with dirt, worn patches and holes in the felt roof. 'Tom Nowt's old hut,' she told him. 'He called it his hunting lodge.'

'You used to go there?'

'Oh, a lot. He was good at lending it to us. We went there when we were young. Me and the vicar's sons.'

'The one you married or the one you loved?'

'Well, quite honestly, both of them.'

'You went there, I suppose, for picnics?'

'Not really.' She was further down the slope and looked back up at him. 'We went there to fuck.'

He was saved from deciding how to react by a cry from the mobile phone in his pocket. Kate's voice, young, clear and irritated, sounded in his ear. 'Wherever've you got to? Penry's trying to get hold of you.'

'I've been canvassing,' he said. 'Quite interesting. I'll tell you all about it.' But he wouldn't, not all.

# Chapter Seven

W.R.F., the letters standing for Worsfield Road Furnishings, illuminated the sky over the largest building in the town's trading estate. Terry Flitton stopped at the gate, gave his name and said, 'To see the Chairman.' A list was consulted, a bar rose into the air and he found a parking space outside the factory where his father had spent his entire working life and never caught sight of the Chairman.

Kate's call had ordered him back to headquarters where Penry and Nabbs M.P., the controllers who had temporarily lost control of him, were speaking in the low, excited tones of those who have extraordinary news. The Chairman of W.R.F., not hitherto known for his left-wing opinions, was considering offering them telephone-canvassing facilities on a part of his organization's switchboard. A condition of this munificence was, however, an immediate meeting with the candidate, in private.

'One on one,' Penry said. 'His P.A. Lorraine, very pleasant-sounding girl, made that perfectly clear.'

'He wanted to see the cut of your jib.' Nabbs M.P. spoke dolefully, as though fearing that Terry's jib would not be found satisfactory.

'An old-fashioned expression,' Penry explained to the far younger candidate. 'I imagine they were the words of the Chairman. Not the sort of thing Lorraine would come up with.'

'We're letting you off the lead, young man' – Nabbs sounded a note of warning – 'so don't go committing yourself to policies.'

'Just express gratitude and say you're handing over negotiations to us,' Penry advised.

'Have you spoken to this Chairman?' Terry was bold enough to ask.

'We have dealt with the matter,' Nabbs had to admit, 'only at P.A. level at the present time.'

'But Lorraine's given you a seven o'clock appointment. Tell them on the gate that you're for the Chairman.'

The entrance hall was echoing marble. Soon he was going up in a lift with Lorraine and walking down silent corridors to an outer office which was meticulously tidy. She was a pale, sharp-featured girl with the fixed smile of an air hostess and the decisive movements of a dental nurse. 'A little bit of paperwork for you, Mr Flitton. I'm going to ask you to sign this formality. Then if you'd be good enough to take a seat.'

The single sheet of paper invited Terry to treat the forthcoming meeting as entirely confidential. If he reported anything that was said, all offers of support for his campaign would be withdrawn. Lorraine departed, scrutinizing his signature as she walked. Terry was left alone with a back number of *Highwayman. The Journal of Road-Mending and Motorway Improvement.* He found himself thinking only of the dilapidated hut Agnes had shown him in the woods and had an uninvited picture of her palely naked, lying on an old blanket on the damp and rotting floor. The vision faded when Lorraine reappeared at the door and said, 'Will you come this way now, Mr Flitton?'

He found himself in a boardroom, dimly lit. There was a long table on which pads and pencils had been set for a meeting. At the head of the table, as though the host at some spectral dinner party, was a man he had seen hundreds of times on television screens and caricatured in newspapers and whom he had been brought up, since his earliest student days, to hate like poison.

Lord Titmuss said, 'Sit down, young man. Where've you been hiding yourself?'

'You're not the Chairman?' This was all Terry could think of to say.

'I am not. I do, however, have a certain amount of influence in this company. The offer of a part of their telephone switchboard is perfectly genuine. I just hope your people are up to making good use of it.' Lord Titmuss's pale eyes stared at the Labour candidate without a blink. His knotted hands were joined in front of his face in what might have been an attitude of prayer. He looked like an ascetic monk who had risen to become a Prince of the Church. Terry felt that his world had suddenly swung upside-down.

'You know I'm the Labour candidate?' The question sounded silly as soon as he had asked it.

'I don't care if you're the Maoist Revisionist Anti-Rat-Hunting candidate for Free Love and Acupuncture. I take it you want to defeat the Tories?'

'Of course.'

'And you're one hundred and one per cent determined to do so?'

'Absolutely.'

'You see no possible alternative to winning?'

'None!'

'Then you'll suit my purpose admirably.'

'Is your purpose to defeat your own party?'

'My party? Are you suggesting that little traitor Willock, that damp, fawning, Europe-loving git whose true occupation is selling strings of onions off a French bicycle, that three-legged coward who stood with his dagger out during the assassination of the greatest Leader we ever had, his hand shaking and afraid to strike, that vacillating voice of the Prime Minister's movement for mediocrity, belongs to my party? I tell you this honestly, young man' – And here Lord Titmuss disconnected his hands and laid them, pale palms up, on the table, in the manner of someone showing his cards – 'To call Timothy Willock a member of my Party is to throw mud in the face of Margaret Thatcher. Is that what you want to do?'

'I wouldn't have minded,' Terry admitted, 'in her day.'

Leslie Titmuss greeted this confession with a long, penetrating stare, and it crossed Terry's mind, as the legendary politician rose to his feet, that he was about to be seized by the throat and shaken like a rat. Titmuss, however, moved into the shadows and said, in a voice which came with an added rasp, 'You've got guts, at least. You'll do.'

'I'll do for what?'

'Driving Wee Willie Willock out of Hartscombe and Worsfield South. Sending him back to his villa in Spain with his tail between his wet little legs.'

'Has Willock got a villa in Spain?'

'It would be entirely typical.'

'And I don't really know what his policy on Europe is, do you?'

'No.' And Leslie Titmuss added darkly, 'But I can guess!'

'Hartscombe's a safe Tory seat.' Terry was honest about his problems.

'I thought I'd explained.' Titmuss's patience was becoming exhausted. 'We haven't got a Tory candidate. You'll beat him all right. I can make you win!'

'*Make* me?' Terry felt relaxed, the old man was dotty and probably harmless.

'Correction.' Standing, Titmuss smiled, which made him look, a political journalist once wrote, like an alligator about to bite off a particularly toothsome leg. 'I'm going to help you beat him.'

'We're tremendously grateful for the telephone service. That's extremely generous.'

'The telephone service is only the start of it.' Titmuss found another chair and sat, this time so close to Terry that their knees were touching. 'I'm going to teach you how to do it.'

Shifting his legs slightly to avoid contact with a bony knee, Terry had to admit, 'I'm sure you know a lot more about politics than I do.'

'Politics' – Leslie Titmuss started his first lesson – 'is simply about winning.'

'My politics' – Terry's tone was now slightly superior, even condescending – 'are about beliefs.'

'Beliefs come into it, of course. I take it you believe in "Socialism", equality, full employment, the minimum wage and free seats at the bloody opera house for the workers?'

'Something like that.' Terry was still smiling.

'And you would agree that to have such beliefs, without doing anything to put them into practice, is pure emotional self-indulgence?'

'I suppose so.' Terry felt he had taken a step on to dangerous ground. 'Yes.'

'And the only point in having such beliefs is to affect society, as you would say, for the better?'

'Well,' Terry conceded, 'that must be right.'

'And the only way you can affect society is by winning elections. You and your party.'

'In a democracy, yes.'

'Well, we're living in a democracy, aren't we? This isn't bloody Iraq.' Lord Titmuss, having decided to adopt the winning ways of a pussy-cat, seemed to feel a constant temptation to turn back into an alligator.

'No. Of course we're in a democracy. Thank God!' Terry reaffirmed his credentials.

'Then if you want Socialism, beat Willock!'

'That's what I intend to do.'

'And if you want Socialism, don't mention the word during your campaign. Or at least only use it to abuse it. Willock's lust for Brussels, you might say for instance, will lead us straight to one-state European Socialism. Government interference in industry. The death of freedom.'

'I couldn't possibly say that.'

'Because you don't want to win?' Titmuss seemed about to sneer.

'Because it wouldn't be true to my beliefs.'

'Of course it would.' His Lordship sighed and rose wearily to his feet as though about to explain an obvious point to a particularly thick House of Commons. 'You'd be doing your beliefs the greatest possible service. You'd be giving them the chance of a lifetime. Then, if you beat Wee Willie and your party wins the next general election, you can come up red as roses. Be as bloody Socialist as you like!'

There was a silence as Titmuss moved away to a far end of the boardroom, so far that Terry had to raise his voice. 'You're prepared to take that risk?' he bellowed.

'I'm prepared to take any risk,' Titmuss called back, 'for the sake of punishing the likes of Wee Willie Willock!'

Terry thought about it and felt he had to say, 'That's extraordinary!'

'Not extraordinary at all. Revenge is one of the few remaining pleasures of old age.'

He got something off a table set against the wall and returned to sit knee to knee with Terry. 'Do you know who you remind me of?'

'No.'

'Me!'

Terry, unflattered, asked why.

'Both of us. Pushy young men. Pulling ourselves up by our bootstraps. Believing in ourselves and knowing we were going to take power away from the toffs and use it for ourselves. My father was a clerk in Simcox Brewery. Every night of his life, when he'd finished up his tea, he'd push away his plate and say to mother, "That was very tasty, dear." I know what your father did.'

'He worked here.'

'So you say.' Titmuss had collected a copy of Terry's election leaflet and now quoted from it. ' "Terry Flitton is a local boy made good. His father was a worker in W.R.F., who spent his life on the shop-floor." Excellent working-class origins! By the way, you don't mention the fact that your father became some sort of personnel officer. Middle management. No doubt voted Tory. You kept that dark, didn't you?'

'There wasn't the space to go into every detail.' Terry realized the lameness of this excuse.

Then he felt the Titmuss hand on his knee and heard Leslie's reassuring voice. 'Of course, you lied. Exactly what I should have done myself. I think we can work together. But for the moment . . .'

'What?'

'You're just another Labour no-hoper. You agreed that this conversation would be entirely off the record. If you mention it to anyone I'll deny every word and no one will believe you.'

'That's probably true.'

'Good. You're beginning to show some political sense. At last.'

'But we can have the switchboard?'

'I don't see why not. Of course, it's got nothing whatever to do with me.'

As Terry left, Lorraine asked him how it had gone. 'Very well,' he told her. He had no intention of running his campaign under the orders of an enemy general, long ago retired, but having been asked to do so was none the less flattering. Titmuss had, whatever he said, spotted him as a potential winner. If he could ever be persuaded to endorse Terry openly the publicity would be the most astonishing news of the week. Meanwhile he had given away nothing and taken over part of the telephone exchange in the great organization which had fed his family and produced enough traffic cones to clog the motorways of England.

As he drove away from the cone factory he remembered that Agnes had invited him and Kate to supper. With the optimism of many men in such situations he hoped that the two women would get on together.

Agnes said, 'I really am terribly sorry.'

Terry said, 'No, really! There's no reason why you should have known.'

Kate said, 'I don't want to be a nuisance.'

Agnes said, 'Could I just give you some of the potato off the top of the shepherd's pie?'

'Isn't it cooked with the meat?' Kate was doubtful.

'Well. Yes. If I have to be honest.'

'Then, if you don't mind, I'd rather not.'

'She'll just have some of the vegetables,' Terry said. 'That'll be all right, won't it, Kate?'

'Absolutely! That'll be perfectly all right.'

'You can't just eat cabbage! That would be horribly dull. Couldn't I run you up an omelette?'

'Well, I'm terribly sorry. But I don't eat eggs.'

'Really?' Paul Fogarty looked at Kate as if she were a new and interesting inmate of his Young Offenders' Institution. 'Why's that?'

'Cheese!' Terry said it like a man who has found the solution to a problem which had been troubling the world. 'Kate eats cheese! Don't you, darling?'

'Absolutely! A slab of cheese would be marvellous. Don't bother to grate it or anything like that!'

'Are you a vegetarian too?' Paul Fogarty asked Terry when Agnes had gone off in search of cheese.

'Oh no. Terry's carnivorous!' Kate used the word solemnly, as though it were an unfortunate complaint, like incontinence or asthma.

'So you cook him meat?' Paul was determined to get to the truth of the matter.

'No. But he wolfs it down when he's out to dinner. Like tonight.'

'I do want to see Skurfield Young Offenders' – Terry did his best to get the conversation off the Flittons' eating habits and back to social issues – 'From all I've heard, you're doing a marvellous job there.'

'Imagine I'm running a hospital.' Paul was offering wine to Kate, who put her hand over her glass. 'The boys are ill and I want them to come out cured. Tim Willock wants to turn it into an infected area, a place where they'll catch far more serious criminal diseases. I'd be interested to know what your position is?'

'We're tough on crime and tough on the causes of crime,' Terry came out with the party line in a way that Des Nabbs would have been proud of.

'Presumably you only have to worry about the causes.' Paul Fogarty, with half-closed eyes and his head on one side, was gently probing. 'Get rid of the causes and you'd get rid of crime, wouldn't you say? I mean, you can't separate them, exactly. You read Darwin, I suppose? On the survival of the fittest?'

'Of course,' Terry answered, although it was not strictly true.

'If you're a chimpanzee you do well if you can push a stick into a hole. Better if you can bring it out covered with nice succulent ants. Best of all if you can indulge in a few primitive acts of deception. The process of evolution in the South London jungle.'

From the moment they had arrived for dinner ('Nothing in the least grand. Just shepherd's pie in the kitchen,' Agnes had said) Terry had felt strangely threatened by the governor of Skurfield boys' prison. Paul Fogarty had seemed to be master of the household, so much in charge, opening and pouring out the wine, lighting candles in china candlesticks on the kitchen table, filling the butter dish from the fridge, that Terry was driven to the uncomfortable conclusion that he was Agnes's lover. He was suitably older, intelligent and with a face creased by experience. Terry felt a stab of unreasoning and unexpected jealousy and was at first inclined to argue with Paul, to challenge him and win. But Agnes clearly wanted her new friend and her old friend to like each other, so he smiled encouragement at the prison governor and agreed with him.

'Of course you're right,' he said, looking across at Agnes, in black silk trousers and a white shirt with full sleeves, who was grating cheese, over and above Kate's demands, and making a salad. 'Get rid of inner-city squalor, hopeless schools, no chance of a job, and boredom and you'd go a long way . . .'

'Boredom!' Paul agreed. 'That's the problem. What can we find that's more interesting than joy-riding and nicking car radios?'

Agnes was coming back to the table, holding the salad bowl in both hands, looking down at it as though it contained precious liquid which was not to be spilt. Terry breathed in the warmth of the kitchen, the smell of herbs and wine and olive oil, and thought of how many things in his life there were of far greater interest, and might provide even more dangerous excitement, than the tedious theft of car radios. He watched Agnes put down the bowl on the table and helped Kate to salad, smiling as though seeing to the comfort of an invalid or a child. Then she sat, poured out wine for both of them and he drank, feeling irritated by Kate, whose hand was forever closing her glass to pleasure. Paul was asking him how the campaign was going.

'It's pretty successful. W.R.F. are giving us part of their switchboard.'

'Big business behind you? Willock'll be furious.'

'Amazing, isn't it? My dad worked on the shop-floor and there was I sitting in the Chairman's office, kindly allowing them to help us.'

'Don't let them seduce you.' Agnes's hand was on his arm. 'I hope you didn't make any promises.'

'Absolutely none. It's an offer with no strings attached.'

He didn't tell them he hadn't told Penry, or Nabbs the gloomy M.P., who it was who had been waiting for him in the Chairman's office. He had come back with a deal, a token of favour from the business community, and they had looked at him with a new respect. Only he knew that the arch-enemy, the harsh voice of right-wing *realpolitik*, had spoken to him and offered him advice. It was absurd, of course. The old man was past it, off his trolley, soured by years as a hermit in the wilderness. Terry scarcely knew why he had come away flattered, proud of the secret he was careful to keep. Sometime, who knows, he might be able to make use of the old devil. It would be a fitting end to Titmuss, if the old war-horse were harnessed to the great Labour bandwagon.

'Agnes said she showed you round our rural heartland. What's left of it.' Why did Paul have to say that? Terry looked to see how Kate took the news and was relieved to see her eating salad, apparently unperturbed.

'I volunteered to do a bit of canvassing,' Agnes told Kate, 'among the lonely ladies who drink brandy with their elevenses.'

'It's beautiful up there towards the Rapstone Valley,' Paul told them. 'The best way to see it's from a horse. I don't know if either of you ride?'

'Ride?' Kate shook her head and laughed, as though she had been asked if she spent much time at the spinning wheel or potted meat. 'Well, not a lot actually. Terry used to. Before I met him.'

'Not very well.' Terry had, in his last term at university, fallen in love with a girl who turned out to love horses. She had taken him riding and, with the fear washed away by the years, he remembered the experience as strangely erotic.

'Ride up to Hanging Wood and look down the valley. If you turn your back on Fallowfield Country Town, it's still breathtaking.'

Terry wondered if Paul Fogarty kept a horse stabled in the prison yard, fed and watered by the young offenders. 'No. Betty Wellover at Hartscombe stables lets me take out her hacks. She's got a boy at Harrow with marked criminal tendencies and I think she wants to keep in touch with me in case he ends up as our guest in the Y.O.I.'

Terry stayed late at Agnes's, ignoring Kate's sighs, yawns and occasional reminders that he had to be out early canvassing the next day. After Paul had left to go back to prison, and when Kate was in the loo, he was, for the first time in that long evening, alone with Agnes. He asked, 'What is Paul, exactly?'

'Well. He's governor of the Skurfield nick.'

'I know that. But what is he as far as you're concerned?'

'My friend. About my best friend, I suppose.'

'Only that?'

'Only that. What did you think?'

'The way he opened the wine and got the butter out. The way he knew where everything was. I thought perhaps he was your lover.'

'Hardly.' She was laughing at him. 'He's not exactly that way inclined.'

The governor was gay, Terry was relieved to discover.

'Don't say that to anyone, will you?' Her hand was on his arm again. 'It'd be all up with his job if the prison service knew. So ridiculous! He cares about the boys more than anyone. Quite platonically.'

'Of course not. I won't breathe a word.'

'Bless you.' Her face was near his, and he thought she might have kissed him gratefully, but there was a sound of rushing water and Kate returned to the room.

'"You can't just eat cabbage. That'd be terribly dull." I could see what she had me down as – a really boring cabbage-eater.'

'She offered you an omelette . . .'

'To "run me up" one! With a sort of symbolic sigh. Just because I don't like chewing on dead animals!' Kate, cleaning her teeth, was calling from the bathroom. Terry was already in bed. He thought of pointing out that an omelette isn't necessarily made with dead animals, but decided against it. Too vigorous a defence of Agnes, he was afraid, might betray his feelings and even arouse Kate's suspicions. She came into the bedroom, smiling, her hair and eyes shining. 'We won't have to ask her back, will we?'

'I think we'll be too busy.'

'That's right. You're going to be much too busy and important.' She was in bed now, her legs wound about his, her head on his chest. 'If she came we could have pasta. Then I'd offer to run her up a chop at the last moment, with a heavy sigh. Should I do that?'

'I shouldn't bother.' The idea of a comfortable friendship between Kate and Agnes would have to be abandoned. In future the carnivore and the vegetarian would have to be entertained separately. Terry switched off the light and, while Kate slept, lay for a long while staring into the darkness.

# *Chapter Eight*

The Millichips' living-room was done out in clear pastel shades, filled with eau-de-Nil sofas, white rugs, white-legged, glass-topped occasional tables and paintings of boats in Mediterranean ports. In this room Linda Millichip moved silently, like a huge and extremely expensive yacht, gliding from her moorings. Her solemn, frequently sulky little-girl's face was supported by a formidable body, swathed in the folds and frills of a white négligé. Jewels, twinkling in the autumn sunlight, nestled in her ears and were embedded in the flesh on her fingers. As she watered green and white house plants, breathing heavily, there was a barbaric splendour about Linda Millichip which had in no way been shared by her husband, the late and not much lamented Member for Hartscombe and Worsfield South. Since his death all traces of his existence had been removed from the house, and not a single framed photograph, not even a snapshot, of him remained.

She was interrupted at her task of nourishing the camellias with a mixture of Phostrogen and tepid water by an insistent tapping at the French windows. She looked up, blinking in the low sunlight, and narrowed her eyes to focus on the blurred outline of a tall man, darkly dressed, with a high, naked forehead. She opened the glass doors to admit him.

'This is a private visit,' he began, with an air of mystery he seemed to relish. 'So I came round the garden way.'

'Do come in, won't you? What will you have? Tea? Coffee? A

drink or something? It's not too early for a drinkie, is it? As I say, it's never too early! And won't you make yourself comfortable on the sofa?'

'Thank you. I prefer a hard chair.'

'What can I pour for you then?' Linda set off towards the white-legged, glass-topped drinks table, on which the bottles had their names on porcelain labels which they wore like necklaces.

'Nothing. I'll take nothing, thank you. I've had a substantial breakfast. As I habitually do.'

'Well, then. I'll have to take a teeny one for both of us.' She poured a slug of Cointreau in the bottom of a brandy glass and made herself luxuriously comfortable on the sofa, plumping cushions before she was finally settled. Lord Titmuss, meanwhile, loomed above her in an upright chair he had pulled over from the wall. 'I got your letter,' she told him, 'when Peter died.'

'I would have written more,' Titmuss told her, 'if I'd known more. I never got to know your husband well. Tell me about him.'

'He was a complete pain in the backside.' Linda raised her drink to her lips, and he saw her face, for a moment, distorted in the glass balloon. 'But we mustn't speak ill of the dead, must we?'

There was a silence, in which Titmuss registered no surprise. 'Was he a good swimmer?' he asked.

'He wasn't a particularly good anything. He made money, of course. But that's fairly easy, isn't it, if you happen to be born into a family of merchant bankers? I don't think they trusted him with anything that required more than simple adding up. No good about the house. Ask him to mend a fuse? You'd be wasting your time.'

'You don't seem to have liked him very much.' The Leslie Titmuss rasp, emotionless and only slightly amused, filled the air.

'I didn't. And if you wanted to know the reason, I wouldn't tell you. Not even if you were here from the *Daily Fortress* with a cheque for a cool 50k.'

'I respect your secrets and I certainly wouldn't offer you money for them.' The Titmuss voice had now acquired its note of throaty sincerity.

'Thank you for that, Lord Titmuss. I'm very grateful.'

'I only wonder how your husband managed to drown in the pool. It must be quite a hard thing to do. Even if he could only swim a few strokes.'

'I told you. He was incompetent about the house.' She gathered up the folds of her négligé and rose into the air like a monstrous swan. 'Put a washer on the tap in the *en suite* bathroom? Forget it!' She sailed away to the drinks table and recaptured the Cointreau bottle.

'Had he knocked himself out on the side of the pool or anything like that?'

'I wouldn't know. I didn't examine him all that closely. The years when I used to examine Peter Millichip closely were over. If you want to know the truth.'

'But you found him, in the pool?'

'I woke up early. The damned birds round here make such a racket. They've got no consideration, have they? I opened my bedroom window and there he was. Floating.'

'So you rang for the ambulance?'

'No.'

'The police?'

'No.'

'Who, then?'

'I rang Sir Gregory.'

'Why him?'

'Peter Millichip always said, if he ever got into any sort of trouble, the first person to ring was the Party Chairman.'

'And he was in trouble?'

'He was dead.'

I must be, Agnes said to herself, mad even to think about such a thing. Of course I'm old, past it, out of the race; this is because I'm a woman and our shelf-life is somewhere between the milk and the yoghurt. At my age, at the age I've reached, I'm expected to be on the boards of charities and babysit for the grandchildren. And he has a young wife who is beautiful, I have to admit, even though she has conscientious objections to most types of food and fans the air with her hand if I dare to light up a fag. If he were married to me he would dream of fucking her and would do so with only an occasional twinge of guilt whenever the opportunity arose. Married to her, the idea of fucking a woman seventeen years older than himself and something like twenty-seven years older than his wife would seem merely bizarre.

Given all that, why did he look at me the way he did when I carried salad across the kitchen to his wife? Why was he so delighted to discover that Paul Fogarty's gay? Why did he look disturbed and interested when I told him the use we had for Tom Nowt's old hut? He sort of quivered. Imagine that! A man who can fight for Socialism and the just society in complacent Hartscombe quivering when he heard that long, long ago, I made love in a hut in the woods. What's he doing now, I wonder.

She was in bed with a cigarette and a cup of tea and had a vision of Terry and Kate, engaged in early-morning love. She saw Kate's face, flushed with youthful enthusiasm, and decided to get up before she could imagine her clear and girlish whimper of pleasure. She decided to open the bookshop, rearrange the entire fiction section and not think about Terry again, at least until lunch-time. As she made this decision she told herself, 'I hope to God he doesn't guess any of this. If he did he'd laugh at me and I'd feel a complete idiot.'

Lying in the chipped bath in the upper reaches of Penry's house, in water which was rapidly cooling and had never been really hot, looking at the greying cream walls and the mugs over the basin full of assorted toothbrushes, Terry thought, 'At least she admires me.' He found this flattering because Agnes didn't give away admiration easily. Since the evening of shepherd's pie she had come to the office to stuff envelopes and had volunteered to go out canvassing again. He had called at the bookshop and she'd made him coffee, and her rapid assessments, not only of his opponent Willock and the Lib Dem woman, but of Penry and the M.P. Nabbs were brief and withering. He was delighted to discover that he was one of those rare beings of whom she approved, himself and the prison governor, but Paul, happily, could now be dismissed from the equation. And Agnes's approval came from a long line of authorities, from the C.N.D. marches and the books on her shelves, Orwell and Tawney and E. P. Thompson and perhaps even, although he was more doubtful about this, Oscar Wilde. More than that, politics with Agnes, usually a grimly serious business having much to do with committees of local activists and Nabbs' party line, became entertaining, glamorous, almost raffish. Agnes, of course, had no idea he was lying in a cooling bath thinking about her, that he thought about her now most of the time and that, even in the grim surroundings of the W.R.F. works she had come, naked and available on the floor of a hut, into his mind. Had she known all that, he was sure, she'd have laughed in his face.

'This is Terry Flitton, your Labour candidate. Time for the train. Time for a change!' Kate Flitton, now commuting to the S.C.R.A.P. office in London, heard her husband, like the voice of God, booming across Hartscombe station and smiled contentedly. She shared none of the pessimism of Penry or Nabbs. For her Terry's victory was as inevitable as the banning of cigarettes in public places, the minimum wage and the end of fox-hunting. She was the child of school-teachers, a father and mother who moved quietly, smiling with confidence, about the bright classrooms of a successful suburban comprehensive, convinced that the truth was great and would prevail once the Nativity play was abolished in favour of the enactment of multi-ethnic legends and Afro-Caribbean history took the place of grim reminders of Henry VIII and the British Empire.

They didn't, as they always said, push their only child towards their dearly held beliefs, but they allowed her to absorb them, together with a diet strong in pulses, which contributed to her perfect health. She also grew up with a beauty which provoked dangerous and anarchic thoughts in men, but her quiet certainty on almost every subject cooled and often disconcerted them. What her friends and contemporaries called 'having sex', or even 'a bit of a fling', she would call 'a commitment', a word which produced serious thoughts, and sometimes hesitation, in the men to whom she took a fancy and who found her, at first glance, extremely desirable.

There were a good many of these males, both at the school in which her parents resolutely showed her no favour and at London University. She got her first job in the press office at S.C.R.A.P. and helped in arranging press interviews and television appearances for Terry whenever a rain forest was threatened or the oceans seemed capable of overheating. He was always polite to her, sometimes charming, but it wasn't until he drove her home after he had done 'Any Questions' in Grimsby that it happened. They were both in a high mood, the adrenalin flowing after the way Terry had put down a junior Foreign Office minister ('Hot air from politicians will do nothing to reduce global warming'). She paused and raised her face to him before she got out of the car, and he kissed her with the expertise he had acquired thanks to his ten-year start in life. He went upstairs to the flat she shared with two girls in Tufnell Park. By the morning they were well on the way to making a commitment.

Three years had passed, during which they would both have called themselves happy. Kate's commitment was as single-minded as religious faith, and freer from doubt. Terry was proud of the youth and beauty of his wife and allowed himself to enjoy the envy of all the men in S.C.R.A.P. who had promised themselves and each other, at lunch-times in the pub, to seduce Kate, from the first day she appeared in the press office. And Kate had no doubts about her husband, although she had noticed, in the last year, moments when he lost interest in falling trees. He seemed, even when they were alone together, to be following thoughts she couldn't guess at, pursuing distant dreams or engrossed in secret discontents. Although he never complained, she had the feeling that the universe was no longer enough for him, and he was ready for the more particular and immediate concerns of Hartscombe and Worsfield South. Victory in the by-election, Kate assured herself, would be quite enough to make her husband happy during the years to come.

So she sat, contented, waiting for the train to jolt into life as the Hartscombe commuters, dark-clothed, determined, unsmiling people carrying briefcases and newspapers, hurried down the platform. She saw a surprising number of them stop to accept leaflets from a woman in a leather jacket, who smiled at the many she seemed to know. Kate recognized Terry's new friend, who had made a salad for her and grated cheese and brought it with the careful cheerfulness with which a nurse would approach the terminally ill. This woman was, she supposed, important in the constituency. Clearly she had a lot of friends, which was why Terry had turned on all his charm for her. Kate just hoped that, when the seat was won, they would have no more suppers in the overheated kitchen where everyone drank too much and vegetarianism was made to sound like a disease only to be spoken of in whispers. Now she saw Terry come up and join the woman, and the dark figure of Nabbs was hovering in the background. The woman left then, and she saw a smiling Terry approach a couple of business girls, who stopped, listened to him and smiled back.

Then the door of the carriage opened and the woman was there, pushing a leaflet at her. 'Terry Flitton. Your Labour candidate. Have you thought about voting for him?' she said, and then, 'Oh, it's you! How stupid of me. It must be encroaching Alzheimer's.' It only proved what Kate had suspected all along, that when it came to working for the Party, Agnes Simcox was a complete amateur.

Officers of the Inniskilling, the Guards regiments, the 52nd and the Royal Artillery, together with allies from the 1st Prussian Army

Corps and Kellerman's Cuirassiers, the enemy being represented by the Emperor's Old Guard, were being carefully dusted by the Chairman of the local Conservative Party and returned to the glass shelves of the illuminated cupboard where they pranced in attitudes of deathless war. Sir Gregory was just cleaning up a major in the reserve cavalry (under the command of Lord Uxbridge) when his wife trilled from the doorway, 'Darling, Lord Titmuss has come to pay us a call!'

'Thank you, Dorothy. Nothing secret, but I'd like a confidential word with Leslie. Politics, you know. Don't want to bore you to death.'

So, dismissed with unusual politeness, Lady Inwood left the two men together.

Titmuss found another hard chair and sat. He had kept on his dark overcoat, telling them he'd only be staying a few minutes.

'Campaign's going well, I think.' Sir Gregory put the little, bright, sabre-waving horseman lovingly back on his shelf. 'We're relying on you to finish it off. Like the Old Guard.'

'The Old Guard, I'm sure I don't need to remind you, lost the Battle of Waterloo.'

'Of course.' The Chairman looked flustered. 'Not a particularly happy phrase, I'm afraid. But you'll help us win it. Willock's a first-rate candidate.'

'Is that your opinion?'

'I expect you heard him on local radio?'

'I denied myself that pleasure.'

'All about juvenile crime. How it doesn't do to mollycoddle the little buggers. What happens, even if they do get locked up, which is rare? Television. Compact-disc players. Erotic pin-ups in every cell. From all I can see, it's a damned sight more comfortable than Eton!'

'I'm afraid I wouldn't know.' The Titmuss smile was particularly glassy. 'I never went to Eton. And this young man Flitton. Do you think he's a good candidate?'

'I think he's making some serious mistakes.'

'Such as?'

'I expect we'll get him for being soft on crime. I hear he's making friends with the do-gooder who runs the young offenders' lock-up. Willock's line plays much better on the housing estates round Worsfield. Murder and mayhem stalk the streets round there, as you well know.'

'I don't know. But you're a constant visitor to the Worsfield housing estates, are you, Chairman?'

'To be quite honest with you, Leslie, I've never been there in my life. But I can assure you, Tim Willock'll make a bloody good constituency M.P. Just as good, in his way, as Peter Milli-chip.'

'You thought Millichip was good?'

'First-rate.'

Titmuss looked amused, in a way that the Party Chairman found strangely alarming. 'I've been talking to his wife. I don't think she'd agree with you.'

'You've been talking to Linda?' Sir Gregory folded his duster neatly and moved to put it away in the bottom drawer of his study desk. 'Terribly nice girl, but fighting a losing battle against Cointreau, you noticed?'

'I never noticed that she was particularly nice, and certainly not a girl.'

'You don't mince your words, Leslie. Perhaps Millichip wasn't up to your high standards of public service. But I'm sure Willock's an excellent replacement. As you know, he was a parliamentary secretary before he lost his seat.'

'A parliamentary secretary who voted in the leadership election of 1990.'

'Well. All M.P.s did that. Including you, Leslie.'

'Some of us,' Titmuss was looking steadily out of the study window in a way that the Chairman found unnerving, 'did our duty. That's not what I came to talk to you about.'

'Of course not.' The Chairman seemed relieved. 'Now, how can I help you?'

'Not me. I just wondered. How did you help Linda Millichip?'

'Help her?'

'She relied on you, didn't she? I mean, she rang you and not the police or the ambulance. When she saw her husband floating . . .'

'She did, yes. Of course I went round at once.'

'How good of you.'

'What else could I do?'

'I don't know. Was he in the pool when you got there?'

'Yes, he was.'

'She'd left him there?'

'Well, I don't expect she could fish him out exactly.' Perhaps it was the dreadful memory that made the Chairman take refuge in dry, nervous laughter, which he stifled almost before it escaped him.

'Was he dressed?'

'What?'

'I mean, I thought he might have been doing something round the pool and fallen in accidentally. Did he have his clothes on?'

'No. No clothes.'

'Just swimming trunks?'

'Well, actually . . .' The Chairman hesitated. 'He had nothing on at all.'

'He swam naked?' Titmuss made it sound like an accusation.

'Well, it was pretty early. Before anyone arrived. I mean, the cleaning lady, or the gardener.'

'So you were the first on the scene?'

'First, after Linda.'

'Oh, yes. Of course. So you rang for the ambulance?'

'For the police. It was too late for anything else.'

'Because he was dead.'

'I'm afraid he was. All that came out at the inquest.'

'I looked up the report in the *Sentinel*. It talked about a naked body with some bruising.'

'Not serious bruising.'

'But some on his wrists. How did that happen?'

'I've absolutely no idea. But the verdict was . . .'

' "Accidental death!"' Titmuss managed to put a pair of mocking inverted commas round the words. 'Well, of course, there are all sorts and kinds of accidents.'

'It came as a shock to us all. Deeply distressing.' Sir Gregory tried for a quick summing-up.

'It must have been.' Titmuss had risen and was standing looking out at the wintry, leaf-littered garden of the grey-stone rectory Sir Gregory had bought when he retired from the diplomatic service. 'Distressing for you?'

'Well, naturally' – Sir Gregory became more modest about his share of grief – 'even more distressing for Linda.'

'But not distressing for Millichip.'

'What do you mean?'

'He'd escaped, hadn't he? He'd gone off somewhere and put an end to all his troubles.'

'I suppose you could say that.'

'You employ a very good gardener.'

A boy was scraping up leaves between two short planks of wet wood and lifting them into a barrow which was overflowing with crisp golden shapes that floated away on a sudden gust of wind. He was an energetic boy with a tuft of hair and a pale, indoor face. An older man, perhaps a gardener or a driver, stood watching him.

'Oh, him.' The Chairman had joined his visitor at the window. 'I have him out from the Skurfield Young Offenders'.'

'I thought you were all for treating them like members of a chain-gang. Lock 'em up and throw away the key.'

'Oh, they get pretty tough treatment when they come to me. No mollycoddling. I get a decent day's work out of them *and* a bit extra.

And of course they get work experience. One likes to do something for the lads.'

'That's very kind of one,' said Lord Titmuss.

# Chapter Nine

The horse Balaclava had, Terry thought, a mad appearance, with a rolling eye and strong yellow teeth exposed in a sneer. 'I'm putting you up on Balaclava,' Betty Wellover at Hartscombe stables said. 'You look strong enough. Don't take any nonsense from him!' Terry wondered what sort of nonsense she had in mind and decided it was the wild rush to death against impossible odds suggested by the horse's name.

Betty Wellover had a brick-red complexion, hair that looked as if it had been gnawed by rats and a voice raised as though she were trying to attract the attention of someone far away in a high wind. 'Agnes tells me you're going to fight Hartscombe for the Reds,' she yelled, as Terry clambered aboard the horse, which now stamped and stirred, impatient for the bugle and the order to charge.

'I'm going to win Hartscombe for the Reds,' Terry panted.

'What's your position on hunting, then?' It was the question he had been advised to avoid. A wrong answer, he feared, might cause a furious Miss Wellover to whip up Balaclava and send him galloping suicidally into the traffic. He played for safety with, 'We're going to allow a free vote. It's a matter for the individual conscience.'

'Well, what's your individual conscience tell you? And stick your leg up, why don't you?' She was yanking at straps and finding new holes for buckles in the regions under Terry's thighs.

'I really haven't made up my mind.'

'Make it up then! Tell him, Agnes.'

'Leave him alone.' Agnes, straight-backed and perfectly relaxed, wearing jodhpurs, while Terry had nothing to offer but jeans, sat on a small brown horse which seemed prepared to obey her every whim. 'He's got more important things to do.'

'There isn't anything more important. Nothing in the world.' With which Miss Wellover shouted, 'Walk!' to Balaclava, who perturbed Terry by tossing his head sideways, trembling as though in receipt of a small electric shock and lurching out of the stable yard as though making for the starting gate.

The campaign had been going in a way which had surprised Penry and Nabbs: Terry's face over the red instruction to 'Vote Flitton' sprouted not only on the Worsfield estates, not only in the windows of doctors and nurses and teachers' houses in Hartscombe, but in some converted-cottage windows in the villages where the morning-coffee ladies had been charmed by Terry's visits. He appeared on the 'Breakfast Egg' programme on Worsfield Radio and listeners phoned in to wish him well and complain that they were tired of waiting for their hip operations or fed up with having to find money for school-books and how come the late Peter Millichip got permission for a swimming pool while they were still stuck in a mobile home? Could it be because they never invited anyone on the planning committee to their holiday villa in Majorca?

So tireless Terry visited factories and comprehensives and did 'Question Time' at his old university. He drank beer and sang rugby songs in the Worsfield Sports Club and drank mulled wine and discussed a new policy for the arts at a musical evening in Hartscombe town hall. He got himself twice on Home Counties Television, once to protest about the threatened closure of a geriatric ward ('We owe our old people a debt we can never repay') and once when he judged the Dog-Who-Looks-Most-Like-Its-Owner contest at the Skurfield Show. In the evenings, when Kate came back from London, they would grab a pizza and go out canvassing.

They looked eager, attractive and anxious to be of help, and few doors slammed on them. He went to matins in St Joseph's, Hartscombe, attended a Worsfield mosque and mass with the Benedictine community in Nunn's Courtny. He addressed car-boot sales, sang at karaoke evenings and wore a ten-gallon hat to a country-and-western evening at the Rotary Club. In his confident moments, and Terry had very few unconfident ones, he told himself that he was taking part in the inspiring process of democracy. And as the time to polling day grew shorter his excitement, and therefore his energy, increased.

He spent a morning at Skurfield Young Offenders' and shared the inmates' lunch. Now he knew that Paul was no sort of challenge, he became a friend of the gentle governor, and they discussed facing the boys with their victims, classes in car maintenance for car thieves and various alternatives to the criminalizing effect of prison. They nodded in agreement, and Terry promised to make his government, when it was in power, discover a better way, and Agnes, when she heard about these conversations, looked at him with increased approval and smiled.

He talked to local Labour parties, S.C.R.A.P. supporters, focus groups and countryside protectors, and he still had words to spare for Agnes. The best times were when they met for a quick sandwich and a beer in the Water-Boatman, the pub by the river at Hartscombe, with its fading photographs of eights, fours and single scullers, huge young men in blazers and caps, and when the river was high the water would lap over the little landing stage and sometimes seep under the bar door. There was an old piano with yellow keys and a husky tone at which Agnes sometimes sat and sang songs her father had taught her, like 'Abdul the Bul Bul Amir' and 'The Daring Young Man on the Flying Trapeze'. When Paul joined them he knew the words too, and when he couldn't come Terry remembered them, and when, at the end of a song, the barmaid or an odd drinker (the Water-Boatman downstairs was not popular at lunch-time) clapped, Terry thought it was no bad thing that the Labour candidate was caught singing in a pub. He asked Penry to fix up a photo opportunity for the *Sentinel*.

His early experience in far-left politics at university, at a time when the political skills of Castro and Colonel Gaddafi were much admired, meant that Terry had, beneath a thick coating of charm, authoritarian instincts. He listened carefully to his Party Executive, the Lady Chairperson and even to the M.P. Nabbs and, having listened, he would make his own decisions. He hadn't encountered much dissent so far, but if he did he intended to make it quite clear who the candidate was and who were his willing, enthusiastic but finally obedient helpers. He rose to the top at S.C.R.A.P. not only by being indispensable to the Chairman, but by deciding that those who weren't for him were against him. And those who were against him found themselves, sooner or later, looking for jobs in other organizations.

So when he told Nabbs that he intended to take an occasional afternoon off during the campaign, he didn't expect any argument. When the M.P. asked 'Why?', he said, as shortly as possible, that if he worked eighteen hours a day he might go mad and fail to attract the voters. He had to have fresh air and exercise.

'Exercise? What sort of exercise?' Nabbs said the word as though it were a dangerous substance.

'I'm not sure yet. Perhaps squash, or jogging. Riding, maybe.'

'Riding?' Nabbs was puzzled at first and then said, 'You'll be going out with the cycling club, then?'

'Something like that,' Terry said. 'So it's agreed, is it?' He was careful to say nothing about horses.

On this, his first ride out with Agnes, by good luck rather than good management, Terry managed to stop Balaclava getting any mistaken order to charge. When the horse walked he half-trotted, and when he trotted he broke unnervingly, as soon as he touched soft ground, into a swerving canter. Terry gripped the front of his saddle with one hand and managed to smile as though enjoying it and not fall off, although the clear blue sky of a crisp November day was visible between his legs. Luckily Agnes saw little of this. She rode in front all the time and assumed, he hoped, that he was riding as casually as she was, swaying hardly at all, sitting down at the canter and keeping, as his university girlfriend had so often yelled at him to do, her bottom on the plate.

They took to the lanes and looked down over garden walls, on to dying Michaelmas daisies and frost-charred chrysanthemums, broken toys and quietly rotting wicker chairs. Agnes slid off her horse to open a gate for him, and he felt slighted because she hadn't waited for him to do it for her. Through the long wet grass in Plashy Bottom, where the outskirts of Hartscombe, the untidy backs of houses and shops, were still visible, Agnes called, 'This is where we gallop.' Terry was white-knuckled, clutching his saddle. Divots of earth flew up from her horse's hooves as they were going up the bridle path between the hedges to Jim Eyles's farm, achieving what was, in Terry's case, a sort of untidy rhythm, but a rhythm all the same. Intoxicated by his skill, he tried to shout, but found that all he got was a mouthful of wind, and no audible sound emerged. He looked down at the pigs nosing around corrugated-iron shelters and smelt the slurry on the wind at Eyles's farm, and then the path took them out on to the high common at Nunn's Courtny. There Balaclava, tired out, fell into a long, triumphant slope, as though back, unwounded, from battle.

On a loose rein Agnes found a cigarette and lit it as her horse sauntered to a stop. From far off they saw the dark smudge of Fallowfield Country Town, a menacing encampment which would be lit up with a false, sulphurous daylight quite soon in the early darkness. And then they clattered through Skurfield and up the side of a ploughed field into Hanging Wood. And there, as Balaclava became lethargic and Terry's confidence grew, he toyed with some childhood fantasies; he was Robin Hood, Dick Turpin, a knight errant, pictures in the history books his mother had given him, which still had her name and the crayon scrawls and torn pages of her childhood. He quite forgot that he was the serious New Labour candidate, dedicated to saving Hartscombe and Worsfield South for social justice. These childish dreams persisted until the horses stopped and Agnes kicked her feet out of her stirrups in front of Tom Nowt's collapsing hunting lodge.

'So long since I looked in here.' There was a rusty padlock hanging uselessly beside the door. Agnes pushed it open, and Terry followed her across damp and creaking floorboards. 'It's amazing that no one's applied for planning permission to turn it into a desirable second home, christened it Deer's Leap and put in a sauna.' There was a work-bench under the blurred window, a table and the remains of a couch, exposing its stuffing and springs like a sheep with its stomach ripped out. There were signs of recent occupation, tins in a dark corner, a newspaper and an empty gin bottle. Terry was confident enough to think he knew why she had brought him there, and his belief was confirmed when she said, 'Romantic little spot, isn't it?'

'Romantic enough.' He put his hands round her face and turned it towards him. She looked up at him, amused but not at all surprised. When he kissed her he found her lips dry and felt her fingers cold on the back of his neck. They stood in a long embrace, his hands straying over her. She was quiet, breathing gently in this place where, it seemed, so much had happened to her. Inside her sweater now, he felt her straight back and moved to discover a small breast, free and unsupported. She took hold of his wrists and pulled his hands away. 'Not here,' she said.

'Why?' He became jealous of departed men. 'Because of who you used to meet here?'

'No, you idiot! Because it's too cold and damp and the floor's probably covered in dirty needles. We'd be far better off at home.'

The Stealth Missile zipped across the car park of the supermarket outside Hartscombe, causing small children to laugh and clap their hands, girls to skip as though threatened by mice and sparks to

shower from the latest, most costly firework on sale for that Guy
Fawkes Night.

Lady Dorothy Inwood emerged from the self-opening glass
doors; she was wearing brown corduroy trousers and a Barbour as
protection against the gently sifting rain. Her grey curls had been
permed that afternoon, her spectacles hung round her neck on a
chain, and she pushed a loaded trolley, on which her handbag
perched, towards the Volvo Estate. And then the Stealth found its
target against her trolley wheels and finally exploded with an ear-
splitting crack. For a second the blow to her face seemed to be a
shock from the firework, but then she saw a long Pluto head
and was punched in the stomach. Donald Duck, Popeye, Elvis and
Madonna, bright colours against the dark sky, danced before her
eyes. She heard a voice call 'Slippy!' and didn't know if it was a
warning or a command, and then her feet were kicked from under
her and she fell to the concrete. The masked boys, whooping
with triumph, danced away with her supermarket trolley and her
handbag stuffed with money. No one stopped the thieves; the
shoppers stood helpless and silent, as though the incident were too
common for comment or they didn't believe it had happened at all.

It was afternoon and the swollen river was shrouded in mist, above
which the bridge rose apparently without support and through
which the black-beaked head of a swan occasionally penetrated.
Anyone passing what was once the doctor's house, its windows
overlooking the water, might have heard, if they stood listening,
two people laughing. Terry had never associated laughter with
making love.

Before they were married, stealing a long lunch-hour from
S.C.R.A.P., Kate, sliding into bed with an expression of serious
commitment, had warned him: 'Please. Don't make jokes.' But
Agnes, it seemed, had no such rules. Terry, in the white bedroom
with fluttering curtains and books piled against the walls, with a
bottle of off-licence champagne on the floor and Agnes naked,

warm between cold sheets, her body almost unmarked by time and only her hands, quick and competent, showing the length of her experience, felt he had strolled into a world he had never known before, a place where sex was entertaining and called for skill but was not, or only at your direst peril, to be taken over-seriously.

But when it was over, when they were damp and resting and he had got over a feeling of amazement, she lay in his arms, her head on his chest, as though she were still young enough to flatter him, and said, 'I know you're going to win.'

'Thank you. I think I will.'

'You read it, didn't you?'

'Read what?' He was alarmed, feeling she was going to try to teach him something.

'*The Soul of Man under Socialism.*'

'Oh yes, I read that.'

'It'll be good, won't it, if we can get to a state where we don't have to worry about people.'

'I suppose so.' Old habits die hard. He had spent his life in a political party dedicated to worrying about people.

There was a long silence, and then she said, 'Wilde said a map of the world which doesn't include Utopia isn't worth even glancing at.'

'Did he?' Terry had not remembered this and was uncertain how to react to it.

'It's what I like about you. Your map's got Utopia.'

'It'll be a different world,' Terry told her, 'when we've won the election.'

'That's not the point. The point is what you've got marked on your map.'

He felt he had been corrected, and so he thought, suddenly and uncomfortably, about Kate. But Kate was in a different world. A solid, serious world from which he was taking, and surely he deserved it, time off. There was no connection between Kate and Agnes and therefore no rivalry, so he comforted himself, forgetting that there was a connection and he was it. He looked at his watch, untangled himself and started to dress. She said goodbye to him casually, as though nothing much had happened at all.

When he got into the street he heard a van approaching in the mist and his opponent's voice booming, 'Mugging in Hartscombe supermarket! Build the boot camps! Vote Willock and crack down on youth crime! For zero tolerance, vote for your Conservative candidate!'

Terry walked on, towards Penry's house and his political advisers.

# Chapter Ten

'What my listeners will want to know is what your lot are going to do about it. How are you going to hit these lads where it really hurts?'

'You mean, turn them into harder criminals?'

'Mugging the Conservative Chairman's wife outside Hartscombe supermarket! Kicking her to the ground! What're you going to do to save respectable elderly ladies from rape and robbery?'

'I don't believe she was raped.'

'Well, not this time perhaps. But there have been cases.'

'Of course.'

'So what are *you* going to *do*?'

'I've written to Lady Inwood to express my sympathy . . .'

'Very nice of you, I'm sure. But that's not going to stop them.'

'Of course it isn't.'

'All right. Tell us, then. What will?'

'Let me tell you, Ken. We've got to look for causes. We've got to look at the schools, and the clapped-out buildings on the Worsfield estates. We've got to ask why this government has reduced the number of bobbies on the beat . . .'

'And while you're looking at all that, how many more elderly ladies have got to be mugged?'

Kenny Iremonger, of the Worsfield Radio 'Breakfast Egg' show, was hatchet faced, beady eyed, with a small ginger moustache. He had been playing a Pulp number, 'Common People', smiling, shaking his shoulders in time to the music when Terry was ushered into the hot little cell which smelt, he thought, of stale sandwiches and unwashed socks. He even muttered something encouraging like it being time for a change before Pulp reached their climax and sang about going to bed with common people. But now Terry was being stared at with studied distaste by an outraged ginger judge, eager to damn him. 'For God's sake,' a voice inside Terry protested, 'it's not *fair*. He's treating you as if you were already in government.' And then he thought that was, in a way, a kind of compliment. His courage returned. He was going to be in government soon, a regime which would give effect, in so far as it could, to the aspirations of Agnes Simcox and Paul Fogarty. Didn't he owe it to her, if not to himself, to prepare Hartscombe and Worsfield South for the shock? From the dock he did his best to offer the judge a friendly smile.

'Hang on a moment, Ken. You and I know there aren't any quick and easy solutions. We're facing the consequences of a government which has put the widest gap ever between the rich and poor, the haves and the have nots. A regime that thought money was the only thing worth having. We've got to start by understanding the nature of the problem. Let me tell you something interesting . . .'

'About young thugs?'

'About chimpanzees. The ones survive who can push a stick down a hole and bring up some nice juicy ants for dinner. It all depends on which particular jungle you're born in.'

'Hang on, Terry.' Kenny Iremonger's smile was merciless. 'I'm going to throw you open to the public. Just try putting on the headphones.'

*'I don't know why you're on about perfectly decent chimpanzees. I'd call this lot hyenas!' 'Six of the very best when I was at Rugby. Put me off buggery for the rest of my life!' 'I blame the Common Market. The teachers are powerless to hit back.' 'It's the parents that ought to be in prison. I hold the parents responsible.' 'No children allowed out on*

*the streets after six o'clock.' 'None of this would have happened if we hadn't gone all soft in the sixties. The only things today's teachers learnt at school was finger-painting and how to make a model kibbutz out of yoghurt pots. How do you expect the kids to have any respect?' 'Eight years old and of course they're capable of evil.' 'Police cautions? Don't make me laugh!' 'As I say, six of the very best and they'd have nothing left to smirk about.' 'You expect that sort of thing in Worsfield, but this was Hartscombe. In broad daylight!' 'Good morning, Terry. This is Colin Wythenshaw calling from Nunn's Courtny.' 'Good morning, Colin. And how are you?' 'Perfectly fine, thank you, Terry. And quite honestly, would you be saying the same thing if they'd raped your mother?'*

Listening to the phone-ins on the 'Breakfast Egg' in his office, Paul Fogarty called Clifford and made sure, for the fifth time, that Slippy Johnson had been safely in his cell at the time of the supermarket assault. And Agnes, warming her hands on a mug of black coffee, rejoiced because Terry had, against all odds, pointed out the route to Utopia.

Spirits were not high in Penry's office. An opinion poll had given Tim Willock an eight-point lead, and Des Nabbs was drafting a Private Member's Bill to ban fireworks.

At the weekend Kate and Terry went canvassing. Their little band of helpers knocked on doors, and when they met at the end of the street they were quieter than usual. The tide of hope on which Terry had launched his campaign had retreated, leaving him beached on the hard rock of the Hartscombe mugging. Doors which had once opened to him stayed shut, although inside 'Match of the Day' could be heard booming. When the doors were opened, reluctantly, they were held almost closed, to create a slim channel for voices at one with the phoners-in to the 'Breakfast Egg':

*'Heard you on the radio and I didn't agree with that at all.' 'Tim Willock. That's the one that's got my support.' 'Keep the little buggers marching. Make the little sods dig out deep holes and fill them in again.'*

'*Clever chap, that Kenny Iremonger. Got the better of you there, didn't he?*'

Des Nabbs joined them to announce, with gloomy satisfaction, that he'd been down all the streets between Queen Alexandra Road and Tow Path Lane and Terry's face had vanished from no fewer than thirty-nine windows. Tim Willock, framed in blue, seemed to have taken over the high street; only the Dust Jacket bookshop remained ostentatiously loyal to the cause.

Terry found support from where, perhaps, he least deserved it. 'In their hearts they know you're right,' Kate told him. 'Those kids know nothing better than a society that told them all you need for human happiness is a mortgage, two cars and a holiday on the Costa del Sol. If the Chairman's wife got mugged she should blame it on her ghastly government.'

'I don't think they mugged her for a holiday on the Costa del Sol.'

'Stick to the message. That's all you've got to do.' Kate was quietly impatient with what she thought was a moment of unnecessary doubt. 'Think of the committee meeting last night. They were rock solid behind you, Terry.'

He tried not to remember all fifteen members of the local Party crouched uncomfortably at children's desks in Skurfield school. The grey-haired couple who could hardly get a sentence out without mentioning Nye Bevan, the aloof lady who'd opened the gourmet cheese shop in Nunn's Courtny and sat shivering in her poncho, a young couple of house agents who'd heard that property boomed during the Harold Wilson era and were prepared to be on that happening again, the dedicated band of door-knockers and envelope-stuffers who were not particularly looking forward to another day at the front. Nabbs, addressing the meeting, had decided to guillotine all discussion. 'Some of you,' he rasped, 'may have seen a bit of rubbish in the form of a leading article in the *Sentinel* expressing criticism of our candidate's views on the treatment of juveniles. Some of you may have tuned in to the candidate's chat on the "Breakfast Egg".' Here the committee nodded, as Terry thought, gloomily. 'All I have to tell you is that the treatment of juveniles will be decided by a Labour government after the general election, which the Tories can't postpone much longer.' Here the couple who remembered Nye Bevan were seen to smile vigorously. 'I suggest we deal with this matter shortly. Will anyone who wishes to criticize the candidate at this stage please show in the usual way.'

Only one hand was raised, that of the cheese-shop owner who, in the accents of old Bloomsbury, suggested a law to make the provision of organically grown meals compulsory in the Youth Offenders' Institution, it having been demonstrated by science that an injection of pesticides and chemical additives into the food chain led, invariably, to an increase in crime. This suggestion having been ruled irrelevant and out of order, the motion standing in Nabbs' name was carried, he told the meeting, 'unanimous'.

Terry remembered these events, and that Penry had looked particularly cheerful. Was his agent, Terry worried, relieved because the awesome possibility of victory had vanished and life in the local Labour Party could return to its normal state of peaceful protest?

Now, having knocked on the last unsympathetic door, he was grateful to Kate for her invincible certainty. She was faithful to him, and he had been unfaithful to her, but that seemed, as they stood together at the end of a windy street, to be an event far from the steady progress of their lives. It had been a dream, a momentary diversion, a night out, a party he shouldn't have gone to, something she need never guess at, even if the worst was going to happen and they had to go back to London, back to S.C.R.A.P., and wait and hope for a more sympathetic seat than Hartscombe and Worsfield South. They had walked together to the last of a row of Victorian cottages, now bright with the neon sign of a fish and chip shop. They went in to buy supper and mingle with the natives and hoped to find someone who didn't listen to the radio and who might be inclined to vote Labour. So Terry, his confidence ebbing away, forgot the other woman who also had faith in him.

'What the hell,' Agnes asked herself, 'did I think I was up to?' She sat in the bookshop behind the window still decorated with the Labour candidate, vainly trying to read an interminable tale of espionage and sudden death. The elderly people of Hartscombe, whose lives were, on the whole, singularly uneventful, loved to lose themselves in a world of treachery, moles, double-crossing, scenes of sex and torture and unexplained bodies found floating in the canals of Amsterdam. She hadn't, had she, taken up with Terry simply because his wife had objected to her Gauloise? Had she, though? 'I'm allowed to smoke and I can also fuck your husband.' She tried this accusation, presented the arguments forcefully and acquitted herself. Unpredictable she might be, but not, thank God, trivial enough to have sex as a result of an argument about a cigarette.

But what was the song she'd heard on the car radio? 'Common People'. Was that about her, an ageing middle-class snob, the doctor's daughter, the famous novelist's ex-wife, sniffing around the town wanting to have sex with common people? Was the Labour candidate in the coming by-election her bit of rough trade? She made herself think about it seriously and wasn't convinced. To begin with the director of S.C.R.A.P., with his two-piece suits, and one, she had noticed, fashionably unstructured, was hardly rough trade, in spite of the factory-worker father, spoken of, perhaps too prominently, in his election leaflet. Besides which, you had, hadn't you, to be a stinking great snob to want to talk about 'common people'. Although she would admit to smoking too much and drinking, sometimes, without particular restraint, although she indulged in irrational dislikes, used to enjoy knocking things and had, no doubt, fucked around more than was called for, she refused, absolutely, to own up to being a snob.

She had been attracted to Terry, she told herself, because there was a sort of innocence about him, a kind of purity which had touched her when he first came into the bookshop and was confirmed, as far as she was concerned, by his fearlessly unpopular answers on the 'Breakfast Egg'. He had behaved like a man who knew he was right and didn't care what those with time on their hands to phone in thought about it. Was there something, she asked herself, about her beliefs which made her think politicians admirable only if they lost gallantly? She considered this charge and dismissed it also. One of the reasons she had taken to Terry was because he was determined to win, and she longed to cheer his victory when the returning officer read out the number of votes cast.

'But be honest' – Agnes could be fairly tough with herself – 'don't kid yourself, because at your time of life, it's not seemly.' From the moment she directed Terry's attention to the top shelf of old-style Socialist literature she had fancied him, she had to admit, something rotten. There had been times in her life when she had found herself, almost to her surprise, sleeping around, as they called it in the seventies. They were times when she was passionately in love, first with one Simcox brother and then with another. Those were years when sex was an everyday part of her life like breakfast, reading books, going to the movies and hunting, in the morning, for the last one in a packet of fags. Then came times during which, as her father would say of similar periods in his own life, she lay fallow. This restful activity was inappropriately interrupted by a farmer, a television presenter, a persuasive ear, nose and throat specialist from Worsfield and a barrister so self-regarding that she decided he needed no other company. For some time the man she loved most was a gay prison governor whose tastes and terms of employment cut him off from sex of any sort. She had wanted Terry and taken him to Tom Nowt's hut in order to put ideas into his head.

What about Kate then, the beautiful young wife she knew all about from the outset? Kate, she told herself, and she was perhaps prejudiced enough to find the answer convincing, was perfectly safe. Agnes was not daft enough, surely, to imagine that Terry would leave a wife for whose beauty he was envied for a woman who, given an early teenage pregnancy, might have been his mother. Anyway, he wasn't going to tell Kate. He was far too sensible to risk a row, a scandal, perhaps talk of a divorce before polling day. Kate was the candidate's wife, he would stand with his arm round her waist as they both raised their arms to acknowledge the cheers, and then she would be the Member's wife and never know anything of the suggestion made in the hut in the woods. And so the three of them would live on in safety and protection, two in knowledge and one in ignorance.

None of these comforting thoughts relieved her loneliness. Since the 'Breakfast Egg' broadcast Terry had fallen silent, was away somewhere else when she turned up for knocking on doors and seemed to be avoiding her.

If he were to lose, Terry was afraid, it wouldn't be the work of the Tories but through the efforts of children. Since the mugging of Lady Inwood they seemed to have cornered the news, squeezing the progress of a home counties by-election out of the daily papers. A twelve-year-old was said to have achieved his hundredth burglary, a raiding posse of children managed to strip a multiscreen cinema of a length of carpet, twelve seats and a machine for making popcorn, a fourteen-year-old boy fled to Bermuda with his supply teacher, a Citizens Advice Bureau in Leeds was set on fire, the tyres were removed from a school bus in Luton and sold to buy dope, a boy said to be helping the police with their inquiries was found to have hanged himself, the entire skeleton of a dinosaur was dismantled and removed by children from a museum in Huddersfield, and a twelve-year-old girl on a package tour got secretly married to a Turkish policeman. The children of England, it seemed, were desperate to prove Tim Willock right, and in order to do so had boarded the Tory bandwagon.

Terry had been to a Saturday antiques market in Hartscombe

town hall. The stall-holders, wearing scarves and bobble hats and mittens, crouched behind their stuffed birds and wispy antique dresses on coat hangers, their china statuettes and garden cherubs and trays of military buttons, barely returned his greetings. A notice at the door read 'Unaccompanied children not admitted.'

As soon as possible he had left the stall-keepers and the elderly customers picking over their dusty relics and was walking beside the river. Midday struck from the church clock, starting up a colony of rooks, floating like scraps of burnt paper on the wind from the bare trees on the opposite bank. In the distance, crossing the road, he made out the threatening figure of Des Nabbs, who was after him, no doubt, with the party line on No Increase in Taxes, for their evening's talk to the Chamber of Trade. As the polls descended, he feared, the old pro would claim increased power over him, and soon every word he uttered would be censored. To avoid his gloomy control and feeling, anyway, in serious need of a drink, he took refuge in the Water-Boatman and, having negotiated the dark staircase to the downstairs bar, was greeted with unexpected smiles, a warm handshake and a heartfelt, 'Thank you for talking sense to them at last!' from the Governor of the Skurfield Y.O.I.

Paul and Agnes were together in the downstairs bar. It was his day off and everyone had gone to the antiques market and deserted the bookshop. They were drinking rum and had ordered sandwiches. Agnes held up her face to Terry, and he kissed her cheek. He remembered the bedroom over the old surgery, the piles of books, the bottle of champagne on the floor, the cold sheets and the windows looking out on the river; the one sure success, he felt, of his election campaign so far. He was glad to be with friends.

Red-beef sandwiches came, and they ordered more rum and Simcox bitter. 'Bloody children!' Terry was almost ready to laugh. 'If only they'd co-operate and give us a chance to get into government.'

'I'm afraid,' Paul admitted, 'they're all little Tories at heart.

Great believers in private enterprise and the free-market economy. But thank you again for the "Breakfast Egg".'

'It wasn't a huge success with the audience,' Terry had to tell them. 'We're down nine points now in the *Sentinel* poll.'

'You don't mean you regret it?'

He knew he could give Anges only one answer unless he wanted the smile over the glass of Simcox to turn to what he feared might be merciless contempt. 'Of course not. It had to be said. I just hope . . . we can go on to other issues.'

'It had to be said.' Paul Fogarty was very hopeful. 'And when they think about it they'll know you're right. Boot camps are just an expensive way of turning out tougher villains. You get a much lower reoffending rate with some sort of treatment in the community . . .'

'You said it' – Agnes had little interest in the economy of boot camps and not, it must be said, detailed views about care in the community – 'because you have to. Because you've got the map with Utopia marked on it.'

However long and dangerous the journey, Paul was prepared to drink to Utopia. As they raised their glasses to this remote and inaccessible resort the door on to the landing stage opened and there, among the ducks who came squawking out of the icy river, a dark-haired girl in a padded jacket raised a camera, which flashed at them triumphantly.

'I'm June Wilbraham from the *Sentinel*,' she said. 'I saw you come in here. Lovely old bar, isn't it? I knew you wanted a picture.'

Terry remembered telling Penry that the Water-Boatman would provide a photo opportunity for him drinking with the voters. That seemed a very long time ago.

He supposed he should have expected it. On his way back to Party headquarters the phone bleated in his pocket. He stood outside Boots with the little instrument to his ear, and the voice which came rasping out of it seemed unusually amused.

'You really need help, don't you? There's still time. Just about.

Why don't you turn up around six? Rapstone Manor. Park at the back of the house and use the tradesman's entrance. No one'll notice you. Tell your gang you've got a date with the doctor. Nasty attack of foot in the mouth disease.'

# Chapter Eleven

'So, you fell for it! The Left's passion for defeat. So much more
comfortable, isn't it? Lie on your back and let them walk over you,
so long as you can complain eloquently of the terrible injustice of
the world.'

'I wasn't doing that.'

'What the hell did you think you were doing, then?'

'Saying what I honestly thought.'

'That is pure self-indulgence! A dangerous luxury which you
can only afford when you retire to write your memoirs. That's what
I'm doing.'

'Saying what you mean?'

'And doing what I want.'

'Which is . . .?'

'Trying, against all the odds, to get you back into the bloody
battle! Top up your dry little Socialist soul with a gallon or
two of fighting spirit. Do my best to cure your fear of success.
Sit over there, where I can see you. I shan't be offering you a
drink.'

Had Terry, in fact, come like a man driven to the doctor? Not
the regular G.P. who had shaken his head, not held out much hope
but advised him to stay at home and keep taking the tablets, but the
brilliant old sawbones who had, so the legend went, stretched
out the invalid England on the operating table, applied the knife
ruthlessly and produced a new, muscular, slimmed–down and ener-

getic entrepreneur. Or had he been out of his mind to answer the mobile's command?

What was he doing exactly, risking the admiration of Kate and Agnes, courting a vote of censure from the Worsfield Central Committee, a report to Walworth Road from Nabbs and the certain end to a once-promising political career? He could hardly be blamed for losing a safe Tory seat. There would be compensations. The love and sympathy of the two women. The party for the supporters: 'Thanks for all your tireless help and we damn nearly made it.' The sausage rolls and the real ale and 'The Red Flag' in its entirety, sung now with greater confidence in defeat. That wasn't what he had come to Hartscombe for; it was a party he never intended to be at. So he had told Penry that he wanted to go home early and get ready for the Barbarians' dinner. He had taken Nabbs' written orders for his after-dinner speech and driven down the lanes to Rapstone Manor feeling like a villain, hardened perhaps by boot camps, taking a get-away car to the scene of the crime.

It was dark when he drove round to the back of the house and parked among the trees. There was an area of rural mess, a wired-in chicken run, a broken-down Transit van, dustbins and a locked door. He knocked and waited impatiently, as though afraid of watchers in the bushes, and then he heard shuffling footsteps, the door opened a crack, and the pale face of an elderly woman was staring up at him, apparently finding it difficult to suppress laughter.

'His Lordship warned me you'd be coming,' she said. 'And I'm to bring you straight through.'

He noticed how little her dashing lipstick fitted her mouth, and then she led him down draughty passages, economically lit by forty-watt bulbs.

Titmuss said, 'The editor of the *Sentinel* got a picture of you, sharing a joke and a glass with the governor of Skurfield Young Offenders' Holiday Camp. He's not going to use it.'

'Really? Why not?'

'Because he phoned me for advice. And because he owes me

something. And because a picture of you cosying up to Fogarty would be just about handing the election over to Wee Willie Willock with a pound of tea.' His Lordship was lying, uncharacteristically, with his long legs stretched out on the study settee. He held, resting on his stomach, a dark glass of whisky with only a little soda, a drink he had mixed for himself when he denied one to Terry. He was wearing the trousers of a suit, a flannel shirt and the sort of cardigan seen on men in old peoples' homes. His shoes had been kicked off under his desk and a little circle of white toe was visible at the end of his sock, Mrs Ragg's care of him being sometimes more emotional than efficient.

Terry sat on an upright chair, underneath an overhead light which shone with a hundred-watt bulb, regardless of expense. 'You know I did a radio interview?'

'Of course I know you did a radio interview. That was a near-fatal accident. Now we've got to start patching you up. And it's going to take some pretty drastic surgery. You'd better consult me before you do any more dangerous chat shows.'

'Des Nabbs is advising me from now on. He says it's a Party directive.'

'If your Party takes Des Nabbs' advice it'll be out of office for another eighteen years. Labour politicians will be an endangered species, like the white whale, and your precious S.C.R.A.P.'ll be campaigning to save the last living Nabbs from extinction. We have to discuss what you're going to do next.'

'You mean, what I should say about youth crime?'

'Nothing.'

'What?'

'I don't think you should say anything. We can't send the little buggers up chimneys. Or deport them to the colonies. No one knows what the hell to do with them. So shut up on the subject. Everyone has ideas what not to do with them, however. So what I suggest is this . . . You ask a few questions. Rather publicly.'

Terry denied his new adviser the pleasure of being asked, 'What questions?' A silence followed, during which Titmuss emptied his glass, rose from the settee with only a little difficulty and padded across the room in his stockinged feet.

'I know it's become the practice among the damp New Right only to ask questions for ready money, but I'm giving you a few free of charge. Try this one on for size. 'Why is the Chairman of the Conservative Party so keen on easing the lot of Slippy Johnson?'

Terry looked up at the wandering politician, failing to understand.

'Is the Honourable Would-be-Member for Hartscombe inquiring as to the activities of a certain Slippy Johnson?' Titmuss was mocking.

'If you like.'

'Not if I like. The information is entirely for your benefit. The youth Johnson is part of an extended family of house-breakers, safe-openers and more-than-semi-skilled thieves. He has a string of convictions, the last being for extracting money from a row of allegedly impregnable slot-machines in the Fallowfield Park Amusement Centre. He still has six months to go at Skurfield, provided they manage to keep him there that long.'

'What's this boy Slippy . . .?'

'Slippy Johnson. Christened, I believe, Alan.'

'What's Alan Johnson got to do with the Chairman of the Tory Party? Tell me.'

'No.' Titmuss stood, his hands in his pockets, taking his time, apparently enjoying the obscure game he was playing. 'I'll tell you nothing. But I'll ask some further questions, which you may care to repeat. At convenient moments.'

Terry waited. The former favourite of his Party's one-time heroine was choosing his words with care.

'Try this. Slippy, at a tender age, is a habitual criminal. Police cautions, probation, community service, have proved as effective as a fire extinguisher filled with petrol. According to the penal theories of Wee Willie Willock, Slippy should be chained to a log, fed once a day on watered gruel and regularly birched. Instead of which, Willock's boss, the Party Chairman, has him out regularly and asks him only to help with a little light gardening. Why?'

'You want me to ask that?'

'Something to that effect. We'll use it. When the time is ripe.'

'Why, exactly?'

'It'll wrong-foot them. Stop them in their tracks. Make the punters wonder if they really mean what they say.'

'Will they wonder that about me?'

'Let's hope so. If they think you didn't mean the rubbish you talked on the "Breakfast Egg", that will be entirely to your advantage.'

Terry decided to let that go. Instead he asked, 'Are there any other questions?'

'One or two. We might leave them for later.'

'Such as?'

'The attack outside the supermarket. The police got a witness statement from a shopper who thought he heard one of the masked boys shout out, "Slippy". Yet Skurfield's records show Slippy Johnson wasn't at liberty at all that day. Are the records wrong? If so, what's the Chairman doing taking out a boy that mugs his wife?'

'We can't prove the records are wrong.' Terry had no desire to get Agnes's friend into further trouble.

'That remains to be seen. Further inquiries are being made.'

'You've talked to the police?'

'Of course I've talked to the police. What do you think I do here all day? Chess problems? *Petit point?* Breed orchids? Keep myself informed so I can provide you with questions. I hope you're grateful.'

'I understand,' Terry told him. 'I'm simply the instrument of your revenge.'

Titmuss did a surprisingly theatrical bow and bobbed up again, still smiling. 'That is the role,' he said, 'which you have the honour to perform.'

Terry nodded, clear about the arrangement. 'Anything else I ought to ask?'

'Some time. Perhaps. Yes.'

'What exactly?'

Titmuss moved away now and seemed to be intent on examining the photographs of himself with world leaders. He spoke casually, as though engaged in a conversation about the weather or the quickest route to Worsfield. 'Someone might remember the occasion when Millichip, the sitting M.P., was found drowned and was fished out of the water.'

'What about it?'

'That was an early morning when the Chairman had young Slippy out of the nick.'

'You're sure?'

'Perfectly sure. The police inquiries were commendably thorough.'

There was a further silence. Titmuss was dusting the silver frame round Ronald Reagan with a clean handkerchief. This was another area, it seemed, where Mrs Ragg failed in her duties.

Then Terry asked, 'So what's that supposed to mean?'

'Quite honestly I haven't the faintest idea.' Reagan was clean now, and propped back beside the Queen Mother. 'But somebody may have. The time might come when they ought to be asked.'

Was that all, Terry wondered. All the ammunition. He had no idea when to fire it, or at whom. But he felt he'd been let into some secret and trusted to carry out Titmuss's revenge. He remembered the Barbarians, slid back his cuff and tried to look at his watch without his informant noticing.

'So you're anxious to get away from me?' Titmuss had noticed.

'I just wondered, when I should leave. The Barbarians' dinner . . .'

'There'll be some there it'll be worth persuading. The editor of the *Sentinel*. Chief Constable. Bishop Roger. Chancellor of

Worsfield University. You could do yourself quite a lot of good this evening. You'll be dressed, of course.'

Was he to sit down with a naked Chief Constable and a Bishop with his kit off? Or did a point come, late in the evening, when these dignitaries stripped off and the closed circle of jobfinders for fellow Barbarians and funders of many children's charities pranced around in primeval woad, living up to their chosen title? 'What do you mean, exactly?'

'Penguin attire. The soup and fish. The Barbarians will want you in black tie plus all the trimmings. I remember well,' Titmuss shivered slightly as though the memory still caused him some discomfort, 'the first time I wore a soup and fish to a formal dinner at the Swan's Nest Hotel. I was then considerably younger than you.'

'I'm afraid I don't possess one.' Not to wear a dinner-jacket, even on S.C.R.A.P.'s most formal occasions, was an article of Socialist faith with Terry, and he had remained entirely true to it.

'The problem is solved. I got Formal Occasions in Worsfield to telephone your agent. He checked on your approximate height and size of collar. You'll find everything in your bedroom. I'm paying the rent. Please accept it as an anonymous contribution to your expenses. No need to tell Nabbs.'

'That's kind but . . .'

'No "but"'. Go in and woo them. Tonight's an excellent opportunity to launch the first question.'

'Which one's that?'

Titmuss stood a while in thought and came out with, 'Why does a so-called Conservative government, dedicated to be cracking down on crime, leave the vulnerable and criminally minded youth of the Skurfield Institution in the care of a homosexual?'

The air in the study seemed to have got suddenly colder. Terry got up and started for the door. 'I couldn't ask that.' He was thinking of Agnes. 'I couldn't ever ask that.'

'In that case,' Lord Titmuss said, 'I'm afraid I can't help you any further.'

# Chapter Twelve

'New Labour,' said Titmuss, 'new dicky-bow.' He said it with a broad smile because he, like all the other Barbarians, guests, honoured guests and fellow members, had resisted any temptation to put on the soup and fish and were dressed, with varying degrees of elegance, in lounge suits decorated only, in so far as Lord Titmuss was concerned, with the chain of office of Master Barbarian elect, the present Master Barbarian being Bishop Roger, famous for his consoling ecumenical approach to the issues of the day (fox-hunting, cigarette-advertising, boneless beef) on Radio Worsfield's 'Pause for Prayer'.

Terry, still flushed with anger and embarrassment, squirmed in a too-tight Formal Occasions dinner jacket which smelt of lighter fuel. The Barbarians' lady guests, wives and partners looked dressed for the Happy Hour on a first-class Caribbean cruise. Newly waved grey hair topped green and gold dresses, a good deal of costume jewellery and faces lightly tanned by winter breaks. Kate, wearing a red silk dress with a high collar buttoned to the neck as a tribute to the Third World, looked like an extremely beautiful Japanese waitress in a restaurant where she loathed and despised the customers.

Titmuss was now on his feet, introducing that evening's honoured guest and visiting speaker. 'I well remember when I wore my first dicky-bow at a Young Conservatives do at the Swan's Nest Hotel. It's going back a bit but Young Conservatives then were different from today. They were all old boy and public school and "I say, I think Jamie Thingummy's been sick in the bogs!" (Moderate laughter from all except Bishop Roger, who was creased up with amusement.) The sort of Champagne Charlies our late and greatest Leader wouldn't give the time of day to. Well, there was I, a young lad, a very junior clerk in Simcox Brewery, doing his best to pull himself up by his bootstraps. Thank God my bootstraps have been long enough and tough enough to yank me up to the Cabinet and the House of Lords (a number of Barbarians called out, 'Here, here!' and there was a fusillade of applause) and I'd never seen a tuxedo except in the films. Bing Crosby wore it in *High Society* at the Hartscombe Odeon. [*Soft and yearning murmurs of 'Oh, yes. Bing Crosby.'*] That was the nearest I ever got to a "soup and fish". And then what do you think the Old-School-Tie Brigade did to me? Only took exception to my formal wear. Only accused me of carrying about on my borrowed finery the smell of mothballs! [*Laughter.*] Oh, yes, fellow Barbarians, they were merciless concerning my dicky-bow. What was wrong with it? So far as I was concerned nothing was wrong with it. It was plain and simple. A black bow which clipped on to the collar. But that was wrong, you see, to those champagne oafs. Because they had the knowledge and the number of formal invitations, and the wealthy family backgrounds, to learn how to tie their own dicky-bows. No doubt some of those young lads learnt to tie their dicky-bows before they learnt to read! [*Loud laughter.*] Anyway, not to tie your own dicky-bow was something so disgraceful that I ended up ceremoniously dumped in the river. [*Cries of 'Shame!', and from the widow Millichip, 'Bastards!'*] And I would say this to you, Honoured Guests and fellow Barbarians. That experience did me nothing but good. [*Murmurs of 'No, whyever?' and 'Outrageous behaviour!'*] Because, and I say this to you, I was determined that, from then on, our great Conservative Party would be for us all! Those who couldn't tie their dicky-bows as well as those who could. And the most important members of our Party, fellow Barbarians and guests, are those for whom dressing for dinner just means asking the wife to iron a clean shirt! [*Loud applause.*]'

'Why are you going to wear it, just tell me why? That's all!' Kate had asked when he opened the box from Formal Occasions. 'You never do. You don't believe in it.'

'We've got an election to win,' he told her. 'Wherever we go we mustn't upset the audience. You took your shoes off when we went into the Worsfield mosque.'

'That was Third World,' she argued. 'That was part of their religion. These are just a collection of ghastly businessmen.'

'Ghastly businessmen have got votes. Anyway, it seems dinner-jackets are part of their religion.'

'Who told you that?'

'Oh, someone who knows.' Terry found cuff-links in a small, plastic envelope; they seemed to bear the crest of the local constabulary. 'I think he was on the committee.'

Now Titmuss was saying, 'That's quite enough about me. [*Negative noises from the diners, indicating that they would be quite prepared to hear his Lordship rattling on about himself for the rest of the evening.*] It's now my job to introduce our honoured guest and visiting speaker. [*Silence greeted this change of subject.*] Now I'm sure Mr Flitton will not mind my saying this, but the fact of the matter is, and he makes no secret of it: he is not a Conservative! [*Some laughter, in which Terry does not join.*] There may be moments of extreme emotion when he calls himself a Socialist, which I take to be an extinct sort of animal, exclusively Jurassic [*Applause.*], but whatever he calls himself, those of you who have had the privilege of sitting next to him at this excellent meal, or next to his good lady Denise [*This led to a whispered interlude with the Secretary, followed by*] Kate. Thank you for correcting me, Malcolm. His lovely wife Kate. We know our honoured guest is a thoroughly bright lad and very much the sort of bright lad I was when I first clipped on a dicky-bow and entered politics. [*Applause, during which several of the lady wives are seen to smile at Terry.*]'

'And may I end these remarks by saying this. Let me return to the subject of the dicky-bow. No doubt our honoured guest now feels, not to put too fine a point on it, a bit of a chump! [*Laughter.*] No doubt he thinks he's put his foot in it. No doubt he's shown his ignorance of the way we manage our affairs and the Barbarians' dress code on formal occasions. But I say this. What he has done shows his respect for our gathering! It shows he wishes to pay tribute to us and our wonderful work for charity. It shows, does it not, how much he honours us that he, who calls himself a Socialist, will put on a dicky-bow for our guest night? [*Murmurs of approval and further smiles at Terry.*] I ask you, fellow Barbarians, to greet young Terence Flitton with applause and listen to him with interest!'

'We won't do anything like that again. Promise me!'
    'I can't.'
    'You can't do anything like that again.' Kate was hopeful.
    'No. I can't promise we won't ever do anything like that.'
    'It was a complete nightmare!'
    'Did you think so? I thought it was rather useful.'
    Kate looked at her husband with bewilderment, as though he had just said something in a foreign language she didn't understand. The horrible hired costume had been thrown in the vague direction of the Formal Occasions box. Terry, stripped to his underpants, was setting the alarm clock. He had a look of contentment which she found treacherous.
    'Useful! They made a complete fool of you. Getting you to wear that ridiculous tuxedo!'
    'Not a complete fool. I thought Titmuss turned that quite nicely in my favour.'
    'Titmuss? If anyone had told me six months ago that I'd not only be in the same room as Leslie Titmuss but eat with him, drink with him, have him tell me what a lucky young chap you were and listen to him talking about President Reagan! If anyone had said

that was going to happen to me, I'd've thought they were certifiably insane!'

'Six months ago we weren't trying to win an election.'

'You think you can win it by eating dinner with Leslie Titmuss?'

'Titmuss is a superb politician.'

'Oh, yes!' Kate's voice rose to a chant of derision. 'He hates foreigners, gays, single mothers, social workers and the poor. He loves Mrs Thatcher, hanging, mandatory life sentences, global warming and ex-President Reagan. Is *that* what you call a superb politician?'

'It's the way he operates that you've got to admire. Forget the political beliefs.'

'Oh, well then. Yes. Marvellous! You can forget political beliefs, can you? Political beliefs don't matter *that* to you.' Here Kate moved to Terry to snap her fingers in his face. His smile remained imperturbable. 'It's just the game that counts, is it? The Titmuss game. Pulling the strings, conning the electors. Winning!'

'Winning matters most of all.'

'Without beliefs?'

'With beliefs. My beliefs. Not his. My beliefs and something of the Titmuss technique.'

'The Titmuss technique!' She turned away from him then and began to undo the long row of buttons on the front of the bright Japanese waitress dress. 'Quite honestly, you disgust me!'

'No,' Terry said, sure of himself. 'I don't disgust you at all.'

They slept together that night, stretched out like a crusader and his lovely wife; but they didn't make love.

'He's had to stop them.'

'What?'

'The Director of the Prison Service got on to Paul after what you said to that weird club. The Home Secretary wants all days out for work experience stopped. He's worried about the by-election.'

'That's ridiculous!'

'Of course it is. But that's what's happened.'

'What I said at that dinner was strictly off the record.'

'Someone told the papers.'

Terry said, 'I can't imagine who . . .' although of course he could.

Solemnly accusing, Agnes asked, 'Why did you have to do it?'

They were alone in the downstairs bar of the Water-Boatman. Outside the rain fell steadily, shining the streets and pimpling the river. His mood had risen since their last meeting, and his confidence had almost returned to its former level. His speech to the Barbarians had been greeted with unexpectedly prolonged applause. He had made a small joke about the soup and fish ('Almost as soon as I arrived I was given two orders for wine and asked the way to the Gents!') which was clearly considered sporting and granted more laughter than it deserved. He had made a careful selection of policies to whet the appetite of the Barbarians. Labour, he told them, was the particular friend of small businesses, but that didn't mean that big business wouldn't also be cherished. Taxes wouldn't rise, but money would be spent more efficiently. The preservation of the beautiful Hartscombe countryside, round which he had had the privilege to cycle in his university days (in fact Terry had been far too hectically engaged in student politics to mount a bicycle and meander down country lanes). And then, as planned, he came to crime, cracking down on it and its causes.

He had, he told them, said something about the causes when a guest on 'Breakfast Egg'. Some of his remarks had been, perhaps, wilfully misunderstood. Now he wanted to make it clear that he had no time for the do-gooders' approach. His tolerance for youth crime, he said, ('And I want to be perfectly frank with you about this') had sunk to zero. When they looked at such appalling incidents as the mugging of Lady Inwood they had to admit, had they not, that those involved, although young in years, were inherently wicked? ('Evil exists, and we mustn't be afraid to face up to it.') This brought a heartfelt round of applause from the Barbarians; only Bishop Roger seemed puzzled by the conception.

'Our hearts go out to Lady Inwood' – Terry, reaching the end of his speech, played out his trump – 'She has undergone a terrible ordeal. But there are, and I must say this to you (Terry borrowed a Titmuss phrase), questions to be asked about the conduct of that heroic lady's husband. The fact of the matter is this. These youths have been ordered into custody, for the safety of such innocent and elderly people as Lady Inwood. And custody, in my book, means lock and key. It means confinement in a safe and secure environment. It does not mean, as the Chairman of the Conservative Party seems to think, allowing young thugs to roam the countryside in order that they may weed his rose beds and sweep up his dead leaves. I am prepared to give this solemn commitment to the people of Hartscombe and Worsfield South. That sort of bending of the rules, that kind of bucking the system in the apparently noble cause of keeping Sir Gregory's garden tidy, would not be permitted under a Labour government. The word "prison", and I give you my word on this, is simply going to have to mean "prison".'

Sir Gregory had not been present at the dinner, nor was Lady Inwood; she had retreated to her sister's place in Marbella for rest and recuperation. But as soon as Terry started on the subject of Slippy's day out, the Barbarians were breathlessly attentive. Not a glass was raised, not a cigar was re-lit. Terry sat down in silence, until Lord Titmuss rose.

'Well, guests, honoured guests and fellow Barbarians. This young lad has certainly given us food for thought this evening. I think you'll all agree that he's made an important contribution, and I'd like you to recognize that in the usual manner.'

The applause which followed had exceeded, Titmuss later told him, in decibels, that accorded to Tim Willock or even the Minister for Agriculture. During the evening Terry had noticed a woman, sitting on the other side of Bishop Roger, to whom he hadn't been introduced. She was dressed more soberly than the wives and partners, wearing a jacket and trousers, with only one large piece of modern jewellery, a red heart with a blue border, pinned like a medal to her breast. Her face was long and pale, her hair dark, and she looked what Terry's mother would have called, derisively, 'well groomed'. During his speech he thought she was making notes on the back of a menu. During the applause she whispered something to the Bishop, got up and left, and Terry didn't seen her again for some time.

So he had survived the disapproval of Kate and her disgust at the Barbarians. He blamed her for failing, quite noticeably, to join in the applause at the end of his speech. The scene in their bedroom afterwards led him to distrust, almost for the first time, the narrow intensity of her politics. There were political ideals, and there was the art of winning elections, and Kate seemed quite unable to keep the two conceptions separate in her mind. Titmuss was skilled in the art of winning elections and whatever his bizarre reason for offering it, his help might lead Terry to victory. If he gave the voters an undiluted diet of Kate's views he was on the sure path to defeat. He remembered her flapping at the air in the Chinese restaurant and her objection to Agnes's Gauloise, which he now found intolerant, and almost excused his infidelity. He knew that if he were going to win he no longer had to please Kate. He thought more and more of Agnes and, forgetting the content of the triumphant speech, wished she'd been there to join in the applause.

There was a report of his speech, to his surprise, in the *Hartscombe Sentinel*. LABOUR CANDIDATE ACCUSES TORY CHAIRMAN OF SOFTNESS TO YOUNG OFFENDERS was repeated in the tabloids and was thought worth a short, on the whole flattering, editorial paragraph in the *Daily Fortress*. When he rang Agnes at the bookshop and suggested a meeting she sounded aloof and unenthusiastic. Finally she agreed to a drink in the Water-Boatman.

When he got there he found that she was as hard on him as Kate, asking him, clearly without sympathy or understanding, 'Why did you have to do it?'

'I'm sure you've noticed' – feeling attacked, he took refuge in disappointed anger – 'I'm fighting an election.'

'Does that mean you have to say the opposite of what you believe?'

'It means I've got to win.'

'At all costs?' She was looking at him, a wide-eyed stare, as daunting as a bright lamp on the desk of a police interrogator.

'You want us to treat youth offenders properly. You want us to keep them out of prison. You want Paul to run Skurfield as a part of the health service and not as a penal colony? You want boys to come out cured? Do you want all that seriously?' he asked her.

'You know I do.' It was, it seemed to her, an unnecessary question.

'The only way that's going to happen is for me to win Hartscombe. And to win it again for a Labour government in the General Election. That's the only way. Power.'

'And tell all sorts of lies to get it?'

'I said what you wanted on the radio and Willock got his biggest lead in the polls. Anyway, I'm not telling lies.'

'You're saying what you don't believe.'

'There are two sides to every question.'

'Are there?'

'I was simply emphasizing the side that's going to get us elected.'

'You mean, deceiving the voters?'

'You know damn well, Agnes, that if we asked the voters tomorrow, they'd have the boys who mugged the Chairman's wife hung, drawn and quartered. You know they're not going to vote for the Paul Fogarty treatment. But they can be persuaded to vote for someone who'll make Paul's dream come true. If I don't shock them before polling day. We've got to live in the real bloody world!' His words may have sounded angry, but he spoke them softly, smiling and looking, Agnes had to admit, exceptionally fuckable. 'If we want all we've dreamt about, all that's in the books on your top shelf, we've got to get the crosses against T. Flitton, Labour. There's no other way of doing it.'

'Is that what you think?' She was prepared to consider it.

'It's what I know.'

'It's a horrible business.' She gave a small shiver.

'I don't know. I'm quite enjoying it.'

'That's what I was afraid of.'

'And we've wrong-footed the Tories.'

'Then I suppose you think I ought to congratulate you.' She was still not persuaded.

'Not necessary,' he told her. 'Just have a bit of patience. Have a little faith. Shut your eyes and hold on tight. You can open them to see the size of my majority.'

'And until then?'

'I've got nothing till 3.30 in the sixth-form college. It's only a short walk to your bedroom.'

She took a gulp of Simcox and seemed to consider it. 'I don't think so. Not yet, anyway.'

'Then we'll do something together. Something you'd enjoy.'

'What like?'

'Go for another ride?' He thought it would please her.

She considered it; put down her beer mug and said, 'All right. I'll ring Betty Wellover.'

So she did, and the next stage of Terry's campaign degenerated into farce.

# Chapter Thirteen

Leslie Titmuss heard the sound of dogs barking, the jangle and stamp of waiting horses. Leaving the memoirs, on which he had been working since dawn, he went to his study window, tightened and retied the monkish cord of his hairy dressing-gown and looked down on the grand sweep in front of Rapstone Manor.

What he saw was a ceremony that had been going on since long before he, or the oldest local inhabitant could remember. It had certainly been in practice when the restored Charles II rewarded the royalist Fanners with their baronetcy. It was alive in the Regency when the profligate gambler, Sir Lorenzo Fanner, took his friends and drinking companions hunting in night-gowns, with lanterns swinging from their saddles, to kill by candlelight. It had long preceded Leslie's late father-in-law, one-time Conservative Party Chairman, Sir Nicholas Fanner, who enjoyed the meet and gave hunters an effusive welcome with mulled wine, port, brandy and slices of pork pie. When the Manor was taken over by a rabbit farm it had been suspended, but Titmuss had revived it. Perhaps it appealed to his strange and sardonic sense of humour. He had got hold of the big house, the seat of the Fanners, the Lordship of the Manor. He, the runaround from the brewery, was Lord Titmuss of Skurfield in the Peerage of England, with a coat of arms to go with it. Why shouldn't his driveway be the meeting place for the Hartscombe Hunt?

The Hartscombe wasn't the smartest of hunts, and wasn't

mentioned in the same breath as the Heythrop, the Belvoir or the Quorn. Indeed, the poshest hunters said that if you hunted as far south as Hartscombe you should keep quiet about it. The most elegant followers that morning, those sticklers for etiquette who wore pink coats and top hats, were a garage manager from Worsfield, the proprietor of Pooh Corner garden centre and the owner of a string of Thames Valley hairdressing salons. Although it might be thought of as down-market by the blue-blooded fox chasers to the north, the Hartscombe meet was an exciting occasion for all concerned, particularly for the antis, the hunt saboteurs, who had parked their vans at the end of Titmuss's drive and were consuming the packed meal provided for them by P.A.L.S. (the Pro-Animal-Life Society), sometimes leaving their vans to shout 'Murderers!' at the girls from the pony club or, more daringly, to stub out their cigarettes on the rumps of horses who had, presumably, defected from the animal world and gone over to the enemy. Excitement was rising in both camps at the prospect of the great pursuit, when the hunt would chase the fox, the saboteurs would chase the hunters, and a good time would be had by all.

By all except the fox? Leslie Titmuss considered the question because it might soon have to be debated in the House of Lords, and he decided that it held little interest for him. He had grown up in a home without pets. When he was a child the sight of animals had often alarmed him, and their habits disgusted him. So far as he was concerned, how foxes lived or died was hardly a fit subject for political debate. Little as he liked foxes, he was quite sure he detested fox-hunters. It was not their killing animals he objected to but their devotion to dumb creatures. They surrounded themselves with horses, dogs, sheep, cows and poultry. They spent fortunes on vets to treat their neurotic hunters and wept when their dogs had to be put down. He regarded them, even the top-hatted garagiste, the garden-centre proprietor and the owner of the Snippers chain, as old-style Tories, nostalgic for a rural past, aping the ways of that patronizing, paternalistic squirearchy Mrs Thatcher had put out to grass. He felt all that, and yet he allowed the Hartscombe Hunt to assemble in front of his house; because, after all, he was Lord Titmuss, and that was the sort of thing they expected from a Lord.

A pony, touched by a burning fag, reared and a girl with a pony-tail and a black riding hat was thrown into the rhododendrons. A saboteur was chased back to his van by a middle-aged woman on what seemed to Titmuss a gigantic horse. What did his Lordship think about sabs? They were anarchists, of course, and anarchy couldn't be tolerated unless it was cunningly disguised and introduced as part of a free-market economy. The sabs were lawless, irresponsible and should be cracked down on like other protesters, mercenaries and rent-a-riot hooligans. And yet he couldn't resist a sneaking sympathy for the sabs. They were engaged in the great cause to which he had devoted his youth, getting up the noses of the toffs and organizing the defeat of those who had criticized his dicky-bow.

The number of hunters was increasing steadily, with women and teenaged girls, farmers, market gardeners and a long-distance lorry driver with money to spare for hunting. The cries of 'Murderers!' grew louder and were also directed at the foot followers, grey-haired couples with rucksacks and walking-sticks, an athletic London vicar and a party of enthusiasts from the Women's Institute.

Nobby Noakes, a small wizened man who rode with his legs stuck out on either side of his horse as though he had dropped in from the sky doing the splits, edged his mount towards that of the brick-complexioned Betty Wellover. He was a dealer in garden furniture, wattle fencing, children's ponies and other things well-off townies feel the need to acquire when they emigrate to the country; and he was so old that he could remember the Rapstone cottages when they were the homes of woodmen and farm labourers. He now solicited Mrs Wellover in a metaphor taken from country sports. 'I say, Betty,' he said. 'Any chance of a gun in your shoot?'

She looked him over and turned him down. 'Sorry, Nobby. I'm fully syndicated at the moment.'

Now, as the number of horses increased, the car followers arrived, old boys from the woods in damaged Fords and dented pick-up trucks who poached, dealt in firewood and scraped a rural living. They were outnumbered by couples in tweed hats, with brandy flasks and dogs in the back of their Saabs and Volvos. Binoculars swung from their necks, and they would do their best to watch the hunt from the roadside. Their presence puzzled the antis, who weren't sure if they were hunt supporters or prosperous members of P.A.L.S., so they didn't shout 'Murderers!' at them but 'Come to watch the slaughter of the innocent, have you, mate?' or suchlike non-committal questions.

The owner of the Pooh Corner garden centre, a business which made a fortune out of those new arrivals in the countryside who like to buy their plants ready-made, was surprised to see Lord Titmuss on the ground below him, offering up a glass of mulled wine and a small segment of pork pie. The legendary politician was wearing an aged car-coat with scuffed leather and a yellowing collar, a tweed cap, shapeless grey flannel trousers and bedroom slippers. The owner of Pooh Corner said, 'Thank you, my Lord,' and, in some confusion, stuffed his mouth with pork pie. The truth of the matter was that Titmuss had been counting the number of the hunt followers and, looking at them simply as crosses on voting papers, thought it might be as well to have them on his side, whatever that side might turn out to be. Ten minutes later the door of a sab's van slid open, and a gaunt face, under the shadow of a tweed cap, looked in offering wine and pie. Titmuss had also seen the growing number of antis as crosses on slips of paper.

Politics were suspended as Blanche 'Blanchie' Evergreen, the Field Master, or Mistress, moved off with a white wave of dogs' backs and wagging tails. The whipper-in and the huntsman shouted and the whole disparate regiment, half cavalry, half motorized transport in various degrees of disrepair, set off for battle, leaving

Lord Titmuss on the driveway of his country seat, chewing a slice of his own pork pie. He heard the accelerators pressed, the grinding of gears, the blasted horns and shouts of the sabs and the regular beat of hooves as the horses broke into a canter. Then the sounds died away in the distance, and nothing was left but the wind in the trees and the distant hum of the motorway.

There was the scent of a fox, which excited the hounds almost beyond endurance, as they came down towards Hookers Spinney; but they followed the scent on a long detour around the trees while the fox, whom they hadn't noticed, escaped across a patch of scrub and darted, missing death by inches, across the motorway. For a long while the hunt was frustrated, but the hounds found a scent again after the long wet grass in Plashy Bottom, and the riders gathered speed up the bridle path to Eyles's farm. The hounds were running fast across the high open common at Nunn's Courtny, and the horses were at a full gallop. Sabs' vans and the cars of the tweed-hatted supporters speeded up the narrow road which bisected the common, and faces, from old Nobby Noakes and weather-beaten Betty Wellover to the youngest pony club girl, were blushed by the wind. And then Blanche, the Field Master, rose in her stirrups and yelled a warning. She had seen a couple of riders, a woman with a straight back smoking a cigarette and a man in jeans and a sweater, ambling across the common in front of the stampede.

Agnes turned her head, kicked her horse and cantered out of the path of the attack. Terry tried kicking also, but Balaclava stood stock-still, trembling like a gigantic leaf, his nostrils dilated and his eyes rolling, awaiting the command for a fatal charge. Then he tossed his head and uttered a ghastly whinny, a sound like the trumpet of death. At which moment, the dogs broke like surf about his hooves. Terry saw men with whips and red coats, a woman on a huge horse yelling at him, words of abuse he couldn't hear above the horses, the baying of the hounds and the thudding of hooves.

Now, Balaclava galloping along at full stretch, and Terry, gripping the horse's mane, pale in the face and white in the knuckles, were up with the leaders in headlong pursuit of a kill.

Months later he lay awake at night re-living the nightmare that followed. He was deafened by the noise, above which he could hear furious voices ordering him to get the hell back, a command which he had no means of persuading Balaclava to obey. He was conscious of tearing up farm tracks, between hedges where branches whipped his face, and through great puddles from which the horses' hooves threw up mud which plastered his face and momentarily blinded him. They thundered through woods, and he had to lie, as though in some horrible embrace, along Balaclava's neck to avoid being swept to the ground, or perhaps decapitated, by low branches. He charged, at breakneck speed, along paths at the edge of ploughed fields and across pasture in which the cows lolloped away in fear.

Then he saw a towering hedge rushing towards him, blocking out the low-hanging sun. Riders around him sailed into the air, sending back a cloud of twigs and leaves. For a moment Terry was sure that Balaclava was about to take off, to aim his cumbersome weight at the sky and deposit Terry, a bag of broken bones, on the other side. But the riding-school horse was not so ambitious. He twisted towards a gap, his hooves struck a cattle grid, a fatal trap all animals are meant to avoid and, by some miracle, wasn't caught and lamed in its iron rungs. With a resonant clang horse and rider were over and in the forefront of the charge up another green field towards the distant shadow of a wood. Far ahead, now the last of the sunlight had returned, he could see a small shadow moving quickly; a fox running towards the trees. He closed his eyes and gripped the mane harder than ever, not knowing what would happen next and whether he would fall into the racing, baying pack of hounds.

What happened was that Balaclava stopped and Terry fell, once again, on to his horse's neck. He opened his eyes and saw other horses standing round a group of hounds, who were consuming a dead fox. The sabs had left their vans and were busy photographing what might appear to be dogs rending apart a living animal. None of this was seen by Terry, who was dazed, mud-spattered, blinking and no longer able to exercise any control over Balaclava, as the horse moved in a lurching walk towards the devouring hounds. There was a flash, and he saw, leaning against a sab van and pointing a camera directly at him, none other than June Wilbraham, reporter, photographer and general run-around for the *Sentinel*. A moment later Agnes, riding up to him, grabbed Balaclava's reins and led him away. She was laughing so much that she was barely able to control the two horses.

Later he was lying in the bath in her house by the river, soaking off the mud and the aching of his limbs and feeling that his arms might, just possibly, settle back into their sockets. He saw her standing naked beside him, still laughing, until she joined him and crouched between his legs in the soapy water. He had never felt fear and love so intensely, over so short a period and, for a while at least, he forgot the election.

# Chapter Fourteen

### LABOUR CANDIDATE IN AT THE KILL

Greatly to the surprise of members of the Harts-combe Hunt, Terry Flitton joined them for a day out yesterday. Scorning the traditional hunt uniform, Labour man Flitton turned out in a sweater and jeans, but he was, old hunting hands say, a fearless rider and was up with the leaders when they killed near Hanging Wood. The informality of his dress surprised those who had seen him turn out in black tie at a recent Barbarians dinner. He left the field immediately after the kill and Field Master Blanche Evergreen was unable to say if he was applying for hunt membership. 'We haven't yet seen his payment for today's outing,' she told the *Sentinel*'s June Wilbraham.

Neither Terry Flitton nor Labour Party head-quarters were prepared to comment last night, although a statement is expected shortly. Tim Willock said he disapproved of blood sports and would, when elected, be one of the Conservatives who wished to see hunting with dogs made a criminal offence. 'Flitton's tally-ho attitude,' Willock said, 'will horrify his Labour supporters.'

It so happened that the *Sentinel* came out the day after the hunt, and the front page had been remade to include a photograph, spread over four columns, of Terry, mounted and muddy, wearing a borrowed riding hat and staring down at a pack of hounds making a meal of a fox. He had no doubt that the story would be picked up and the picture reproduced in every one of the nation's newspapers.

By the time Kate got back from London on the day of the hunt he was bathed, changed and well aware of the difficult time ahead. He laid the table and prepared to cook spaghetti. When she arrived he poured her a drink and told her the whole story. To do this he had to confess that he had taken to riding out with Agnes Simcox, a piece of information he had postponed passing on to her, but naturally he omitted such post-equestrian scenes as that which had recently taken place in Agnes's bathroom.

'You mean, you sat there and watched while the dogs ate an animal?' Kate was more worried about the fox than about Agnes.

'Quite honestly, darling. There was very little I could do about it.'

'You didn't protest? You didn't shout at those murdering bastards?'

'You mean the dogs, or the people?'

'Both!' Her voice rose in anger. 'Of course I mean *both*!'

'The fact of the matter was' – he did his best to explain – 'all the breath had been knocked out of me. I'd been dicing with death.'

'*You'd* been dicing with death? What about the bloody fox?' At which Terry's wife burst into tears. She scorned both spaghetti and wine and remained speechless until she went to bed and lay, in danger of falling out, as far from her husband as possible.

Terry slept fitfully, drifting into total oblivion only around dawn.

When he woke up at nine Kate had gone, leaving him a note telling him that she was staying in London until she'd got over the shock and worked out how she should respond to what he had told her. She needed her own space, she said, and she particularly asked that he shouldn't try and phone her or contact her in any way until she'd cleared her head.

While he was reading this the telephone rang and the voice of Nabbs, querulously gloomy, asked him what sort of joker he thought he was and said that he'd brought not only his campaign but the entire Labour Party into hatred, ridicule and contempt. Walworth Road would be down on him like a ton of bricks, and if he thought he'd ever live to fight again he had another think coming. It was the predictable result of selecting so-called intellectuals from the universities instead of men like Nabbs, who represented the decent, ordinary Labour Party supporter in the street. He'd better issue a press statement at once and denounce the barbaric spectacle which he'd been forced to attend.

'Forced? What do you mean, "forced"?'

'I don't know. You tell me why you were stuck up there on a horse like a bleeding toff.'

'I'll think about what I'm going to say.' Terry tried to respond with dignity.

'Think quick, or I'll have to think for you.'

'If you issue a statement which I haven't approved of I'll disassociate myself from it at once.'

'Suits me if you disassociate yourself from the entire campaign.'

'You know perfectly well I won't do that. I'm going to go on, and I'm going to win. I'll think about my press statement. Call you later.' And he put down the phone. To be fair to Terry, he meant what he said. His determination to win was as strong as ever. This momentary set-back would be overcome, but he was in need of advice.

\*

'You want to appear a complete bloody idiot?'

'I suppose that's the truth of the matter.'

'You're a man who goes out on a horse he can't control, gets swept along by a crowd of people he's never met and finds himself making a clear political gesture in favour of a highly controversial cause with which he doesn't agree. Hardly the sort of clown the good people of Hartscombe might choose to represent them.'

'I suppose it could be made to look like that.'

'That's exactly how you're going to make it look if you tell that story.'

'It happens to be true.'

'That,' Lord Titmuss said, 'is clearly what's wrong with it.' He laughed in a way which reminded Terry, uncomfortably, of the laughter of Agnes. Titmuss the adviser, the final arbiter of the Labour candidate's reaction to this bizarre turn of events, had, strangely enough, suggested a meeting in Rapstone church. The occasion was so momentous, perhaps he had thought, the decision so vital, that no other rendezvous would be suitable. In fact he wanted to make sure no one knew they were together before the press statement and had forbidden Terry even the back door of the Manor. 'Rapstone church is always open for private prayer,' he'd said on the telephone, 'but no one prays privately any more. Shall we say ten o'clock?'

When Terry arrived he had seen, in the subdued light, the back of Titmuss's head, with the bald patch gleaming like a tonsure. He was sitting alone in a pew, reading the *Daily Telegraph*. He was wearing his leather car-coat as it seemed that the church heating wasn't turned on for the comfort of private prayers. So now they sat beside the tombs of the Civil War Fanners whose kneeling children were equally divided in the King's or Parliament's uniform to ensure the survival of the family whichever side won, and Sir Lorenzo Fanner, who drowned in the river at Hartscombe during the Regency, being transported to heaven, wearing boating costume, by marble cherubs and a weeping angel.

'This hunting business,' Titmuss said, 'is extraordinarily tricky. The British *may* be won over to the common currency. They might agree to an independent Yorkshire. They'll put up with the withdrawal of child support and exorbitant charges for false teeth. But they'll never change their minds about fox-hunting. They're either passionately for it, or passionately against it, or they passionately don't give a damn. I belong to the third small and happy group.'

'Willock's declared himself against it.'

'At least that's a powerful argument in its favour.'

'You mean you want me to come out *for* hunting?'

Terry stared bleakly into the future and saw his marriage split apart on the rocks and sinking rapidly. In spite of his growing love for Agnes, the thought filled him with dismay. This was not a moment in his career to start discussing divorce.

'You needn't necessarily come out for it. And certainly not yet.' Titmuss cheered him up a little.

'What's that mean exactly?'

'That there is only one way to deal with this tricky and deeply felt issue.'

'What's that?'

'A full inquiry. An informed debate.'

'So what was I doing?'

'Collecting the evidence, of course. The hard way. Taking part in the experience. So that you could speak on the subject with authority.'

'You mean, I *intended* to join in the hunt?' Such an explanation had never occured to Terry.

'Of course you did. I mean, you're not a complete nincompoop, are you?'

'A few minutes ago you thought I was.'

'Time's passed. Your prayers have been answered, and you have become intelligent enough to deserve my help. For the time being.'

'So the press statement will say I was carrying out a carefully prepared programme of research into the hunting question?'

'You've got it!'

Terry thought it over. 'The Labour loyalists won't like it one little bit.'

'They'll put up with it. It doesn't commit you to anything. And they're going to vote for you anyway. And as for the Conservative pro-hunters. . .'

'What about them?'

'There're quite a lot of them, judging by the crowd in my drive yesterday. I imagine they're fairly pissed off with Wee Willie Willock's anti attitude. There might be quite a few votes worth catching.'

'From blood-sporting Tories?'

'Why ever not? Their crosses on ballot papers are worth just as much as hunt saboteurs'.'

Terry was silent, thinking it over. The church chill seemed to be eating into his bones. He saw, as usual, some sense in the Titmuss approach. But there was a difficulty.

'I told Kate it was entirely accidental.'

'Who's Kate?'

'My wife.'

'Then she'll support you whatever you choose to say about it.'

'I'm not too sure about that.'

'Then you'll have to deal with her.' Titmuss was clearly drawing a line. For all his political mastery, he had never enjoyed a similar success with women. 'I can manage your election campaign. But you'll have to deal with your wife. You'd better start now.'

On his way out Terry saw the vicar, a small, round-faced man in a thick sweater and a glimpse, almost an apology for a dog-collar, busy, for some reason, among the graves.

'I'm grateful to you,' he said. 'So few people take advantage of our open-church policy for the purpose of private prayer.' And, looking round nervously, as though afraid of being overheard by God, he added, 'You can be certain of my vote.'

'I realize that the fox-hunting issue rouses strong and sincere feelings on either side. I am determined to research the question thoroughly before I come to a settled view and decide on political action. For that reason I decided to follow the hunt when I was out riding, and the experience has been of enormous value to me in forming an opinion,' Labour candidate Terry Flitton told the *Sentinel*'s June Wilbraham. 'I'm having further talks with members of the Hartscombe Hunt and with those who view hunting with dogs as morally repugnant. There is much more to be learnt from both sides, and I regret that my Conservative opponent has come to a premature conclusion without, so far as I am aware, ever having ridden to hounds.

'I have been asked why I didn't intervene to save the fox once it had been caught. The Hunt Master had told me that the fox is killed instantly by the lead dog. To stop the rest of the pack eating it when dead could be achieved only by violence and cruelty to dogs. I am determined to investigate this further, and I will come to no conclusion until both sides have had a further opportunity of putting their case.'

'So you see,' Terry telephoned Kate to say, 'I've left the way open for a ban on fox-hunting.'

'That's not how you said it happened at all.'

'That's how I'm saying it happened now.'

'But *why*?'

'So I can have a bit of credibility with the voters. So they'll elect me to do all the things you want.'

'Like stopping blood sports?'

'Of course! In the fullness of time.'

'How full does the time have to be?'

'I suppose, when we get into power.'

'You mean, postponed indefinitely?'

'We can't do anything until we get into government, Kate. You understand politics as well as anyone. We want exactly the same things. You know that.'

'I suppose so,' she had to admit.

'Come back, Kate.' His voice became soft and pleading. 'I can't manage here without you. You know that.'

'You seemed to manage to go riding with Agnes Simcox without me. You could go on lots more disastrous rides.'

'I don't think I'll ever go riding with her again. Come back, Kate. Come back this evening. We'll eat out. At the Chinese restaurant.'

'Will *she* be there? Smoking?'

'I'm sure she won't. If she is, we'll go to the Thai Kitchen. Say you'll come!'

'I'll think about it,' Kate said. 'I'll consider all the evidence.' Then she rang off, leaving him not entirely dissatisfied.

'It's absolutely hilarious!' Agnes had put down the *Sentinel* after reading the column.

'It seemed a sensible way of explaining it.'

'It's an absolutely ridiculous way of explaining it.' She was laughing at him, not without affection. 'Your horse bolts with you clinging on to its mane for dear life and what you're doing is carrying out careful and open-minded research into animal welfare. You must see how wonderfully comic it makes you look.'

'To you, perhaps. Not to the average voter.'

'Thank you.'

'What for?'

'For saying I'm not the average voter.' They were in the bookshop, in an alcove reserved for contemporary fiction. There were no customers about, and she kissed him. He had his arms round her as he said, 'I know you're in favour of fox-hunting.'

She broke away from him, searched on her desk for her packet of cigarettes. 'My father the doctor was neither a criminal nor a sadist. He went hunting because he enjoyed it and could find nothing immoral about it. It provided him, he thought, with an easy death. He said we're all animals, the foxes and us. Hunting is a natural instinct. Like sex. I don't do it much now. I'm afraid of the jumps. Hunting, I mean, not sex.'

'But you'd want to save hunting. You wouldn't want it made a crime . . . like mugging Lady Inwood?'

'Of course I wouldn't.' She lit her cigarette, about, he thought, to lose interest in the subject. But he kept to it.

'By saying all that, I've kept the confidence of the electors. When the time comes I can try to keep what your father enjoyed.'

'By telling a load of lies, you mean?'

'By winning the election.'

She looked at him through a haze of smoke. 'You really are very funny indeed,' she said fondly. 'Is Kate still away?'

'For the moment,' he told her. 'Yes.'

'We could meet this evening?'

'Damn! I'm busy.'

'Something exciting?'

'Boring. My agent . . .'

'Oh, well,' she said. 'Some other time.'

Kate came back from London, and she and Terry had dinner in the Magic Magnolia, untroubled by Agnes's cigarettes. They talked with restraint, about things that didn't matter, as though they had just met and had not been married at all.

As they spread their pancakes with plum sauce and fragments of duck, Terry told Charlie, the Chinese waiter, that the Labour Party would take immediate steps to improve the lot of those, often underpaid and overworked, toilers in the catering industry and gave him a copy of his election pamphlet. Charlie smiled, nodded and, in return, showed Terry a photograph, in colour, of his sister in Hong Kong. But the questions of fox-hunting, and Terry's relationship with Kate and Agnes, were solved for the time being.

# Chapter Fifteen

'We particularly regret the fact that the Home Secretary cancelled the Work Experience Programme.'

'The Home Secretary did that, did he?'

'Through the prison service, of course.'

'Through the prison service, naturally. That must have been disappointing for you. After all the work you've put into it.'

'It gave the boys a sense of purpose and a little self-respect. For a day or two they could think of themselves as gardeners and not criminals. I looked on it as an important step on the road to reform.'

'Nothing like work to keep you on the straight and narrow. I had to work my way up every step of the ladder, which is more than you can say for some of our present masters. Those that sail into government from Eton and Oxford and think they can understand a young lad on a housing estate who's got no hope of a job and whose only way of a decent income is through the sale of crack cocaine.'

Paul Fogarty looked at his guest in astonishment. Had he gone senile or had the man sitting opposite him, after a lifetime recommending penal reform by way of the birch and the rope suddenly, like Lear passing to sunlight through madness, arrived at a plane of sanity? He said, 'I'm very grateful to you for saying that.'

'And I may say it again. In a few influential quarters.'

They were having lunch, dubious meat pie, lumpy mash, soggy peas and a packet of digestive biscuits, served on bright blue plates, with plastic knives and forks, washed down with water in large mugs. It was Paul's habit to invite important people in the neighbourhood to share the inmates' lunch at a table in the corner of the Skurfield canteen. Judges, doctors, magistrates, headmasters, university lecturers and editors of local newspapers had, he discovered, not the remotest idea of what life in a youth offenders' centre was like, and this ignorance was particularly noticeable in judges who, in certain particularly hard cases, seemed to think it beneath their dignity to enquire into the fate of those they found guilty and sentenced. Such matters, they clearly thought, were best left to civil servants and those who carried on the humble profession of prison governor.

Although Sir Gregory Inwood had accepted his invitation and taken a kindly interest in the place, Paul had never felt that there was the slightest point in inviting Lord Titmuss, whose views on crime and criminals were well known from dozens of speeches at Party conferences. But, to his surprise, Titmuss had rung up, solicited an invitation and was apparently in full sympathy with Paul's theory that crime was an illness to be cured rather than a sin to be punished with all possible severity in order to satisfy a public thirst for revenge.

'I can understand' – Paul didn't want to push his luck with his unexpected Lordship too far – 'the public revulsion when Lady Inwood was mugged . . .'

'A bit exaggerated, don't you think?' Titmuss's capacity to surprise seemed inexhaustible. 'Dorothy Inwood's a pretty tough old boot, and it'll've given her a story to bore them all with on the Costa Geriatrica. Of course, it's unfortunate that someone heard a call of "Slippy", and that Slippy Johnson was a boy who'd had a day out at the invitation of her husband.'

'You're remarkably well informed.'

'I regard keeping myself informed as a retirement occupation. I play no golf.'

'Of course, Slippy had nothing whatever to do with the mugging.'

'You're sure of that?'

'Absolutely sure.'

'You didn't see him here yourself?'

'No. My chief prison officer tells me Slippy was locked in his cell at the time of the attack.'

'You can trust him?'

'Clifford isn't exactly Elizabeth Fry, but he's totally reliable. But that's not the whole story.'

'What's the whole story then? I'd be interested to know.' Titmuss pushed away his prisoner's meal half-eaten, while the governor took a brief rest from the lumpy mash to say, 'Slippy's got a trade. He learnt it from his father, 'Peters' Johnson. Neither father nor son have one incident of violence in their records. They'd regard mugging as beneath their dignity. Slippy robs by picking locks, delicately opening car doors, cunningly extracting coins from apparently impregnable machines. It wouldn't occur to him to steal by knocking down old ladies.'

Titmuss was silent. Then he took a tube of peppermints from his waistcoat pocket and put one into his mouth, no doubt to banish the taste of the lunch. He asked, 'When Sir Gregory wanted a boy out for gardening duty, did he mention this young hopeful Johnson in particular?'

'Well, yes. As a matter of fact he did.'

'Sir Gregory had visited your nick a number of times . . .'

'Yes.'

'Because he's interested in penal reform?'

'I'm sure he is. But there was another reason.'

'Tell me.'

'I'm afraid it's confidential.'

'All secrets are safe with me.' Titmuss smiled enigmatically. 'And please remember, I mean to put your case, in influential quarters.'

'That young man over there. Good-looking boy. He's Rosalind in our *As You Like It*.'

135

'Isn't that about a girl pretending to be a boy, or is it the other way round?' Titmuss frowned with distaste.

'Part of it's about that. Well, it's no secret. He's young Alaric Inwood, Sir Gregory's nephew.'

'I see.' Titmuss clearly found this news more acceptable than cross-dressing in Elizabethan drama.

'Public-school drug-dealer with an unusual headmaster who handed him over to the police.'

'I don't suppose his parents thought that was what they paid the fees for. Tell me, was that classy young criminal here when Slippy had his first day out?'

'I think so. I'd have to check.'

'Please do. And had Sir Gregory met Slippy?'

'Oh, yes. He came to lunch and I gave him the history of a few of the boys his nephew seemed to mix with in Association. I told him about Slippy to prove that not all our customers are violent.'

'Told him *all* about Slippy?'

'Oh, yes.'

'All that you've told me?'

'Yes.'

'His talents as a locksmith?'

'I'm sure I mentioned that.' Paul ruefully admitted his own weakness. 'I shouldn't tell people so much about the boys here, but I want them thought about as individuals, people with talents and weaknesses and problems of their own. They're not just numbers in the crime statistics, or a government report on drug abuse.'

'Of course.' Titmuss came out in full support of the governor. 'I understand that. We all get into trouble for different reasons. No doubt this young lock-picker is a likeable enough lad. At any rate, Sir Gregory seems to like him. From what I can discover he had him out to work on the day Peter Millichip was found drowned in his swimming pool.'

There's not much, Paul thought, that you can't discover. 'So far as I can remember.'

'And I suppose he'd made the booking, I mean, reserved the services of young Slippy, some time before that?'

'Well. I suppose so.'

'You suppose?'

'He said he had. He told me he had when he rang up that morning. But I couldn't find an entry. I must have forgotten when he asked me earlier.'

'You're not as efficient as your prison officer?'

'Not as meticulous, perhaps.'

'And you let Sir Gregory take the boy?'

'I thought it would be good for Slippy, and of course Sir Gregory was completely trustworthy.'

'Oh, yes. Completely. Only one other thing. I wondered what time it was. When he rang you?'

'Oh, very early in the morning. In fact he woke me up. I suppose he wanted to get in a long day's gardening.'

'I'm sure that's what it was.' Titmuss looked round at the young offenders, boys of all shapes, sizes and colours, some sullen, some jaunty, some silently angry, some determined to smile, finishing lunch under the eye of prison officers. 'And I'm sure that all your lads will grow up to be excellent gardeners.'

Two weeks to go before polling day and Tim Willock's lead had shrunk to 4 per cent. More importantly, the Liberal Democrat, an intense and desperately well-meaning lecturer in statistics at Worsfield University, seemed to be making a diminishing impression on the voters. Velma Warrington could provide figures from some inexhaustible computer in her head to prove or disprove any argument, but somehow the numbers were not memorable, and cynical voters wondered if she really spent the time travelling the country to discover how many children under fourteen spent over a third of their pocket-money on cigarettes, or the exact proportion of those who, drinking over two pints of beer a day, thereby contracted bronchitis. Although by no means a Conservative, she seemed to spend most of her political energy attacking Terry and thereby confirming his position as the sole opposition candidate.

Penry read of the closing gap with surprise and disbelief. He had expected this Labour campaign to be like the others he had fought, a hard slog leading to an honourable defeat. There had been few surprises in the past, but this campaign was different. He felt he had lost control of his candidate and that the battle was being directed by some hidden hand who might send it chasing off after unlikely enemies, or organize an attack on hitherto unidentified targets. When he was feeling particularly rattled he comforted himself with the thought that 4 per cent was a fairly comfortable lead, and he wouldn't have to face the embarrassment of a victorious Terry, who had taken none of his advice and seemed to have long ago given up speaking to Nabbs.

The list of surprises for Penry, however, was not yet complete. He and Terry were crossing the high street in Hartscombe, on their way to meet a focus group in the Swan's Nest Hotel, when a rich, female voice hailed Terry, a sound which brought back to him the day of his nightmare ride to hounds. It was Blanche Evergreen, the plumpish, smiling, grey-haired woman whom hounds obeyed and who chased saboteurs.

'Thanks for the cap money, Mr Flitton. It arrived at last.'

'The what?'

'The sixty quid. For your day out with the Hartscombe.'

Terry, who was not conscious of having made any such payment, gave his fully committed, charming smile and said, 'Oh, of course. Well, thank you for putting up with me.'

'Interesting style of riding you have. Did you pick it up in South America?'

'Oh, well. From here and there, actually.'

'Anyway. I hope you enjoyed the day.'

'I found it . . . extremely interesting.'

'You're a political chap, Mr Flitton.' Blanche's voice had become more confidential. She moved uncomfortably close to Terry, grabbed the lapel of his jacket as though about to climb up him and said, 'You'll save our hunting. You'll do that for me, won't you, Mr Flitton darling?' And with that Blanche patted Terry, as though he were a horse which had just cleared a dangerous jump, and went on her way.

'Are you making commitments to the hunters,' Penry was bound to protest.

'Not commitments. Just hopes.'

The agent said no more. The week before he had received a contribution of £10,000 from the hunting owner of Pooh Corner, with a letter which said that all lovers of country sports should work for the defeat of Willock. The money couldn't be spent on the election, so he showed it to Nabbs, who recommended it be sent on to Walworth Road without the covering letter but with a note from the nearby M.P. to say that he had managed, while at work in the Hartscombe constituency, to do a bit of successful fund-raising.

'They got you in the frame, Slippy, for mugging my Aunt Dorothy.'

'Don't make me laugh! I was banged up.'

'They don't think you're called Slippy for nothing. They know your reputation with locks. Hope you got a good brief for when they're doing you for Robbery with Violence.'

Alaric Inwood had clear blue eyes, a high, bridged nose and a perpetual expression of ironical and amused contempt. He enjoyed, and even exaggerated, the troubles of his fellow prisoners, and now, as he played ping-pong with Slippy during an Association period when other boys were watching 'Home and Away', he revelled in his opponent's troubles as though he were enjoying a warm bath.

'What'm I meant to have done? Broken out, gone to the supermarket in a funny mask, done over your aunty and picked all the locks to get back in here again? That's ridiculous.'

Alaric relied on the sweeping smash, which often went off the table. Slippy replied with gentler shots, carefully placed, and he was, for the moment, up on points.

'They've got the evidence,' Alaric said. 'One of the blokes shouted out, "Slippy." They've got a witness.'

'That don't mean nothing. How many Slippys do you think there are in the world?'

'Only one, I should think. You're in the frame, old man. One of those bad boys called out your name. You don't think they'd do that if you weren't there, do you?'

'I wouldn't put it past them.' Life had left Slippy with little faith in honour among Skurfield inmates.

'I lay you any odds,' Alaric tried a mean serve which just toppled over the net, 'that you get a call to see the governor.'

Alaric would have won the bet. The next day a regretful Paul Fogarty told Slippy that he was destined for Blackenstock, a grim and poorly run Y.O.I. in the north of England, in which four inmates had committed suicide in the last eighteen months. The best Paul could do was to postpone the move until after *As You Like It*.

# Chapter Sixteen

'Would you like to comment on Terry Flitton's proposal to have a full judicial inquiry into hunting, Mr Willock?'

'Certainly. The fact of the matter is, you can't believe a word that's said by my lying opponent from the Party opposite. He'll say anything to appease any sectional interest. My views on what some people call country sports and I call, in plain English, blood sports, are well known. I don't have to take refuge in a lot of meaningless talk about judicial inquiries.'

There was a sudden silence and a quickening of interest at the morning Conservative press conference in the baptist hall. Representatives of national newspapers, television reporters and political pundits stopped their murmured gossip, raised their eyes from the sports pages and stared at Tim Willock, who was in an unusually abrasive and cocky mood this morning. He sat next to Sir Gregory Inwood and Marcia Turnbull, the Minister for Agriculture, sent down to stiffen the sinews of an apparently weakening campaign, at a table draped with a Union Jack at the end of the hall. The reporters had a suspicion that some sort of news had just broken. A solemn young man in spectacles raised his pencil as though making a bid at an auction.

'Cornelius Vance of the *Telegraph*,' he announced himself modestly. 'Did you just say that we can't believe a word spoken by the Labour candidate?'

'Of course you can't.' Tim Willock seemed to be intoxicated

with sudden unexpected and unusual courage. 'I can prove that Terry Flitton's a liar and has lied deliberately to the electors of Hartscombe and Worsfield South.'

'Mel Rathbone of the *Guardian*.' A girl in the front row took off her glasses to make a bid. 'When do you say Terry Flitton lied?'

'In his election pamphlet. A lie delivered to every household in the constituency.' Willock made the claim confidently. Sir Gregory held the pamphlet in his hand and was getting ready to quote. The Minister half-closed her eyes as though to avoid a disgusting spectacle and looked pained at the stink of corruption.

'"Terry Flitton",' Sir Gregory quoted clearly and slowly, as though reading the charge in an indictment, ' "is a local boy made good. His father was a worker in W.R.F. who spent his life on the shop-floor."'

'Is that a lie?' Mel from the *Guardian* asked.

'It certainly is,' Willock was delighted to tell her. 'Flitton's father was promoted to middle management. Manager in charge of Human Resources. One of the bosses and not one of the workers.'

'Bob Pertwee from *The Times*,' this was a middle-aged man in a tweed suit. 'Doesn't that reflect rather well on Flitton père?'

Sir Gregory took the question. 'We're not really concerned with Flitton père. It just proves that Flitton fils is a stranger to the truth.'

'What's the evidence for that?' Mel from the *Guardian* needed convincing.

'We shall produce full documentary evidence at the proper time,' Willock told her.

'And what's the proper time?'

'Next Wednesday's press conference.'

'But just before polling day . . .'

'Exactly!' Sir Gregory sat back, smiling with satisfaction and, as they passed on to the question of the danger of heart disease from consuming sausages, the Minister for Agriculture was able to breathe again.

\*

Robert Flitton, wearing a dressing-gown and bedroom slippers, sat in a place known as the 'sun lounge', although there was no sun on that grey, autumn morning. He didn't take his turn with the newspaper, nor did he pay any attention to the television, which glowed and burbled in a corner of the room. It seemed to him like a picture, hanging on the wall, sometimes a representation of snowy mountains, or wild animals, but more often of people arguing. He wondered why a picture should be so noisy and wished it could be kept quiet. Sometimes he thought that those arguing might be real people, gathered in a corner of the room and planning to attack him, and then he sat very still so that they wouldn't notice him and would go away. These were alarming moments but most of the time he was not frightened, only a little anxious because the thoughts that flitted through his head seemed to have no meaning attached to them. They were about places he couldn't identify and people he couldn't remember. He saw no possible reason for these thoughts and wondered if they didn't belong to someone else entirely, old Mrs Duckworth, for instance, who, in the chair beside him, had nodded off again. Perhaps they had spilt over from her mind. And then moments came when he had no thoughts at all, the screen in his head was blank, and he felt entirely happy. But now he was worried again. He heard a voice which, for some unknown reason, he felt he ought to recognize.

'Dad,' the voice was saying. 'How are you, Dad?'

'Yes, Dawn,' Robert said. 'How are you, dear?'

Although he could remember none of this clearly, or even obscurely, Robert was speaking to his second wife, Dawn Allbright, whom he had married years after Terry's mother deserted him. Dawn had been an efficient housekeeper, he had thought at the time, clean about the place, reasonably enthusiastic in bed and, unlike Clarice, otherwise known as Susie, polite and welcoming when he brought colleagues home from the office. But Dawn had also fled, puzzled and irritated by the onset of his illness. When he put butter away in the broom cupboard and an office file in the fridge, when he called her nothing but Gladys and later completely failed to recognize her, she told Terry she could cope no longer and was going to live with an uncle in Newcastle. Then Robert was handed over to the Social Services and, at last, came to rest in Evenload, a Worsfield old people's home, a man only in his sixties, divorced from his past and long parted from himself. He turned to where the voice he thought was Dawn's and saw a face which bore some resemblance to the one he looked at each morning, in the bathroom mirror.

'Dad, it's me. It's your son. It's Terry.'

'It's Terry,' Robert repeated the last words obediently, although they had no particular meaning for him.

'That's right! You recognize me. That's very good!' Terry thought how handsome the old man was, his dark curls now grey at the temples but his features still clear, his pyjama collar turned up, his eyes bright and smiling although there were no thoughts behind them. He looked, his son thought, like a film star, ageing but still popular and with world-wide box-office appeal. 'Dad. I want to ask you about your job.'

A nurse passed with a trolley and handed Robert a mug of tea, already mixed with milk and sugar, which had the spoon standing up in it. Robert said, 'Thank you, Dawn. That's very thoughtful of you, dearest.' Terry declined politely when he was offered tea also.

'Dad. About your job. If anybody asks you . . .'

Robert took the spoon out of his mug of tea, licked it and put it neatly in the top pocket of his dressing-gown. 'Forms to be filled in,' he said. 'That'll come in useful.'

'Dad. You were always shop-floor, weren't you? All your life. You were one of the workers.'

'That pen,' Robert asked plaintively, 'where the hell did I put it? Forget my own name next.'

'Remember, Dad? You may have helped out with Personnel occasionally, but you were always thought of as shop-floor. Always

144

one of the workers, weren't you, Dad? Remember that, if anybody asks.'

'Oh, here it is at last!' Robert found the spoon in his top pocket and held it between his fingers. 'Now. Let's get down a few particulars. Name, height and date of birth. That'll do to be getting on with.'

Terry stood up and sighed, 'Bless you, Dad.' When he left, his father was smiling happily, as though conscious of a job well done.

'So you told a lie.' Agnes sounded not angry, but vaguely amused.

'Not a lie. Just a slightly ambiguous statement.'

'You seem to be rather fond of slightly ambiguous statements.'

'Darling. Just try and remember . . .'

'I know. There's an election!'

'Next week. And Willock's gone one more point ahead in the polls.'

'So it's time to be ambiguous?'

'Just for the moment.'

'And when the election's over it'll be the truth, the whole truth and nothing but the truth?'

'Absolutely.'

'You swear?'

'Of course I swear.'

'I don't believe you.'

'Why not?'

'Because after this election there'll be another election and after that, if we get into power, it'll be necessary to win the next election, and the truth's going to be postponed indefinitely. Isn't that how it'll be?'

He didn't deny it directly. Instead he told her, 'He was a shop steward who gave some advice to the personnel department. That's all. He was always regarded as a manual worker.'

'That's what you're proud of?' Luckily she was still smiling.

'Of course. And they can't prove he wasn't.' He said that

confidently, but he wasn't sure that Willock's case couldn't be proved quite easily. Why had he ever said that about Robert? Was it because, like his vanished mother, he was ashamed of middle management? He had cleared so many hurdles; was it fair that he should be brought crashing to the ground by a lie nailed on the last day of the campaign? He said, 'We'll win, whatever cards Willock and his lot think they've got up their sleeves.'

'Shits.' Agnes kicked up a fluttering pile of leaves, almost over-balanced and held his arm. 'They are the most awful shits.'

'Yes.'

'The Home Office. The prison service. Whoever it is Paul has to contend with.'

'Of course they are. What's happened now?'

'Oh, it's just a boy. Ordinary decent criminal. No violence in his record. Paul's done a lot to help him. He's got high hopes of finding him a decent job when he leaves. I don't know, gardening or something like that. So the bloody job'sworth in government who decides these cruelties is going to take the boy away from Skurfield and send him to some dump in the north. Blackenstock. No education, no work experience, nothing to do outside the cells. Just banging up and suicide.'

'I can do something about that, when I'm the local M.P.'

'You will, won't you?'

'You know I will.'

'Whatever you have to do to get there.' She stood in front of him in the wood, her hand on his chest to stop him moving, and instead of accusing him further, she kissed him.

It shouldn't be thought that Lord Titmuss spent his whole time and concentrated all his efforts on manœuvring the candidates and the voters of Hartscombe and Worsfield South. He had, early in his political career, amassed a considerable fortune and, when dealing in the City, had easily been able to outsmart his public-schoolboy associates and partners. Having bought back Rapstone

Manor, his expenses were extremely small. He didn't gamble, buy pictures, own a yacht or keep mistresses. Becoming, with the years, increasingly monkish, he could live without sex, winter holidays or works of art. He drank whisky and soda, increasingly dark as polling day drew near, ate the plainest food (and no one cooked more plainly than Mrs Ragg) and hadn't ordered a new suit of clothes for ten years. He allowed his son a small income to supplement his earnings as a librarian and paid Mrs Ragg a little under the going rate for the district. He employed an elderly gardener and Ted Lumsden, a driver who had been with him since he was first a minister. The large Rover car was one he had bought second-hand from the government when he left it. The Lumsdens got a cottage, which Mrs Lumsden continually complained his Lordship was maddeningly slow to repair, and they had to pay their own council tax, water rates and electricity. Titmuss, however, reminded the couple of the high cost of living, the level of taxation since Mrs Thatcher had been deposed, and pretended that he was writing his memoirs to give him 'Something to buy a crust with in my old age.' The fact that he had so little use for money didn't stop him wanting to make a great deal more of it. He was frequently on the telephone to his accountant and his stockbroker, and such conversations invariably served to swell his Lordship's portfolio. He was still looking for ways to increase his wealth.

Although his life was monastic Lord Titmuss kept his ear to the ground, was an encyclopaedia of local gossip and a frequent guest at cocktail parties where he stood, a gaunt figure, listening keenly, drinking strong whiskies and consuming a record amount of finger food, wolfing sausages on sticks, vol-au-vents and avocado dip as though he hadn't enjoyed a square meal for weeks. Some time ago he had discovered that Hanging Wood might be up for sale.

Tom Nowt's son, living in South Africa, had apparently grown weary of nursing a chunk of the Hartscombe countryside he never saw. He had written to Nobby Noakes, who had enjoyed pints of

Simcox and poaching anecdotes with his father, and asked if it were possible to find a purchaser. Nobby had mentioned the matter to a successful Worsfield builder named Chuffnel and, as they hit upon a plan which would require a considerable amount of capital, they sought an audience with Lord Titmuss.

'This is the most desirable part of the British Isles. Seventy-five per cent of those questioned in a recent poll gave the Thames Valley as their preferred living area.' Gerry Chuffnel was a large man with a fair moustache and hair worn just over the ears, so that he looked like a professional cricketer. He spoke loudly and enthusiastically in favour of the project. 'Fallowfield's just a beach-head, my Lord. Just marking out the territory. We're going to have to meet the need for at least a thousand new homes between here and Skurfield, and the bulk of those will have to go on green-field areas.'

'You mean a green-tree area?' Titmuss, who disliked being called 'my Lord', hadn't taken to Chuffnel; but then he didn't take to many people, his liking for Terry Flitton being something of an exception.

'Green-tree area! Of course. Very good, that, my Lord.' Chuffnel forced a laugh which lasted rather too long. 'Of course we know that it's a O.N.B.' Hanging Wood had been for years scheduled as an Area of Outstanding Natural Beauty.

'O.N.B.s are going. The green belt's a thoroughly out-of-date conception and there are motorways over most of the places of Special Scientific Interest. You know that as well as anybody.' For the purposes of this conversation Nobby Noakes regretted nothing.

'I thought you wanted to save the wood for your precious foxes to breed in.' Titmuss gave Nobby a look of exaggerated surprise.

'If this business goes through,' Nobby was laughing, 'I can buy a place in Leicestershire and join a decent hunt!'

After the whisky had been poured Titmuss promised to talk to his accountant, giving the impression that it would come as a surprise to him if he found he had enough cash for a couple of trees, let alone a wood and the building of so many new houses. They fixed on a date for a further meeting to inspect the merchandise.

Terry had become, Agnes thought, ridiculously cautious. It was not polling day he feared most but the day when he expected Tim Willock, at his press conference, to announce that they had proof positive, an old employee, records and wage slips from W.R.F. to convince the electors that Terry had lied about his father. He saw the statement in his election pamphlet not as a lie but as a pardonable exaggeration and an article of faith. He was proclaiming his commitment to the Man in the Street, the Ordinary Man, the Worker. Of course it could be argued that no man is ordinary, but solidarity with the workers was as much a part of Terry's creed as calling himself a Socialist, a Democratic Socialist of course, a Socialist who could coexist with Capitalism, naturally, but a Socialist all the same, who had first won Agnes's love by his admiration for the books on her top shelf. And he was undoubtedly the son of a worker, a man whose working-class credentials had won him the love of Terry's mother. The fact that Robert had ended up on the third floor, managing Human Resources, was an irrelevant detail, and failing to mention it was entirely forgivable. But Terry knew that Willock, and perhaps the voters, would not forgive it.

The accusation had broken the spell of the fear of success which had kept Penry and Nabbs at a respectful distance. Now they watched over him, kept him on a tight rein and a tighter schedule, convinced that he was a candidate who, given half a chance, would make another fatal blunder. They smiled when they remembered Terry's conviction that he would become the Honourable Member for Hartscombe. Their sole concern, now, was to avoid the sort of massacre which would earn ridicule for the Party and black looks for Des Nabbs M.P. in the Walworth Road.

Terry knew that Nabbs and Penry were watching him, and he began to believe that Willock's men were also taking a close interest in his movements. He got the uneasy feeling that he was being followed, his conversations in pubs listened to and his movements noted down. When he visited the Dust Jacket he noticed a young man in a blazer and a grey-haired man pretending an interest in the books but in fact, he thought, standing listening. He became nervous of visiting Agnes's house and afraid to go up to her bedroom. Once polling day was over things, of course, would be different, he told her. And she, finding herself increasingly fond of him, being what she would have had to call, if she didn't shy away from the sentimentality of the hackneyed phrase 'in love', as she had not expected to be again, forgave him. She was, she had to admit it, lonely, and sitting all day in the bookshop had become a bore. It would be great if they could just have an hour alone together.

Terry had to make a speech at a business college which had been set up in a Georgian house on the river by the new proprietors of Simcox Ales. It was to be an important statement on co-operation with the private sector, and he told Nabbs that he needed to be alone to compose it. He was also desperate for fresh air and exercise. He was going to the woods and the hills.

'Not on horseback, let's hope.' Nabbs gave him one of his most merciless smiles.

'Of course not.'

'And I'll want to see every word of that speech before you utter it.'

'So you shall.' And Terry went off to the lavatory in Penry's house, locked the door and phoned Agnes on his mobile.

So they had driven their own cars and met in the wood where they had first walked alone together, and she mocked him gently about ambiguous statements and told him about the unjust treatment of Slippy Johnson. And as they stood in the leaves, in a patch of winter sunshine, zipped up in warm jackets and muffled in scarves, she stopped him with her hand on his chest and kissed him, and he returned the kiss hungrily and held on to her as if for dear life. They found themselves not far from Tom Nowt's hut.

Deer's Leap. Tom had called it his hunting lodge; the green and rotting shack, with its blind and broken windows, damp smell and the danger that it might have been taken up as a shoot-up centre by the more desperate Thames Valley drug-takers, had once been rejected by Agnes as a refuge for love. Now, as they stood, hungry for each other after a period of abstinence, it seemed a godsent opportunity and a safe harbour. They scorned the wounded and gutted sofa and made a nest of coats and scarves on the wet floor, on to which dead leaves had drifted, and uncovering only as much as was necessary, excited by what they couldn't see, made love with a frantic intensity and agonized delight such as they had never felt before.

Titmuss had seen a Ford Falcon which looked like Terry's, indeed it had so little sense of discretion that it carried a 'Vote Flitton' sticker with a rose on it on the back window, parked not far from an old Volkswagen convertible in the road near Hanging Wood. He and Nobby had got out of Gerry Chuffnel's Range Rover and walked among the trees they might destroy. Hanging Wood slopes, at first gently and then more steeply downhill, and Chuffnel was concerned with the expense of terracing the area. For their exploration they had found themselves splitting up like beaters, and Titmuss had been alone when he saw, between naked beech trees, a lop-sided and ramshackle hut. Outside it the Labour candidate, over whom he had already taken considerable trouble, could be seen locked in a seemingly endless embrace with Agnes Simcox, the old doctor's daughter from the bookshop.

As they entered Tom Nowt's hut Titmuss turned away and, walking back to the Range Rover, wondered if the time had not come to ditch Terry entirely.

# Chapter Seventeen

The time until polling day seemed perilously short and crammed with events. All the candidates were asked to attend the production of *As You Like It* in the Skurfield Y.O.I., but only the Liberal Democrat found it convenient to be present. Neither Willock nor Terry wanted to be publicly associated with one of Paul Fogarty's imaginative projects. The day after Alaric Inwood was to give his Rosalind, and Slippy his supporting Celia, would be the day before the vote, the morning on which Willock had promised to furnish convincing proof of Terry's falsification of his father's job.

Willock had maintained his lead, but Terry told Penry and Nabbs that the Lib Dems, aware that he was by far the strongest opposition candidate, would ditch Velma Warrington, the well-meaning lecturer on statistics, and vote tactically. His political advisers, when he said this, looked sceptical and faintly disgusted, as though they would rather lose than have the purity of their campaign sullied by furtive Lib Dem votes. Willock told Gregory Inwood that the Lib Dems would, on the contrary, vote for him, as the entire population of Hartscombe was determined to keep that Socialist menace, Red Tel, out.

In a feverish burst of activity canvassers on both sides were identifying their supporters and arranging fleets of cars to ferry them to the polling booths in style and comfort. Penry was surprised and a little embarrassed by the huge fleet unexpectedly made available to Labour, including many Range Rovers from hunt supporters in country areas.

To Terry the last days of the campaign seemed to pass in a sort of dream, and what he was dreaming of was Agnes. What had started as a love affair, self-indulgent, enjoyable and interesting, a colourful and unexpected alternative to the wife he had grown used to, had become, since that moment of abandon in Tom Nowt's hut, a continuous obsession. He thought of Agnes constantly, when making speeches, invading doorsteps, taking part in a university Brains Trust and even when he was making love to Kate. The picture of Agnes, her amused smile which contradicted the urgency of her body, hovered always in his mind.

Walking back to Penry's house late at night, after a rally of local Party workers in the baptist hall, Terry took a detour which led him by the side of the river and past her house. He saw a light on in a downstairs room, looked up and down the street and rang the bell. When Agnes opened the door he emerged from the shadows and hurried inside.

'I came to tell you I can't stay.' He stood looking at her, concerned as though a bringer of bad news.

'Well, thanks.'

'I mean, Kate wouldn't understand. She knows what time the meeting was going to end.'

'Well, then. You'd better go, hadn't you?' She was mocking him, he knew, although she put on a look of sympathetic understanding.

'It won't always be like this.'

'Won't it?'

'When the election's over.'

'And you're the Honourable Member.' She said that as though it were a joke.

'I'll come down often. When I do my surgery. Kate'll be up in London.'

'You mean, I'll be another public duty, like your surgery.'

'Of course I don't.'

'I've got this problem, you see. I fancy our local Member and I'm still on the waiting-list. Is that what I'll come and whine about at your surgery?'

'There won't be a waiting-list.'

'You think you'll be able to fit me in?'

'I know I will.'

'A quickie before the pager gets you back for the debate.'

'Will you mind?'

'I suppose I'll have not to.'

'There'll be other times. Foreign travel.'

'You're going to disguise me as a young researcher, fresh out of Manchester University with a First in politics? Might be tricky.'

'We'll think of something.'

'You think of winning. That's all I want you to do.'

She kissed him and let him go. He was thinking how wonderfully well she behaved, and how tolerant she was of Kate; although Kate wouldn't, if she had known, have been in the least tolerant of her. As he left Agnes's house a large black car, waiting by the river, started its engine and switched on dimmed headlights. Terry didn't stop to notice that it was an ancient government Rover.

Neither did he know that Tim Willock had, that evening, made a speech at a Conservative dinner in the Worsfield rugby club. Titmuss was also an honoured guest, and he sat, apparently unmoved, through the Willock peroration.

'Perhaps, in the Thatcher years,' Willock had said, 'we were seen as the hard-faced, hard-hearted Party of big business, ruthless competition and an "I'm all right, Jack" attitude to the poor and disadvantaged. When I'm elected you will be voting for today's and not yesterday's Tory Party. For the Party that stands for One Nation. For the Party that cares deeply for the poor, the handicapped and the single mother. For the Party that abolished slavery and cherishes freedom under the law. For the Party of compassion and tolerance and understanding. When you elect me you will elect a Tory who cares.'

Lord Titmuss sat listening to this in silence, his arms crossed and his eyes closed. But it was then that he decided he would have to back Terry to the bitter end; although the Labour candidate might well put his foot in his mouth and his private parts into a totally inappropriate woman, he was the only contender available to defeat Willock, and Wee Willie had to be defeated. He would have to solve Terry's problems and, pointing his nose in the direction of victory, give him a final shove. Despite Terry's obvious political immaturity and inability to avoid trouble, Titmuss thought it might just be managed. He started by ringing Paul and asking for Slippy's help in dusting the books in the Manor. He expected much to come of this.

'Sorry about the transfer to Blackenstock, Johnson.'

'That's all right.'

'Just watch your step, mind. Don't spend longer there than you absolutely have to. And it wasn't my decision.'

'Not your fault neither.'

'Thank you for that. And there's things to look forward to before you go. *As You Like It* . . .'

'Not much.'

'*As You Like It*, the play.'

'Oh, you mean the concert?'

'I know you always call it that. Looking forward to it, aren't you?'

'I suppose it'll be all right.'

'Anne Hopkins in Education says you're doing really well. You even say some of the lines out of the play.'

'I makes most of them up. Inwood does most of the talking. I just says I'm shagged out, walking through the forest. And that.'

'She says you try hard. I'm grateful to you for trying.'

There was a silence between them. Slippy seemed to be anxious for the governor to leave his cell so he could get on with not doing very much. Then Paul said, 'There's a little ray of hope.'

Slippy was silent, not looking especially hopeful.

'Someone, a man with a lot of influence, doesn't approve of your transfer to Blackenstock. Did you notice who I was having lunch with in the canteen a couple of days ago?'

'Not particular.'

'A very well-known politician.'

'Was he?'

'Lord Titmuss!'

. Slippy looked unimpressed, and Paul had to explain. 'He's very famous. And he's got a bit of pull with the Home Secretary and the prison service and all the powers that rule our lives. Yours and mine. And I know he's interested in you.'

'Why's that?' Seeing he was so deeply uninterested in Lord Titmuss, Slippy couldn't see why his Lordship should be interested in him.

'He wants you out for a day. Work experience. The books in Rapstone Manor.'

'Books?' Slippy looked more alarmed than he had at the prospect of Blackenstock.

'Don't worry. He wants you to dust them. Not read them. You won't get days out for that at Blackenstock, so you'd better make the most of it. And if you can please Lord Titmuss . . .' There was a pause during which Slippy was stony-faced, uncertain of what might be in store for him. 'If you do a good job, who knows, you might be able to stay with us. You'd like that, wouldn't you?'

'I'd like it all right,' was as far as Slippy would go.

The library at Rapstone Manor had been used, during the house's brief and unhappy period as the headquarters of a rabbit farm, as a place to store wire netting, hutches in need of repair and sacks of rabbit food. Titmuss had cleared out the rubbish, but the long room, with its dusty shelves and shrouded furniture, its fading, yellowing globe of the world, steel engravings of the church and the surrounding countryside, its dim green-shaded lamps and portraits of Fanners long dead, was rarely visited, as Titmuss preferred to work on his memoirs in the study, converted from the old estate office along the corridor. The rows of books, unopened for years, had indeed gathered dust, so that the *History of the English Counties*, the *Complete Works of Walter Scott*, the adventures of long-forgotten explorers and volumes bound in crumbling leather by Gibbon, Livy and Herodotus, the stored tedium of sermons, the unremembered lives of Lords Chancellor and archbishops, the careful illustrations of fossils and rock formations, the involved and bewildering history of Byzantium, represented a storehouse of work now wasted and a world of knowledge unexplored.

Now, faced with ten volumes on the Early Fathers and an atlas of the ancient world which he flicked with a duster, Slippy Johnson wished he was back in his cell, comfortably asleep or gazing peacefully up at the ceiling. But then he began to rub industriously at a *Life of Saint Augustine* as he became aware that the tall figure of Lord Titmuss, the man it was in his interest to please, had stolen into the room.

'Working hard?'

'No problem. The blokes that lived here must have liked reading.'

'Probably not. That's why the books are so dusty. I was talking to Mr Fogarty. I told him I might be able to help you.'

'I don't know why you should bother.'

'Don't worry about why. There's absolutely no need for you to understand *why* anything. I imagine you don't want to be transferred to Blackenstock?'

'Not if I can get out of it.'

'Not if I can get you out of it. But you'll have to do something for me.'

'I'm dusting as quick as I can.'

'I'm afraid it's a little more difficult than dusting.'

Titmuss moved to open the window. The room smelt stuffy. The boy was waiting to hear what was going to be demanded of him but suspected it wouldn't be anything he was going to enjoy. 'I want you to tell me the truth.' There was silence, and Titmuss added, 'You don't understand that, do you?'

Slippy shook his head.

'All right. Let's take it in steps. I'm going to ask you about Sir Gregory Inwood.'

'The bloke what had me out to do his garden and that?'

'That's the bloke.' Titmuss gave what was meant to be an encouraging smile, an expression which looked merely threatening. 'He'd met you before that, hadn't he?'

'He came round the nick.'

'And talked to you in your cell?'

'Had a bit of a chat, yes.'

'The governor says he knew you come from a family of lock-pickers.'

'What d'you mean?'

'Oh, yes, you do. Sir Gregory knew your father specialized in cracking safes. And your convictions are for opening a variety of locks without keys. He knew that, didn't he?' Titmuss had moved very close to the kneeling Slippy and seemed to tower over him.

'I suppose so.'

'I'm not interested in what you suppose. I'm asking you to tell me the truth. Did he know that or didn't he?'

'I reckon he knew.' Slippy made a reluctant admission.

Now Titmuss jerked a chair under him and sat, so that his face was on a level with the boy's. 'Do you know why you're being transferred to Blackenstock?'

'I reckon it's the authorities,' Slippy shrugged, 'and that.'

'Would it surprise you to know that Sir Gregory Inwood wants you transferred to a tough nick at the other end of the country with no days out?'

Slippy looked at him, a boy who could be surprised by nothing.

'He wants you out of the way, Slippy. So you don't owe him any favours. But you might owe me something.'

'What you want exactly?' Slippy almost whispered, now convinced the old guy was after sex.

'I told you. I want the truth. About the job he asked you to do that morning when he sent a car for you. Tell me. It won't get you into any trouble.'

'What you want to know then?'

'Let's start with a simple question. Did he take you to a swimming pool?'

And then Slippy, held in the stare of his Lordship's pale eyes and profoundly relieved that no act of love was required of him, began to tell the old politician what he wanted to know. It didn't take very long, no more than ten minutes, and then, having promised Slippy to do his best to keep him in Skurfield, Titmuss left the boy to his dusty books and went to his study to make a telephone call.

The Whips' office keeps files on all the parties' M.P.s, their voting records, financial situations and sexual preferences. Titmuss rang Raleigh Truscott, who had been Chief Conservative Whip when he was in the Cabinet, and asked for confirmation of what he remembered about Peter Millichip. Then he was in a position to launch the attack.

# Chapter Eighteen

It was a quarter to nine in the morning when Sir Gregory Inwood, not troubling his driver and behind the wheel of his impeccably polished Daimler, drove through Hartscombe, up a hill behind the church and away from the river. He had got up early, anxious and unable to sleep, and had bathed and dressed before daylight; but now the wintry sun was shining, the sky was blue with a grey curtain of cloud and in it he saw, as he changed gear and climbed higher, a Red Kite hovering. And he could also see, nearer the sky, the white house, naked of any covering of trees, and its impressive spread. He had no idea why Linda Millichip had invited him to breakfast or why the invitation had been made with such a note of urgency.

He parked on the neat, well-raked gravel and rang the doorbell which, as he knew from bitter experience, chimed. The few notes of *Eine Kleine Nachtmusik*, however, produced no sound of footsteps and shooting of locks. He had been invited for nine o'clock, and it was now seven minutes past. The Conservative Chairman decided to walk round the side of the building. The house was sleeping, there was no sound but the scrunch of his feet on the gravel. He came to a high hedge of leylandii with a small, unlocked gate. He pushed through it and stood blinking at the glitter of low sunlight on the swimming pool.

At first his dazzled eyes saw no one, and then, in the shadow of a striped awning, on a white plastic chair at a white plastic table, he realized a tall, balding man in a dark suit was patiently waiting. Sir Gregory seemed to find this presence reassuring. He called out, 'Is that you, Leslie?' and walked along the concrete path beside the water. It was, he had time to think, rather odd; most people keep their pools covered in the winter.

'So you got an invitation to a breakfast party?' Sir Gregory joined Titmuss at the plastic table.

'Not a party. I think it's just the three of us.'

'Shouldn't we go inside?'

'I think not. Linda's going to bring things out.'

'Won't it be a bit cold?'

'Probably.'

'I wonder the pool's open,' Sir Gregory said as he sat.

'I believe Linda had it uncovered, as more appropriate to the occasion.'

'What occasion?'

'Some sort of ceremony, I think, in memory of Peter Millichip.'

'Not scattering of ashes in the pool?' Sir Gregory looked seriously perturbed.

'I wonder.'

'If the wind gets up they might go anywhere.'

'You mean, in your breakfast?' Titmuss was unsmiling.

'Well, you never know. But now I remember' – the Chairman looked considerably relieved – 'they buried Peter Millichip in Hartscombe churchyard.'

'Then you needn't worry about ashes.'

'No. No worries on that score. But what are we here for exactly?'

'Perhaps a sort of service of remembrance.'

'You mean Holy Joe Fairweather's going to come creeping up here?' Sir Gregory had no particular liking for the Rector of Hartscombe, who spoke about Jesus as though he were the Labour Member for Nazareth East.

'Oh, I think not,' Titmuss reassured him. 'I think any service, if there *is* a service, will be of an entirely secular nature. By the way, how are you getting on with proving that young Flitton lied about his father?'

Sir Gregory seemed startled by the sudden change of subject. He said, 'It's rather odd.'

'What's odd?'

'Half his records seem to have vanished from Worsfield Road Furnishings. They've got his wages on the shop-floor recorded, but all the stuff about his promotion seems to have been pulled out. I wouldn't put that past the Labour Party.'

'Oh, I would,' Titmuss was certain of it. 'They're not nearly well organized enough.'

'We'll get hold of someone who worked with him. We've got a few names. Don't worry.'

'Oh, my worry is quite different. I don't think accusing your opponent of lying was particularly clever, was it? The whole thing may well backfire.'

'Backfire? In what sort of way?'

'Here comes Linda. I'll tell you later.'

The two men rose as a mark of respect to the immense figure which had come gliding out of the house like an overweight soprano about to burst into some ear-piercing lament. She was wearing, that winter morning, a pale green négligé topped with a white fur coat, a number of scarves, earrings, full make-up, and feet zipped into fur boots. She was carrying a tray on which rested a coffee pot, milk and sugar, cups, a large plate of assorted sweet biscuits, the Cointreau bottle and three balloon-like glasses. Sir Gregory took the refreshments from her politely, and Linda apologized.

'Sorry, chaps. I couldn't manage the full English breakfast. The ghastly smell of bacon always reminds me of Peter. But I thought you'd like a nice drinkie and some choccy bics.'

'You want us to have it out here?' Sir Gregory shivered a little as a curtain of cloud closed over the sun. 'Or shall I help you indoors with it?'

'Leslie suggested we meet by the pool.' Linda Millichip looked at the former Cabinet Minister as though for instructions.

'I thought it appropriate' – Titmuss took over the meeting – 'since we're here, to remember Peter Millichip.'

'A thoroughly good sort.' Sir Gregory wished to come to an early and uncontroversial conclusion.

At this Linda Millichip, who had her nose in a glass balloon awash with Cointreau, merely snorted.

'Is that your view of the matter?' Titmuss asked with interest.

'You wouldn't agree?' Sir Gregory frowned, fearing a prolonged discussion.

'A good sort, you said. Doesn't that rather depend on what sort you're talking about?'

'Well, Peter never pretended to be a high-flier.'

'Did he not? I thought he tried to fly pretty high on at least one occasion.'

There was a pause; Sir Gregory looked up and saw the Kite again, a true high-flier. 'I'm not sure about that. Perhaps he'd've liked to be a Junior Minister. At Privatization.'

'I was talking to our former Chief Whip. About the day the gardener here heard a crash in the house and came in to find Peter Millichip lying in the hall with a rope round his neck and wearing rather old-fashioned cami-knickers. I believe with black stockings and garters. I don't think he was after a Junior Ministry on that occasion. He was after an orgasm brought on by partial strangulation.'

'The little creep!' Linda licked the chocolate off her ringed fingers.

'He'd tried hanging himself from the banister railing. Luckily or not it broke. As I remember we had to pay the gardener a considerable sum of money to dissuade him from selling the story to the *Sun*. I think you were away on that occasion, weren't you, Linda?'

'Secretive bastard,' Mrs Millichip agreed. 'Only enjoyed himself behind my back.'

'I know nothing of that.' There was a slight tremor in Sir Gregory's shoulders, as though to shake off an unfortunate memory.

'No. But you know something of the other occasion, when Millichip flirted with disaster and fell for it. You know something about that, don't you, Gregory?'

'I really have no idea what you're talking about.'

'Oh, I think you do. I'm talking about the morning Millichip was found dead in that nice, clean, chlorinated water we see in front of us. I'm recalling the morning when you were kind enough, and public spirited enough, to give work experience to a boy highly skilled in picking locks.'

For a while there was no sound but the water lapping in the wind and the glugging as Linda Millichip replenished her glass. At last Sir Gregory sighed and turned his well-known quizzical smile on Titmuss. 'Really, Leslie,' he said. 'I don't know what Linda's been telling you.'

'Linda didn't tell me. Young Slippy Johnson told me. He came across with the whole story.'

'What do you mean, the whole story?'

'That you didn't get Slippy out to weed roses. You brought him here and showed him something in the shed over there. The one with the sauna bath, I believe. Something you'd fished out of the pool. A man in a woman's leopardskin bathing dress, handcuffed and gagged. Slippy was a boy you knew could pick locks and get the handcuffs off our M.P. before he was dropped back in the pool. I'm sure you thought he'd done an excellent job. Did you help with the gag and the swimwear?'

'It wasn't even my bikini!' Linda gave a mirthless chuckle. 'The little horror must have gone out and bought it for himself!'

'So, by the time the police arrived the Honourable Member was a naked Millichip, back in the pool, unmanacled.'

Sir Gregory crossed his legs, puffed his cheeks, blew out air and decided to meet trouble head on. 'Something had to be done,' he said, 'for the sake of the Party. And Linda too, of course.' He turned and gave Mrs Millichip his charming smile. 'That sort of kinky behaviour wouldn't have gone down at all well in Hartscombe.'

'The fact that you interfered with a corpse wouldn't have gone down very well in Hartscombe either. I'm not at all sure it's not my public duty to let the electors know exactly what you did.'

'You wouldn't do that, Leslie! You've always been loyal to the Party.' Now Sir Gregory was seriously rattled. He twisted a gold signet-ring on his little finger and did his best to look beseeching.

'On certain conditions,' Titmuss told him, 'I might be prepared to keep your secret. And Linda's.'

'What conditions?' Sir Gregory got the whiff of a deal.

'That you behave sensibly and Willock withdraws the stupid allegation of lying against his opponent.'

'You want us to lose the election?'

'I want to save you from making fools of yourselves.'

'Willock's his own man.'

'I don't believe that for a moment. Willock's your man. He'll do exactly what you tell him.'

'What are you getting at, Leslie?'

'Nothing very obscure. A fair fight and a decent result.'

'Aren't you still supporting us?'

'Haven't I agreed to speak outside the town hall?'

'Yes. Of course. And we're extremely grateful.'

'Then I take it we agree. I'll listen to Willock's press conference with considerable interest.'

'The boy Slippy won't say anything?' Sir Gregory was anxious again.

'I'm sure not. We'll do our best to keep him out of Blacken-stock.'

'Then, if Linda agrees . . .'

'Linda has been good enough to organize this meeting.' Titmuss selected, for the first time and with great care, a chocolate biscuit, and bit into it delicately. 'I'm sure, Gregory, she'll be guided by you, as she has been from the beginning.'

'What do you think, Linda?' Sir Gregory was still anxious. 'I don't imagine you want the publicity . . .'

'I told you. The little sod was turned on by death more than by sex with me. I'm not too keen on everyone knowing that. Let's keep it out of the papers.'

'Well, that would seem' – Titmuss, having finished his biscuit, rose to his feet – 'to conclude our business. I'm sure we all know where we stand. You can get the pool covered up again, Linda. No need to remind ourselves of this unhappy incident any more.'

So he moved away from them and Sir Gregory Inwood, in considerable relief, gulped the drink that Linda Millichip poured for him. It was sweet, sticky and rather disgusting, but it restored his confidence.

'I would like to make a statement about the accusation of lying against my Labour opponent.' Tim Willock stood alone at the Union-Jack-draped table at his press conference. No minister had agreed to join him that morning and the Party Chairman was otherwise engaged. 'Our further investigations have shown us that Terry Flitton's father in fact remained a shop-floor employee during his entire working life. His description in the Labour candidate's election manifesto was perfectly correct. I am pleased to withdraw the allegation of publishing an untruth unreservedly.'

When Willock, who didn't look in the least pleased, paused for breath, the journalists made their bids.

'Mel Rathbone from the *Guardian*. Does that mean you're apologizing to Terry Flitton?'

'It means exactly what I say. We withdraw the accusation.'

'Cornelius Vance from the *Telegraph*. So that's an apology?'

'I have already answered that question.'

'Bob Pertwee from *The Times*. Wouldn't it have been better if you'd done your research before you fired off the accusation of lying?'

'I have nothing to add to my previous answer.'

'Are you expecting Terry Flitton to take legal proceedings against you?'

'I think I've answered all your questions on this subject, and time's running short. Can we now deal with Monetary Union . . .'

Realizing they would get no further, the journalists put down their pencils and closed their eyes.

Terry heard the news on the van radio when he was driving with Kate, who had taken the days that were left before the poll off work, and a few volunteers, to canvass the travellers at Worsfield bus station. The volunteers in the van clapped and cheered, and Kate said, 'So that's over then.'

'Yes,' Terry agreed. 'It seems to be over.'

'Thank your lucky stars.'

But Terry thought he knew whom he had to thank.

# Chapter Nineteen

Agnes was looking down at her body, white and pink, shadowed between the legs, lapped in water greened by bath gel. It was a critical assessment. Her legs had grown no shorter, her thighs and stomach had not been distended by the passage of time. She couldn't claim the breasts of a young girl ('young girl' were the words she used to avoid saying 'Kate' to herself), but she was still going to get dressed without a bra. She raised her chin and soaped her neck, fearing loose skin at her throat, feeling for it with forced courage. She would last a little while longer, she decided; her lease of a desirable body might run out, but not yet. How long? How long could she rely on anything? Pressing her breasts she might, any day, discover a lump. She could crash her car, which she drove fast and carelessly, head on into one of the lorries which filled the country lanes bearing precious shit from London Airport to scatter on the fields. She could fall, as her father had, from a soaring horse over a dark hedge, and might, at any time, discover his need to do so. But, while it was still hers, she lay in her bath and thought about her body, and about Terry, who might also be hers for however long or short a time after his passionate love affair with the voters of Hartscombe and Worsfield South released him after election night.

It had been a long, dusty day at the bookshop, reorganizing the second-hand shelves, phoning publishers, dealing with customers desperately anxious to buy books but unable to remember the titles or the authors' names. What she now had to look forward to was

*As You Like It* at Skurfield Y.O.I. She twiddled the hot-water tap with her toe, felt the warm tide flowing up her legs and listened to the five o'clock news programme which boomed and crackled from the transistor on the damp bath-mat. Bob Pertwee from *The Times* was discussing the latest turn of events in the Hartscombe by-election.

'So, Bob,' the anchorlady asked in a sad and serious voice, 'is this retraction going to harm the Conservative campaign seriously?'

'I think it might. It seems to have been a quite reckless allegation, and Mr Willock was obviously extremely uncomfortable when he had to eat his words.'

'Do you think the Labour candidate will sue for libel?'

'He might well have grounds for that, but Terry Flitton told me he doesn't want to drag Mr Willock through the courts. He says he'd much rather leave the decision to the voters on Thursday.'

'Hartscombe has always been a safe Tory seat. Are you saying that Labour are in with a chance?'

'They have an excellent candidate in Terry Flitton. He's got a steep hill to climb, but yes. I think he might just possibly do it.'

'Thank you, Bob. I'm afraid that's all we've got time for. Now, can stiletto heels seriously damage your health . . .'

As the hot water covered her like a warm blanket Agnes's eyes misted. Honour and decency were winning at last, and Terry's refusal to grub for libel damages was a gallant gesture. She loved him the more for it.

That morning Terry had been standing by the steps of the Worsfield Flier, a non-stop bus to London, shaking hands and introducing himself as 'Terry Flitton, your Labour candidate,' when the mobile squeaked in his pocket. He stood with one hand holding the phone to his ear, the other greeting the passengers boarding the Flier, and he heard the familiar mocking rasp. He was grateful to it, of course, but hoped that, after his victory, he would never have to listen to his Master's Voice again.

'I want to see you. Now won't be too soon.'

'And I want to thank you for all you've done.' Terry spoke quietly, looking across at Kate, who was canvassing a couple of drivers who seemed struck dumb by her beauty.

'You may not thank me when you hear what I've got to say. Half an hour. I'll meet you at that damned hut. In Hanging Wood.'

'Sorry. I'm afraid I'm booked up.'

'And if you're not there I'll hand them over to Willock.'

'Hand what over?'

'The documentary evidence. Service agreement. All the details from W.R.F., about your father's job.'

Terry had walked through the wood filled with happiness, on his way to some sort of dream. Now he plodded through the leaves like a man in a nightmare. What was the old bastard up to? Preparing to betray him? Making sure of a Labour defeat? Entertaining himself with some elaborate and brutal practical joke? He had to find out, but he dreaded the knowledge.

He had seen the ex-government Rover in the narrow road, and his heart sank. The hut, when he reached it, seemed silent, empty. Was it all a trick to take him away from pressing the flesh of bus travellers to an empty hut, only for the sake of a sepulchral chuckle? By the time he pushed the rickety door open he'd almost persuaded himself that he'd find no one there, but he was disappointed. The tall figure in the dark coat with a woollen scarf at his throat said, 'Not exactly the bridal suite, is it? Can't quite match up to afternoon sex at the Hotel Splendide in Monte Carlo.'

Terry didn't tell him that, on his last visit, it had seemed more romantic than any hotel. He said, 'It's an old poacher's hut.'

'A good enough place, I suppose, for you to wreck your chances. Anyway, you're five minutes late.'

'I'm sorry.'

'So you should be. After all the damn trouble I've taken over you.'

'I wanted to tell you that I'm extremely grateful.' But should he be? He was about to win, barring all accidents. Should he have to be eternally grateful to a has-been old Tory grandee?

'Perhaps you won't be so grateful when I've finished. Sit down. I want to talk to you.'

Terry looked at the sofa. The escaping springs would stick into him and damp seep into his trousers. He took off his anorak, folded it carefully, and sat on it, alarmed at his own obedience. He said, 'You had some papers.'

'Enough to prove Willock's case a hundred times over.' Titmuss's hand emerged from his coat pocket clutching flimsy and crumpled slips of paper. Terry reached out for them. 'Not yet!' Titmuss restored the papers to his overcoat. 'Not till you've done what I tell you.'

'I'm not exactly under your orders . . .'

'Do you think not? Don't you understand? You've disappointed me. After all I've done for you.'

'I'm sorry . . .'

'No, you're not. You're doing it quite deliberately. Taking the most idiotic risks. Even in this stinking little hut.'

'Risks of what?' But of course Terry knew.

'Becoming a candidate who embarrasses me. Steers himself deliberately on to the rocks. And on to the front page of the *Sun*. What're you going to do when your wife finds out, just before polling day, you've been shafting a middle-aged constituent in the woods?'

'Has she found out?' Terry said as though there were something he could do about it if she had.

'Not yet she hasn't. Not until I tell her.'

'Are you going to?'

'That depends entirely on you.'

'How did you know?' Terry was asking him, he knew, an unimportant question, postponing the demands that were about to be made on him.

'By using my eyes. And with a little help from others.'

'You had me followed?'

Titmuss was clearly not in the least ashamed of it. 'Of course. As I say, I've put a lot of time and effort into you. I had to keep an eye on my investment.'

'It's my private life.'

'It's mine now. And it's your public's.'

'What if I told you I was in love?'

'With the daughter of a Socialist doctor? With a starry-eyed Leftie? With a fag hag who makes friends with a do-gooding prison governor? With a considerably older woman?'

'Yes. With all of those. What would you say?'

'I'd say you've got to break it off before it gets into the tabloids. Kate, or whatever her name is, 'll look so pretty in the photograph. She'll touch the readers' hearts.'

'What do you want me to do?'

'Break it off. Before it's too late.'

'You mean, tell Agnes it's over?'

'You'd probably make a mess of it. I want you to do more than that.'

'What do you mean?'

'Make her hate you.'

'She won't.'

As they stood there, in the damp and rotting hut which had been the scene of so much love, his monstrous helper, the dark presence that seemed to have taken control of his life told him: 'Do what you said you'd never do. Tell the world that the governor of Skurfield Young Offenders' Institution's got a taste for boys.'

'I can't.'

'Yes, you can. You must, to make sure that stupid so-called love affair's over.'

'And if I don't?'

'I told you. Wee Willie Willock gets the evidence he wants.'

Terry looked into the smiling face of the old man. 'You're just doing this to show you can control me. You're doing it for power.'

'You may be right. You should understand as well as anybody that power is a great deal more interesting than love.'

'It's quite unnecessary' – Terry tried to sound reasonable – 'to attack Fogarty.'

'I've decided how it's got to be done. So it seems that you'll have to do it. She won't forgive you.'

'What do you want me to call him?' Terry was angry. 'A faggot? A poofter? A fairy? What was the expression they used in your time? Queer? A pansy?'

'Use whatever words you like. Only make sure she understands.'

There was a silence between them, and then Terry said, 'I'll think about it.'

'If I were you,' Lord Titmuss made the impossible supposition, 'I should think very hard indeed.'


'If I were a woman, I would kiss as many of you as had beards that pleased me, complexions that liked me, and breaths that I defied not; and, I am sure, as many as have good beards, or good faces, or sweet breaths, will, for my kind offer, when I make curtsy, bid me farewell.'

So Rosalind spoke her epilogue in the play, a girl no longer dressed as a boy or, in reality, Alaric Inwood, public-school drug-dealer, now dressed as a girl, and he said the words as they were written, and as he, more than any other member of the cast, had learnt them. On the stage at the end of the Y.O.I. gymnasium Duke Senior and the melancholy Jaques, Orlando and Jaques de Boys, Touchstone the clown and Charles the wrestler, William the country fellow and Audrey the country wench, Celia, Rosalind's friend now dressed as a girl, Silvius and the vicar Sir Oliver Martext, stood on a stage decorated with branches shedding their leaves, a stag's head on loan from the Swan's Nest Hotel, and bowed in more or less embarrassment as Alaric performed a creditable curtsy. An unShakespearean voice in the audience called out, 'Good on yer, poofter!', and was seriously warned by a prison officer. The audience applauded warmly.

The gym was packed, but a wide gap divided the inmates from the visitors, the friends of the Offenders' Institution, who had bought raffle tickets, paid up when the boys' artworks were auctioned, lent furniture, supplied make-up or prepared and served the vegetarian meal. They applauded as loudly as the inmates, told each other that it was really very good and indeed better than the production set on an abandoned building site at Stratford that year. They felt strangely excited at being in a prison, having been let in by men and women with jangling keys, with iron gates opening and clanging behind them. The education officers, the social workers, the instructors in pottery and transcendental meditation, being used to the prison, clapped less loudly than those in the voluntary sector and did not whisper such facts as that the melancholy Jaques had been the leader of a gang rape and that Orlando had robbed for heroin. In the front row the governor sat between Anne Hopkins the English teacher who was the play's producer, and Agnes, who wore, unusually, a black dress, high heels and jewellery for the occasion. She held her hands high in the air and clapped, applauding not only the actors but the high achievement of her friend's liberal and enlightened regime. Agnes and Anne went for a drink in the governor's office. The inmates were taken back to the cells. The visitors were escorted down corridors, through doors unlocked and locked again, and down concrete paths through a prison garden rimed with frost, towards the gate.

They were admitted, in a shivering, chattering group, into a brightly lit no man's land, between custody and freedom. Trevor Marlowe, a prison officer with a beard, and P.O. Sheena Gamble were in charge of this final stage of the visitors' journey. These two were tired after a long day and the overtime entailed in the production of *As You Like It*. They were also much in love and anxious to get back to Sheena's Worsfield flat, into which Trevor had just moved, leaving his wife and children in Fallowfield. Sheena glanced casually at the little knot of women visitors, fur coats, anoraks and scarves over their cocktail dresses, who chattered their teeth and called out to be released to their warm cars. She locked the bars behind them and Trevor opened the small door in the main gate.

Among the departing women was one skirted, cloaked figure, whose head and ears were protected by a tartan scarf. When she was out in the car park she approached no car but made for a dark corner of a wire fence and started to climb. The scarf slid back as Celia/Slippy wriggled over the top of the fence and slipped back into freedom at last.

By the end of the evening Terry had made up his mind. He hadn't come so far in the struggle for Hartscombe to throw the prize away now and, he told himself, he had to protect Agnes. Titmuss had to be told and told quickly. He phoned his Lordship and got no reply. Finally he scribbled a note – 'I have decided to denounce P.F. I see no alternative.' – signed it and after *As You Like It* drove round to the Manor. Nobody answered his ring so he put his envelope through the letter-box and went away, dreading what he had to do.

# Chapter Twenty

Nabbs had said, 'You're strangely honoured. The big guns never arrived to help Des Nabbs win Fallowfield. Reckon they thought I could fight my own battles. Well, I also reckon they were right. What you've done to make yourself the blue-eyed boy, God knows!'

'If God knows,' Terry thought, 'I hope he keeps it to himself.'

So, on the morning before polling day he sat at his positively last morning press conference between the big guns Nabbs had wondered if he deserved. These heavy howitzers came in the shape of a man and a woman. The man was Eric Feldman, a short, plump, bald, bespectacled Bermondsey sparrow who had carried the nasal twang of his South London accent (he was the only child of a successful greengrocer) through London University and all the way up to the Shadow Cabinet. He was a favourite of cartoonists, who saw him as an irrepressible little bird whispering advice, usually to take devious and daring action, into his Leader's ear.

The other big gun was the dark-haired, pale-faced, immaculately dressed woman Terry had seen, but hadn't spoken to, at the Barbarians' dinner. She was wearing, that day, a large brooch in the shape of a scarlet dagger and, as she gave the candidate a firm handshake, she said, 'Hannah Mortlock'. Then Terry knew who she was – a Midlands M.P. and the Leader's political adviser – and he understood why Nabbs M.P., in greeting her, had allowed himself the bow which he would never have made in the presence of Royalty.

They sat in front of a large screen which was not red, or even pink, but a pale shade of green on which a single rose was depicted. The usual suspects, Bob from *The Times*, Mel from the *Guardian* and Cornelius from the *Telegraph*, sat in the front row, and the cameras flashed as Eric Feldman told them that notice would be served on the Conservatives the next day. There would be a Labour government after the general election, which had to come before the summer, and the Tories had better save up their cash for questions as retirement money. They'd be sent home, provided they could find a privatized train still running to take them. He spoke slowly, as though to explain his jokes to an audience of children whose first language was not English. Terry thought that the Shadow Home Secretary's heavily underlined irony was disliked by Bob, Mel and Cornelius, who didn't crack a single smile, although June Wilbraham of the *Sentinel* laughed politely.

When Eric sat down Mel asked if Terry intended to live in the constituency were he to win the next day. Terry had just opened his mouth to reply when Hannah Mortlock's husky voice of authority came out with, 'Terry Flitton's a local boy, as you know. His heart is in Hartscombe, and he's absolutely committed to moving here with his wife after his victory. Terry also tells me he'll be starting a family. If there are no more questions, I think that just about wraps it up.'

As the hall emptied Terry said goodbye to Hannah. 'Thanks for telling me about the family,' he said. 'It's the first I've heard of it.'

'It's what we usually say,' she told him, 'to make sure they don't think you're going in for a sex change or anything embarrassing.'

He said, 'I didn't get a chance to say much.' She was smiling at him, exposing slightly protuberant front teeth. To his surprise he felt a disturbing moment of sexual attraction.

'Until the voters have been counted,' Hannah told him severely, 'it's much better that you don't say anything at all.'

But Terry knew that he'd have to say something very soon indeed.

*

It happened as soon as he got back to headquarters in Penry's house. Nabbs had stayed to make the most of the big guns and escort Hannah Mortlock, with a quasi-royal flourish, to her car. Penry was busy organizing transport to drag potential Labour voters, kicking and screaming if necessary, to the polls. The big downstairs room looked a tip, with lists, pamphlets and paper cups covering the table-tops, but no overflowing ashtrays owing to the presence of Kate, who had answered one foolhardy male Party worker who had asked, 'Do you mind if I smoke?' with 'Do you mind if I die?' A question which he neither wanted nor dared to answer.

'For you,' a red-headed girl in tartan trousers handed Terry a phone.

'Yes? Terry Flitton speaking.'

'Oh, Mr Flitton. It's Kenny Iremonger from Radio Worsfield. I suppose you've heard the news?'

'No. What news?' Terry had a moment of irrational dread, a vision of Agnes's Volkswagen smashed and shapeless in front of a shit wagon, blood on the road and a shape covered with a blanket. It came as a relief when the voice said, 'We've just got the release. There was a break-out last night at Skurfield. One of the young offenders got clean away.'

'Oh, really?' Terry felt detached, uninterested, until he remembered what Titmuss had called upon him to do.

'We don't know who the particular lad is. We have heard that it might be one of the louts that mugged Lady Inwood. We just wondered if you'd care to comment?'

The terrible moment had come. 'Well, yes,' Terry said. 'Yes, I'll give you a quote.'

'We're quite ready,' Kenny Iremonger said over the phone. 'Mr Flitton. What's your comment on the Skurfield break-out?'

'The present Home Secretary must accept responsibility for the slackness at Skurfield. And the inappropriate appointment of that particular governor.'

'You're saying that Paul Fogarty isn't up to the job?'

'I should have thought that was obvious. Mr Fogarty may have many virtues but he's clearly not a suitable custodian of young boys.'

'Why not exactly?'

'He is . . .' In the seconds of a pause Terry's mind was whirling. Couldn't he win now without Titmuss? He could face Willock, he could swear undying loyalty to Kate. He could say no more and fight the battle to the end. But the risks seemed too great, and panic overcame him. Titmuss had got him to the point of victory and now Titmuss could destroy him for ever. He made a dash for safety, as his dark Lordship's obedient servant. He heard his voice, as though it were the voice of a stranger. 'He is . . . unmarried.'

'What's that meant to mean?'

'What I have said. His sexual orientation makes him unsuit-able.'

'Thank you, Mr Flitton. There's nothing else you want to add to that?'

'Nothing.'

He put down the phone with a dry mouth and a feeling of having stepped into darkness. If he hadn't lost the election he had certainly lost Agnes. And then he managed to persuade himself that if he could only speak to her he could find some form of words, some reasonable-sounding explanation which would surely convince her. Even though Kate was in the room he called Agnes's number, but there was no reply; nor was he able to speak to her in the days to come.

'And now, ladies and gentlemen. On the eve of a poll which may prove to be one of the more important events in Hartscombe's history, when this dear old town of ours decides whether to stick to a sensible, businesslike government with increasing prosperity and low inflation or take a risk on the big dipper to Socialism, let me introduce the man who has, for so long, been the heart and soul of the Conservative Party, Lord Titmuss of Skurfield, with a message which I know will hearten and inspire us all.'

What had been planned was an outdoor rally in the early dark of a cold evening. It was to be an echo of a nobler political past, when Disraeli climbed on to the portico of a Beaconsfield hotel or when Gladstone addressed the cheering multitudes in Midlothian. By careful planning the Tory workers had produced something like a multitude, bussing in Young Conservatives from outside the constituency, rounding up Party activists from as far away as London and Birmingham, organizing a number of parties after the event and handing out hot wine to warm the crowd. So the square in front of the town hall looked packed and Sir Gregory, apparently not in the least put out by the discussion of his poolside activities, stood in his overcoat and a fur hat with ear flaps, which he had bought for a mission to Moscow, and introduced the Party's heart and soul.

And then, like some gaunt pontiff about to deliver a message to the faithful, Titmuss emerged from the entrance of the town hall and stood on the top step, bathed in the false sunshine of the television lights, and quoted scripture from a note he held in his hand.

'To every thing there is a season, and a time to every purpose under the heaven. A time to be born, and a time to die; a time to plant and a time to pluck up that which is planted . . . A time to weep, and a time to laugh; a time to mourn, and a time to dance. A time to get, and a time to lose; a time to keep, and a time to cast away.'

There was, at this solemn beginning, an ecclesiastical silence, broken only by a single cough from an elderly supporter who had been dragged out of bed for the occasion.

'So, my friends and fellow Conservatives. What is this time for? This time, when we stand on the verge of a great decision? Is it a time to dance?'

The loyal crowd, which hadn't considered the possibility of dancing, didn't answer this question.

'No, my friends. This is damn well not a time to dance!' Was this a joke? To be on the safe side the audience met it with a ripple of laughter. 'I would suggest to you, in all humility, that we have very little to dance about. Not long ago our Party saw the assassination, the betrayal, the deposition, in a mean-minded back-stairs plot meanly carried out, of the greatest Leader our Party has ever known. I needn't repeat her name. Her name is engraved on the heart of every loyal Party supporter.'

Here the audience clapped, leaving it unclear whether they were applauding the Great Leader or her assassination.

'Among those who carried a dagger, even if was only a small dagger, rather blunt, and he wasn't much good at stabbing, was our present candidate Mr Willock. He was then the not entirely Honourable Member for Pulford. Mr Willock now claims, as his reward, your votes and the seat of Hartscombe and Worsfield South!'

Here the crowd began to realize that this was not to be an enthusiastic endorsement of the Conservative candidate. But then Titmuss was back in Ecclesiastes.

'A time to cast away stones, and a time to gather stones together; a time to embrace, and a time to refrain from embracing . . . A time to rend, and a time to sew; a time to keep silence, and a time to speak. My friends. Fellow Conservatives I have kept silent. After all, I told myself, I'm a retired politician. A bloke kicked upstairs to the House of Lords. An old foot soldier in the service of our late Leader, who has fought his battles and is busy examining his scars and polishing his medals in the retirement home.'

At this a red-faced man with a moustache called out, 'Rubbish, Leslie! You'll always be a fighter!'

'Thank you very much. There may be some truth in that! Well, as I say, I thought it was a time for silence, but now I know it's a time to speak. And you know me. When it's a time to speak I speak my mind. I can't help it!'

Sir Gregory, who thought he knew what was coming and feared

it horribly, moved back into the shadows. Whatever Leslie was going to say about the late Member's death, he was prepared to deny. But once again the sad, sing-song voice quoted the Bible.

' "A time to cast away stones and a time to gather stones together." And which stones should we cast away? Those that pelted our Great Leader! My friends. It's a time to speak, and a time to speak plainly, because there is a time to get and a time to lose. And, in all honesty, I suggest that this is a time to lose!'

The crowd, after a quick intake of breath, was stunned into a profound silence. If Lord Titmuss had stripped and done a full frontal dance on the town hall steps they would not have been so astounded or, indeed, embarrassed.

'And why is this a good election to lose? So we can take stock. So we can get back to the tough old truths we stand for. So we can cast away the stones that tell us to become softer, trendier, more "compassionate", which means trimming our sails and standing for nothing very much. I've been asked here to endorse a candidate. All right, I'll endorse one. Young Terence Flitton calls himself a Socialist. He's not doing himself justice. He's no more a Socialist than I am. Believe you me, that young lad has got his head screwed on. He's not afraid to say what he thinks. You heard what he said about the do-gooding attitude to young thugs. Let's give him a chance, shall we? I reckon he'll do, just until we can pluck out the weeds in our Party and come back and fight for the real Conservatism, the tough old policies we know and love. Fight for them and win! Goodnight and God bless you all.' At this his Lordship turned and, like some character in a melodrama leaving the stage, disappeared into the entrance of the town hall. On a distant hillside a bus hooted. The crowd remained silent.

Standing near the steps, a dark-haired young man wearing a leather coat with a sheepskin collar shouted, 'Good old Titmuss!', and started to clap. Confused but obedient, and because they had always applauded him in the past, the audience gave Titmuss an ovation which was neither loud nor prolonged. He didn't reappear to take his curtain call.

Inside the Town Hall he went to the Gents, took off his overcoat and jacket and washed his face and his hands carefully. He combed what was left of his hair in a spotted mirror and dressed up warmly again. He was not surprised, when he emerged into the marble hallway, to find no sign of the candidate, the Party Chairman or any of their supporters. He heard other footsteps, however, echoing towards him and saw a young man holding out his hand.

'Garth Inwood,' he said. 'I think you got a sighting of my delinquent young brother in the nick. I just wanted to say I thought that was a terrific speech. Agreed with every single word of it. We need a period of peace to regroup and then, Wow! Won't we show them!'

Titmuss stood still, examining the boyishly enthusiastic young man, and then he took the proffered hand. So they stood linked together, like people who have reached an agreement.

# Chapter Twenty-One

The Hartscombe ballot boxes arrived first for the count in the town hall, and then the Willock bundles were stacked higher after the tellers had sorted them. The Conservative candidate had an early lead; the Labour was a distinct second, the Lib Dem third in the field; National Front, Animal Rights, Sterling Protection and Monster Raving Loony were nowhere very much. Terry and Penry, Sir Gregory and Willock, Velma Warrington and her team moved edgily round the hall, peering critically at the tellers, doing sums on the backs of envelopes and, in a common agony of suspense, got together in a sort of companionship, as girls in a slave market might make friends and chatter, trying not to think of the indignity of having to be sold off cheap. Only Terry stood apart, nursing a mug of tea, answering his wife shortly even when she smiled at him. He felt, as that long evening wore on, like a man who has lost everything, and he returned, again and again, to the events of the last twenty-four hours hoping to find some glimmer of consolation.

Titmuss's speech had jostled wars, earthquakes, famines and genocide off the front pages of the national papers; but Titmuss was now the enemy Terry could hardly bear to think about. Among Terry's workforce the terrible words he had been made to utter seemed to have created little impression. Nabbs, it's true, said he'd better watch out for libel actions; but Terry didn't think of Paul as at all likely to sue for damages and comforted himself with the honourable nature of the man he had agreed to dishonour. Even

Kate seemed strangely unmoved by the incident, although she did ask him, with a note of pity in her voice, if he hadn't become a bit homophobic, as though it were a painful and probably incurable disease.

'It's not that I mind in the least about his sexuality. It's just that the boys might be at risk.' He lied to her and she seemed to accept it. She assumed, apparently without difficulty, the old-fashioned feminine role of the comforter, the sensible one, the supporter and tower of strength who got on with things, while her man, a bundle of fears, doubts and nervous dread, stood in the shadows holding a mug of tea he didn't drink, afraid to look at the piles of votes in case the news might be bad.

It was true that Terry had given up looking at the arriving ballot boxes or the growing piles of votes counted. He was re-living, as he would have to in the months and years to come, the agony of the hours since he had commented on the escape of Slippy Johnson. He had gone to his mobile as an alcoholic goes to the bottle and called Agnes again and again at home and in the shop but got no reply at either number. In a wild moment of frustration he had considered ringing Paul Fogarty at the Y.O.I., but wisely decided that was out of the question. The day before he had passed the door of the Dust Jacket and found it open. He had pushed his way in and seen, to his delight, smoke rising from her desk behind a bookcase, but when he got round it he was staring at a plump, jovial, dark-haired woman who twinkled at him in a roguish way and said, 'Oh, jolly good! Have you come in to buy something?'

'Agnes!' Terry cried out for help. 'Where's Agnes?'

'Not here, I'm afraid.'

'Where then? Where is she?'

'Gone off on holiday. Such short notice and so like her. She rang me up and said she was off to the sun somewhere and would I hold the fort. I'm her partner, you know. Jilly Bloxham, if it makes any difference.'

'What sun? Where's she gone, did she say?'

'Oh, Majorca. Martinique. Mombasa. Could it be Mombasa? I'm sure she'll send a postcard.'

'I do need to know. It's quite urgent.'

'Oh, I'll tell her you called. Soon as I hear something. I say,' – She was looking at Terry as though she had detected something wrong with him, egg on his chin perhaps, or a zip undone – 'aren't you one of the candidates?'

'Yes.'

'Oughtn't you to be out canvassing or something?'

'Not exactly, but I've got to go . . .'

'Are you one of those Liberals?'

'My poster's in your window.' Terry did his best to sound calm. 'I'm standing for Labour.'

'Oh, I say, bad luck! Agnes is frightfully Labour, of course. She always backs losers.'

After a long day of frustration Terry called in at the Magic Magnolia for a take-away he could share with Kate as they worked the telephones in Penry's house. The restaurant was full, and Charlie, gliding between the tables, gave Terry a knowing smile. At last the spectacled proprietor, wearing a suit instead of a white jacket, handed Terry the warm bags of seaweed, duck, sizzling beef and mixed vegetables, with fried rice and prawn crackers. He also gave him two bills. The first was for the take-away and entirely reasonable. The second was a blank bill sheet on which was scribbled '£500'. Terry asked what the hell that might be for, had someone given a party in his name?

'Votes.' The restaurant boss made no attempt to lower his voice.

'What?'

'Twelve of us in the Magnolia. We live upstairs. You been asking for our votes. I bring them for you tomorrow.'

Disconsolate, Terry paid only one bill. The line had to be drawn somewhere.

\*

Midnight on polling day and the First Baron Skurfield, tieless, in his old cardigan with his shoes off, lay on the sofa in his study nursing a whisky. On an outsize television screen three pundits, Bob Pertwee, Eric Feldman and Barry Geering, the Home Secretary, a bulky and imposing man with a plummy voice, were filling in time before the Hartscombe result. Mrs Ragg, wearing bedroom slippers because of problems with her feet, squatted uneasily on the edge of the study chair, Leslie having invited her up to watch the result, sipping a small sherry. She was doing her best to follow the thoughts of the pundits.

Eric Feldman said, 'We're not expecting miracles, but we've got a first-class candidate. If the Lib Dems are serious about defeating the Tories they might switch to Labour. But I'm not over-optimistic.'

Barry Geering said, 'Hartscombe's a safe seat for us. I think Tim Willock's home and dry.'

The presenter said, 'What do you think's been the effect of Leslie Titmuss's extraordinary intervention?'

Bob Pertwee said, 'Titmuss is regarded as a bit of an old dinosaur by the Party nowadays. I think the voters in Hartscombe were embarrassed by his speech, quite honestly. I very much doubt if it'll affect the result.'

Mrs Ragg said, 'We are going to win, aren't we, sir?'

Titmuss said, 'It depends on who you mean by "we".'

Mrs Ragg said, 'Well, sir. The Conservatives.'

Titmuss said, 'Then I have to tell you. We are not going to win. I am going to win.'

In Rambo's, the disco on the river, the young clubbers danced, waved their arms, undulated trance-like as their pale faces shone and faded in the flashing lights. They downed Strongbow, parched after taking tablets, and their hands strayed over their partners as they shouted their secrets over the music. Very few of them had bothered to vote.

In the dark, dripping silence of Hanging Wood the deer slept and badgers snuffled in the undergrowth.

Paul Fogarty had the television on as he sat in his office and wrote his letter of resignation. He didn't want his days in court, his libel action, his inquiry into Slippy's escape, his further years of incarceration. He had served, he thought, his time. He wanted to get away from the rattle of keys, the clang of gates, the pervasive smell of cooking and central heating. He wanted to walk free.

The television announced that it was now going over to Hartscombe for the result. The governor had already been to the polling booth. In spite of everything he had voted Labour.

'The number of votes cast for each candidate is as follows.' The town clerk stood in front of the microphone. The candidates were lined up, smiles plastered on their faces and cheerful rosettes fastened to their lapels. Kate held one of Terry's hands, and he dug his nails into the other palm. He didn't dare believe what had become clear since the ballot boxes had to come in from the country areas. He heard a voice; it seemed a long way off.

'Busby, Grace Caroline (Animal Rights), 407 votes. Downey, Robert Cuthbert (National Front), 250 votes. Fortescue, James Catesby (Sterling Protection), 60 votes. Flitton, Terence Robert (Labour), 18,612 votes.' Cheers from the audience. 'Sutch, Screaming Lord (Monster Raving Loony), 115 votes. Warrington, Velma Phyllis (Liberal Democrat), 3060 votes.' Cheers from the audience. 'Willock, Timothy Manningham (Conservative), 13,105 votes.' Cheers. 'And I, declare Terence Robert Flitton duly elected as Member of Parliament for the constituency of Hartscombe and Worsfield South.' The cheers were prolonged. Terry Flitton had got what he wanted.

He thanked the returning officer and the police. He held Kate's hand up high and kissed her. He shook hands with the other candidates and spoke to the television and the radio and June from the *Sentinel*. He heard Penry and Nabbs congratulate each other on a surprising result. 'I had to put a bit of work into it,' said Nabbs, 'among the grass roots. But I always thought we'd do it.'

Then Terry left quickly in the direction of the Gents, but ran out of the town hall and down to the river. And there he saw a light in an upstairs window and was filled with hope.

But when he rang Agnes's bell the light went off immediately, and no one answered his ring, or his knocking, or his final, hopeless shout. A crowd of clubbers from Rambo's came down the street and stared at him. He stood in the shadows, flat against the wall, and felt the pricking in his eyes and a huge emptiness.

The black river was just across the street, but he didn't look towards it. Instead he took a deep breath, pulled himself together and went back towards the town hall and his victory party. Contrary to all reasonable expectations he had passed over, and all the trumpets would be sounding for him on the other side.

# Part Two

# Chapter Twenty-Two

The Red Kite, drifting over the Millichip spread on another late-summer afternoon saw no drowned bodies, dressed or undressed, manacled or free, but something as alarming and as much to be avoided by right-thinking people in the area. A fleet of cars was assembled in the driveway. Indoors the chatter, rising to the ceiling like the sound of a seriously disturbed aviary, rose in volume as the drinks were poured and the canapés, handed round with paper napkins to dab the crumbs from lips and wipe sticky fingers, were consumed as blotting paper for the ever-flowing stream of alcohol.

As the Red Kite, with a stroke of its wings, soared away into a high bank of cloud, Linda Millichip, flashing jewellery, proud of her freedom from the late Millichip, stood like a gracious but overbearing barbarian queen among her loyal subjects, who were gratefully drinking her champagne and manœuvring large Thai chicken balls into their hungry mouths.

'I want you to meet our Minister. This is Andrew Poyser.' And Linda Millichip added with a note of awe in her voice, 'The writer.'

'Minister?' The writer was a small man wearing a tweed suit with a waistcoat, his bald head, plump cheeks and pursed lips made him look like a well-bathed, powdered and contented baby. 'Baptist? Methodist? Seventh-day Adventist?'

'Prisons,' Terry Flitton answered, not solemnly. And then he said, 'Excuse me,' leaving the writer, who had opened his mouth to ask in a jocular sort of way for some further explanation, speechless. But Terry was threading his way through the crowd of Linda Millichip's new-found friends towards the woman he had seen standing under the colourful acrylic painting of boats in a Mediterranean harbour, her head bowed over her lighter as though it were some vestal flame. She was with Jilly Bloxham, her partner in the bookshop, and when he penetrated the crowd and arrived beside her she looked up, blew out smoke and said, 'Oh, hullo,' as though he hadn't missed her, longed for her, pursued her fruitlessly since the election night and his promotion to government.

He said, ignoring Jilly and not caring what she thought, 'I just wanted to explain.'

'No explanations necessary,' Agnes said. 'You simply behaved like a complete shit. Let's leave it at that, shall we?' The extraordinary thing, to Terry, was that she said it without rancour.

The New Labour M.P. for Hartscombe and Worsfield South was, when he took his seat, strangely overcome with nerves and excitement. As on his first day at school he looked on the other backbenchers, most of whom had been there at least a term, with mingled envy and suspicion. Nobody told him what to do or where to go, and he could be seen walking purposefully down corridors, trying hard to give the impression that he was going somewhere important. He voted the way he was told to, dreaded the displeasure of the Whips and, to his surprise, didn't manage to feel at all powerful.

In Hartscombe, however, it was different. Sitting in his surgery each week he could hand out reassurance to the anxious, hope to the unjustly treated and at least a patient hearing to those who complained they were having their sexuality undermined by the colouring in soft drinks or their minds disturbed by the power leaking from electric sockets. To his constituents he was wise, judicial and determinedly on their side. He would write letters to housing authorities, hospitals, schools and ministries demanding justice and attention in the peremptory tones to which he was sure a Member of Parliament was entitled, and if nothing much came of it he could tell his clients, and himself, that he had done all he could and no better could be expected under a Tory government. But as soon as his surgery was over he went in search of a past which, as he looked for it, seemed to grow in importance and deepen his sense of loss. He felt helpless, disappointed and, quite unreasonably, betrayed.

He went to the house by the river but found it dark and empty. He called at the Dust Jacket and found Jilly Bloxham always in charge. He questioned her eagerly at first and then as a sort of hopeless duty. Although her answers were by no means direct he understood, in time, that she knew where Agnes had gone but was instructed not to tell anyone and in particular not to tell the local M.P.

After a while he saw that her house was occupied and a strange car was parked in front of it, and he heard the sound of children. He discovered that it had been let for a year to an airline pilot who had no idea where Agnes was and paid the rent to a local solicitor. Terry called on the solicitor in question but, although he flashed all his credentials as the people's chosen representative, the man refused to divulge his client's address. He was almost desperate enough to ask Paul Fogarty, with impossible apologies, if he knew where Agnes was, but he soon discovered that Paul had left Skurfield not, apparently, with his career wrecked but having been offered a job, his reputation as a reforming governor having so far preceded him, running a boys' detention centre in Australia. So, at last, Terry had become reconciled to the fact that Agnes was lost, as completely as though by death.

What he had most men would have envied. Kate, in a year, had grown even more beautiful. She was proud of being the wife of an M.P. and, the position giving her more confidence, she was more relaxed. She treated her girlfriends at work more warmly, making it clear that Terry's new fame hadn't changed her in the least. She supported him, listened admiringly to his maiden speech (on the uncontroversial subject of rural post offices) and helped type out his numerous letters when they were too much for his shared secretary. She watched over him as he became a year older, less anxious, more secure, with a small part of his ambition realized and a great deal still to be achieved. They never quarrelled, but fell asleep more quickly and made love rather less often.

It was true that at first not many days, later not many weeks went by without Terry thinking of Agnes. It was as though he had been given a glimpse of another country, unexpected, extraordinary, anarchic and sometimes beautiful, which had suddenly been withdrawn from him, its borders closed and his visits clearly unwelcome. As time passed he almost forgot why his adventure with Agnes had ended, and his memories became more enjoyable, less infected by guilt. At moments he allowed himself to feel sorry for her because she had lost him, so it seemed, for good.

The other character who had dominated the Hartscombe by-election had also withdrawn from Terry's life. He avoided Rapstone Manor, and his mobile phone no longer bleated to relay Lord Titmuss's commands. During the general election in the spring after Terry's autumn victory Titmuss was surprisingly absent. Was he on a book tour publicizing his memoirs which, serialized in a Sunday paper, did so much to undermine the then Prime Minister's credibility? If so, his success was extraordinary. Terry doubled his majority and was swept back to power on a great wave on which so many young Labour researchers, party activists and think-tank secretaries joyfully surfed.

But by that time Terry was ahead of the game. He'd been noticed in the tearoom by Eric Feldman, the Shadow Home Secretary. 'I remember you,' he said. 'Never forget a face. Fullerton, isn't it?'

'Flitton.'

'Fallowfield constituency?'

'Hartscombe and Worsfield South.'

'That's right! Photographic memory. Something I was born with. Bloody useful! Never forgot the price of Brussels sprouts, when I was brought up in a greengrocer's shop. And I can tell you, if you can sell Brussels sprouts you can sell policies. You'll be standing again at the general election?'

'Yes,' Terry said. 'I'll be standing.'

'Think you'll win?'

'I'm sure of it.'

'Good. Very good. If I remember your campaign, you talked a certain amount of good common sense about prisons.'

'I'm glad you thought so.' Terry didn't attribute anything he said about penal matters to the inspiration of Lord Titmuss.

'Bit short of ideas in the Shadow Home Office team,' Eric Feldman had to confess. 'Some of them seem to find prison an embarrassing subject, like death. I'd welcome a bloke with strong old-fashioned views on the subject. That's what the voters like. Good dependable iceberg lettuce and none of your fancy rocket. Would you like to join the team? No extra money and precious little gratitude. What do you say?'

Terry said, 'I'd be delighted to do anything I can to help.' But in spite of this he expected a reward.

Terry's career advanced further when he went to a party given by the Elizabeth Fry Society on the terrace of the House of Commons. He made it his business to keep up with prison reformers as well as governors and probation officers, and also to those in his Party who believed in three convictions and that's your life. He was listening to a grey-haired and puzzled woman whose son was doing time for a rape, when Hannah Mortlock came up to him, a huge green star winking like some Ruritanian Order on her trim black jacket, and said, 'Well done you for Hartscombe. Take me to lunch some time. I want to know *all* about our Shadow Home Office team.' When Terry said he'd been asked to think up some new ideas, she was enthusiastic. 'The tabloids are telling the Great British Public they can't put their noses out of the door without being mugged, raped and probably buggered. They'll expect us to tell them the answers.' They were sentiments he'd last heard expressed, less vividly, by Tim Willock during the Hartscombe by-election. And then Hannah said, 'How's old Eric doing, in your opinion?'

It was the first time since he had taken his seat that anyone in the House had asked Terry for his opinion. He smiled and said, 'Oh, Eric's great fun. He keeps talking of selling policies like pounds of Brussels sprouts.'

'I know. It's rather worrying.' Hannah looked serious. 'No one buys Brussels sprouts by the pound any more. They come in packets, don't they, in the Asda freezer? In fact greengrocer's shops have definitely had their day. Keep in touch.' After that, she smiled at him in corridors, occasionally spoke and once instructed him to take her to lunch in a restaurant near the House. She ordered oysters and steak tartare, discussed her husband (in merchant banking), opera and which members of the Conservative Cabinet it would be possible, without taking painkillers, to go to bed with. Her pager went before the pudding, and she left him to pay the bill.

On the day after the general election Terry hung about near the telephone in his London flat. When it rang he leapt at it, answered breathlessly and was noticeably short with the friends, people at work or well-wishers who wanted to congratulate him at length and chat. When Kate was rung by two of her girlfriends he, unusually, lost control, shouted and told her to get off the line. It wasn't until seven o'clock in the evening that it happened. He picked up the telephone, now resigned to the back benches, and heard a sprightly girl's voice say, 'Is that you, Terry? Number Ten here. I've got the Prime Minister for you.'

When the call was over he yelled triumphantly for Kate. He was Minister with Responsibility for Prisons, and the Home Secretary, he was not particularly surprised to hear, was not Eric the green-grocer's son but Hannah Mortlock M.P., the Prime Minister's close political adviser.

*

Looking back on it, Agnes thought of her period of exile as a ridiculous overreaction.

Had it been worth it or, more accurately, had Terry been worth it? She had spent a large part of her savings and often missed Hartscombe, the sun rising out of the mist, the grey bridge and the damp smell of the swollen river. On the other hand she had turned a golden brown, being as reckless about the rays of the sun, feared by so many who covered themselves with various creams or even wore special clothing designed to block out its death-dealing rays, as she was about inhaling nicotine. Moreover, she had, she thought, on the other side of the world, achieved some sense of proportion. Out of his sight she could at last see Terry for what he was, someone to be understood if not forgiven. She could now, she felt in her more optimistic moments, grow up, even if that meant sooner rather than later growing old.

Henry Simcox, the angry young novelist who had been her husband before he turned into a crusty old blimp and left her, had a publisher, a gentle and sensitive soul who could no longer stand the brutal behaviour of such authors as Henry and who had retired to live in a house among the cork trees to the north of Toulon. Agnes, whom he had always fancied and frequently invited to stay, fled at first to this house, lay in the sun, cooked in a kitchen which smelt of olive oil and burning logs and lost count of time. Then, because she missed him and because she felt she had to atone for the unforgivable attack her lover had made on him, she went to stay with Paul Fogarty. In fact, Terry's words, which had shattered their affair, had hardly damaged Paul. The prison service had either wilfully ignored or else forgotten them and the job in Australia was still open. There was a house outside the boys' prison near Avalon, handy for the North Sydney beaches where the sun shone most of the year. Agnes joined him, officially as his housekeeper, some suspected as his mistress, but in truth as his friend, nursing him after a wound which had hardly proved fatal. She spent her days in delicatessens and becoming expert on such wines as Devil's Lair

Chardonnay and Plantagenet Shiraz. And then she told Paul she was going home. He drove her to the airport, and they kissed, two friends who might never, for all their promises to each other, meet again. So she came back to Hartscombe, cleaned her house, helped Jilly with the bookshop and didn't go looking for Terry when he, after so long, had given up looking for her.

She knew she'd meet him some time, and the idea no longer made her nervous. And yet she felt a faint tremor of excitement, a feeling that life might become more interesting, when she accepted the invitation to Linda Millichip's cocktail party.

At the party Betty Wellover from the Hartscombe stables looked round the crowded room and said to her hostess, 'How Peter would have adored a party like this! In your beautiful home.'

'You're quite wrong,' Linda Millichip told her. 'This wasn't the sort of thing that turned Peter on at all.'

'Oh, really? What sort of party did Peter like then?'

'I think,' Linda Millichip was smiling but not in a kind way, 'he liked to enjoy himself on his own.'

'Oh. A very private sort of person, was he?'

'On that subject,' Mrs Millichip said firmly, 'my lips are permanently sealed.'

'All the same' – Betty Wellover thought it wise to ask no further questions – 'we do miss him terribly.'

'There, my dear,' Linda told her, 'you speak entirely for yourself.'

June Wilbraham from the *Sentinel*, who had been invited along to take photographs, heard this conversation and decided, as a good journalist, that she should set about finding out exactly what it meant.

Having been called a complete shit, Terry stood smiling, looking round the room, checking up. Kate was out of earshot, talking to a small group of youngish wives, women he had canvassed and whose votes he had won in what was left of the rural areas. She was at ease, speaking with a new authority, saying something that made them laugh, and she laughed with them. At the French windows which opened on to the terrace and the swimming pool, a new guest had arrived. Lord Titmuss was talking to a young man with dark, carefully arranged hair, wearing an open-necked shirt and a sweater and laughing, as Kate's audience laughed, at some solemn sarcasm from his Lordship.

Terry turned back to Agnes and said, as though they were alone and her partner Jilly, standing close to her, didn't exist, 'We must meet again soon.'

'I honestly don't know why.'

'I want to find out what happened to you.'

'Let's say, I had a long convalescence. I'm better now.'

'You were ill?'

'Don't worry. I've got over it completely.'

'Then I'll ring you.'

'We're terribly busy in the bookshop these days. Aren't we, Jilly?'

'Oh, rushed off our feet.'

Terry had the uncomfortable feeling that Jilly Bloxham was also laughing at him. As he left with Kate he had to pass Lord Titmuss, who said, 'So, they've given you a job.'

'Well, yes. It's a great honour, to be in the government.'

'Not so much of an honour, I think you'll find, as the way they have of making sure you keep your mouth shut. Do you know young Garth Inwood?'

'We haven't met.' The young man held out a hand. 'You lot must be pretty cock-a-hoop, for the moment.'

'The public showed quite clearly what it wanted.' Terry took the hand but returned it as soon as possible to its owner.

'Conservative lot at heart, aren't they, though, the Great British Public?'

Terry was disturbed to see that Titmuss was looking at this youth who, he thought, could be dismissed as some over-eager, upper-class twit, with something like pride.

'Young Inwood's keen to set out on the bumpy road to political fame,' Titmuss said. 'Just as you were not so long ago. You two have got a lot in common.'

So, it seemed, Titmuss had found a new pupil, another plaything. Terry was thankful he was now out of that chilling shadow and that he was his own man entirely. He took Kate's arm, and they left together.

# Chapter Twenty-Three

'Well, now you've got power, what're you going to do with it?'

It had taken Terry and Agnes some time to get into a position where such a question might even be asked. He had left her at Mrs Millichip's party and, although she had told him how little she thought of him, she was perversely displeased that he hadn't stayed with her longer. However, when the phone rang in the bookshop the next day she had known that it must be him and grabbed it before Jilly could get to it. He would be down at his surgery the following Thursday, he told her, and how about a pint of Simcox and sandwiches in the downstairs bar at the Water-Boatman? It would be quite like old times.

'It wouldn't be at all like old times,' she said.

'Why not?'

She turned her back, lowered her voice and hoped that Jilly wasn't listening. 'I believed in you then,' she said. 'I suppose I loved you, in some ridiculous sort of way.'

'And now?'

'I told you exactly what I think of you now.'

'So you won't come for a drink in the Water-Boatman?'

'Why not? I don't get so many free drinks nowadays.'

After that she was surprised he turned up or that she bothered to go. But he did; they both did.

\*

'Oh, hullo,' she said in her most uninterested voice when they met again after so long. She sat on a bar stool and, keeping quiet, lit a cigarette.

'I wish I could explain,' he said after a silence. 'Why I did it.'

'I wish you could. But you can't.'

'It wasn't my idea.'

'But you adopted it.'

'It was someone else.'

'Who?'

'Someone who was advising me.'

'They thought it was a certain vote-winner, to say Paul was going to lust after juvenile offenders?'

'Not that exactly.'

'Then what exactly?'

'They wanted to distance me.'

'From who?'

'From Paul, I suppose. From his friends.'

'You mean from me?'

'Perhaps they had that in mind.'

'Then they certainly succeeded. I distanced myself. To the other end of the world.'

She told him what she had done. He took it as a compliment. Such a precipitate flight over such a vast distance was surely, wasn't it, a sign of love? He said, 'But now you're back.'

'Yes, I am.'

'We're both back. Drinking in this bar by the river. We can go on where we left off.'

'We can't.'

'Why not?'

'I told you. Because now I know you're a shit.'

He looked at her, pained and deeply disappointed. He thought she must have changed her mind when she agreed to meet him and now, it seemed, she hadn't changed her mind at all. 'Because I said what I said?' he asked, as though suggesting her judgement was unfair.

'Because you said what no decent, honourable person would ever have dreamed of saying.'

That silenced him, and she smiled, apparently sorry for him, and said, 'It doesn't matter. Paul's got a good job, and it's better I know exactly what you're like. Some people are quite fond of shits. Some people even fall in love with shits.'

He looked at her, by no means cheered up. 'Why do you say that?'

'No particular reason. It's just a general truth, that's all. A well-known fact about human nature. Was it your wife?'

'Was what my wife?'

'Your wife who wanted to separate you from Paul's friends?'

'Of course not.' He came back to life and was positive again. 'Kate knows nothing at all about us.'

'Now, there's not much to know.'

'She never knew. And she mustn't.'

'Of course not.' She smiled again, as though humouring him. 'It's something that happened at another time. In another world. A sort of dream. Nothing to do with us at all.'

'I could never explain it to Kate.'

'Of course you couldn't,' she agreed.

'I only wish I could explain it to you.'

'Explain what?'

'Why I said that. About Paul. The day before the election.'

'You said it because you wanted power,' she told him.

'Yes. That's it.' He was eager to agree with her. 'You understand!'

It was then she said, 'Well, now you've got power what're you going to do with it?'

'What do you want?'

'What about Socialism?' She was, he was sure, only teasing. 'I'm not asking much. Don't let's go mad. Just a taste. A very small one, with ice and lemon and absolutely drowned in Perrier water. I mean, I don't want to be greedy, but couldn't you do something quite small.' She looked inside her sandwich, 'Like nationalizing mustard.'

He looked at the yellowing photographs of old rowers, at the barman crouched, as though in prayer, over the racing pages. Through the glass door he could see sunlight flash across the river and a single sculler, his body seeming far too heavy for the slip of a boat, the long oars just touching the surface of the water, so that the whole contraption looked like one of those skimming insects who have only a day to live. Perched on a bar stool, he saw a new arrival, the elderly cherub Andrew Poyser, reading the *Literary Review*. Terry's voice sank to a low murmur, and he said, as though it were some secret and sexual suggestion, 'Boot camps.'

'What do you mean?'

'Junior glasshouses. Short sharp shocks. Yelling sergeant-majors. Square-bashing. Banging up. Solitary. No privileges. For the Young Offenders at Skurfield.'

'That's not going to happen?'

'It might. The Tories had the idea. Our Home Secretary seems to find it rather sexy. But as Minister with Responsibility for Prisons, I've got the power . . .'

'To stop it?'

'Paul Fogarty would have hated boot camps, wouldn't he? The idea of military police, put in charge.'

'Of course he hates it.'

'So I can stop it, for his sake.'

'And for the boys also, perhaps.'

'So that's something I can do, with what power I have.'

'Let's get this clear.' She looked at him. 'You attack Paul in public. Put his whole career in danger. He leaves the country, and now you want to stop the Skurfield boot camp. Just to please him.'

He said, very quietly, not to be overheard, 'And to prove something to you as well.'

'What?' she asked. 'What exactly do you want to prove to me?'

'That it was worth it. Getting me elected.'

'Worth all that trouble?'

'Yes.'

It seemed that she had difficulty suppressing laughter. Then she looked at her watch, said she had to get back to the bookshop and finished her drink.

'Shall we meet again?' he asked her.

'It's been very amusing,' she said. 'And I don't really see why not.'

He let her go and paid the barman. As he followed her the pink face and watery blue eyes looked up from the *Literary Review* and the writer said, 'Snug little place this, isn't it? Just right for an intimate conversation.'


'I suppose you want to poke your nose into my sexual proclivities?'

'Not at all, Lord Titmuss. I wouldn't dream of such a thing.'

'Oh, yes, you would. I know your sort. Open the newspaper any day of the week now and what do you find? No news. Not a scrap of news. Newspapers don't deal in news any more. What you buy is assorted opinions, usually with a little snap of one of you girls at the top, and mostly dealing with the matter of sexual proclivities.'

'Quite honestly, Lord Titmuss, we want a straight interview with you about your distinguished political career.'

'Just as well. For I have to tell you, young lady, my sexual proclivities are completely dormant. Permanently hibernated. Let us say, lost interest entirely, which is a fact that will save both of us a good deal of anxiety.'

June Wilbraham wouldn't have dared admit it to the legendary politician she had interviewed, but her ambition was to end up with her photograph at the head of just such a column as he had described in a classy Sunday newspaper. In her sad moments, when she saw the years stretch out in front of her and feared she would end her days on the *Hartscombe Sentinel*, she told herself that her nose was too long, her chin too sharp and her eyes too close together for such a photograph to be printed, but when she was in an optimistic mood and thought of what could be done with a wide grin, a concealing fringe and soft focus, she knew she would get her column in the end. She owed it to herself for all her hard work in the provinces, and she owed it to her father 'Pud' Wilbraham (so called because of his insatiable appetite for baked jam-roll and Black Forest gâteau) who had, for many years, been a crime reporter on the *Daily Planet* until he was promoted to the Tittle Tattle column, where he became known and loved for his outrageous, frequently libellous and often funny stories about the great and the good. He had lately been fired and replaced by an old Etonian who specialized in revealing the bonking habits of television personalities. June's father, now unemployed, wandered sadly round the bars of Fleet Street and Ludgate Circus, trying to pretend that the newspapers hadn't moved to the Isle of Dogs. He would boast to similarly abandoned hacks of his June's magnificent start on the *Hartscombe Sentinel* and her imminent ascent to a national daily. It was her dad's suggestion that June should write perceptive profiles of local celebrities for the *Sentinel*, and her editor, a sleepy little man whose Rambler column dealt largely with gardening hints and bird-watching, liked to have the rest of his paper written for him.

'I know you young people think a lot of sex.' To June's surprise Titmuss had readily agreed to be interviewed, and Mrs Ragg had brought them tea and substantial sandwiches in the newly tidied library. 'I'll have the snap taken in here,' he had said. 'Books in the background. So your readers'll think I'm half-way educated.'

'We don't think about sex *all* the time.' June tried a seductive little grin, calculated to lure his Lordship into some sort of in-discretion, but he stared at her blankly.

'Some people,' he told her, 'find sex rather a painful duty.'

'Are you speaking of yourself, Lord Titmuss?'

'No, young lady. I am not speaking of myself in any shape or form. But I well remember when old Ted Applegarth was at the Welsh Office he thought he ought to have sex to keep up with the young ravers in the government. So he visited some woman in Putney on Wednesday afternoons for the purpose. Poor old Ted! I remember him telling me how much he dreaded Wednesday coming round, when he'd have to trail off to Putney. No doubt about it. Sex is a painful duty for some.'

'Applegarth? How are we spelling that?'

'We're not spelling it at all. What I've told you is strictly off the record.'

'I'm sorry.' June stored the information for a future diary item when the name wouldn't have to be spelt, as in 'Who was the former government minister who found Wednesday afternoons such hard graft?', and she moved on to less intimate questions.

'I suppose you were very upset by your Party's defeat in the last election?'

'There, young lady, you suppose wrong.' Titmuss bit into one of Mrs Ragg's sandwiches, of the sort which, in her childhood, June would have described as 'doorstep'.

'But you can't enjoy the Tories being in the wilderness?'

June looked up from her notebook and her tape recorder (the belt and braces of her nervous trade) as Titmuss started to intone in his new-found ecclesiastical voice. ' "Then shall the lame man leap as an hart, and the tongue of the dumb sing: for in the wilderness shall waters break out, and streams in the desert." I don't suppose you read your Bible?'

'I'm afraid not.' June's dad had regarded God as one of the powerful and pompous characters he mocked in Tittle Tattle, and her upbringing had been entirely secular.

'You should do,' Titmuss told her. 'Full of good stuff, the Old Testament. And God's completely ruthless. I rather like that about Him.'

'So the wilderness . . .?'

'The Party had become dumb and lame. Here I'm quoting the Prophet Isaiah, who could speak sound sense on occasion. A period in the wilderness may do wonders for them.'

'You mean, waters shall break out?' June from the *Sentinel* wasn't slow to catch on.

'Perhaps there's already a bit of a trickle.'

'You mean, your Party might be ready to take power again?'

'It might. Sooner than you think.'

'But there's a huge Labour majority.'

' "And the Lord God of Hosts is He that toucheth the land, and it shall melt." I don't suppose you're overfamiliar with the Prophet Amos?'

'Who's the Lord God of Hosts? Is that you, Lord Titmuss?'

'Certainly not!' Titmuss answered modestly. 'I wouldn't presume. But let's say that His work might be done by the new young recruits to our Party. When they come out of the wilderness they'll obliterate the enemy. "And though they be hid from my sight in the bottom of the sea, thence will I command the serpent, and he shall bite them." I like that bit very much,' Lord Titmuss added with relish.

'But doesn't the Labour victory reflect a general view in the country?'

'I don't think the country can be bothered with a general view. It waits to be told. Then it acts on the right mixture of bribery and fear.'

'Did it come as a surprise to you when Hartscombe went over to Labour?'

There was a silence. Titmuss chewed his sandwich. From some distant recess in the house Mrs Ragg's was playing sweet and forgettable music on Radio Two. June thought that he had forgotten her, so she asked again.

'Weren't you surprised when Terry Flitton won the seat at the by-election?'

'As a matter of fact, not surprised at all.'

'Of course, you endorsed him in your speech outside the town hall.'

'There was, to some extent at least, a laying on of hands.' Titmuss used these ecclesiastical phrases with his own particular brand of glee.

'Why did you do that?'

'I thought he was the best man for the job.'

'And do you still think so?'

'Until a better man comes along.'

'Out of the wilderness?'

'That's probably where he is at the moment.'

'And what will happen when he emerges?'

'The Lord giveth and the Lord taketh away.'

June consulted her notes. Then she asked, 'Didn't you think there was something rather strange about that by-election?'

'It was well organized. The Labour Party are learning their trade.'

'That's high praise from you. But when Willock accused Terry Flitton of lying about his father and then withdrew it . . .'

'I seem to recall something about that.' Titmuss was clearly searching his memory.

'I mean, why did he change his mind?'

'A hopeless candidate,' Titmuss had no doubt on the subject. 'All he had in his head was a little white flag of surrender which fluttered when the wind changed.'

'Can I quote you on that?'

'With the greatest of pleasure.'

'I suppose Willock's one of those chaps you'd send down to the bottom of the sea to be bitten by the serpent?'

'I'm very glad,' Titmuss looked down at her from his throne-like library chair with approval, 'that you're getting to know your Bible.'

'I mean, you would have thought' – June wasn't a reporter's daughter for nothing – 'that the records at W.R.F. would have proved what job old Flitton did, without a doubt.'

'Yes. You'd've thought that, wouldn't you?' The idea seemed to have occurred to Titmuss for the first time.

'I thought,' June from the *Sentinel* confessed, 'that I'd interview Terry Flitton after I'd done you.'

'That's an excellent idea!' Titmuss smiled with approval.

'A study in contrasts?'

'Is that what you think?'

'But can I go back to the beginning.' June became brisk and businesslike. 'We know you were born in Skurfield.'

'The First Baron Skurfield. Born the son of a clerk in Simcox Brewery. Read all about it.' Titmuss unfolded his legs and walked, a little stiffly, to a table on which unsold copies of his memoirs were piled. He opened one, inscribed it to 'Joan, an eager young reporter', and signed it with a flourish. He took the book to her, and she read the title, printed in bold letters over a photograph of the gaunt and brooding politician: BY MY OWN BOOTSTRAPS: THE LIFE AND TIMES OF LESLIE TITMUSS.

'Thank you very much,' she said. 'What are bootstraps, by the way?'

'Straps, I suppose, at the sides of your boots. It's a phrase they use for people who have to fight their way up the ladder. I hope you'll do that too.'

'I don't really have bootstraps.' June was smiling.

'Doesn't matter. You can still fight. By the way, Joan, a word of advice.'

'Yes?'

'If you're interviewing Flitton, it might pay you to do some pretty thorough research beforehand. You might dig up rather interesting information. About his home life, for instance.'

'Thank you very much.' She was genuinely grateful and, wondering whether to tell him that her name wasn't Joan, decided against it.

# Chapter Twenty-Four

Two brothers sat drinking Godfathers, a near-fatal mixture of whisky and Amaretto, at the chromium bar of Rambo's, the Hartscombe disco, unheard in the heavy beat of the drum 'n' bass music, unnoticed by the dancers whose set faces and far-away looks showed a fierce concentration of small, hardly significant movements. The older of the two was Garth Inwood, who had once congratulated Lord Titmuss on his speech outside the town hall and who had since attracted his Lordship's notice and apparent approval; the other was Alaric, still young enough to be a Youth Offender, who had swapped drugs for money in a Great Public School, acted Rosalind and done time in Skurfield.

'So he wants you to have it?' Alaric had moments when he took a strong interest in his elder brother's career and times when his mind wandered to other, more personal concerns. That night, although they had met by chance in Rambo's, he was being attentive and respectful of Garth's achievements.

'He said something about me coming out of the wilderness.'

'What wilderness have you been in, exactly?'

'I'm not sure.'

'I mean, I thought you'd just been living in Clapham and working in Zorkins bank?'

'Well, so I have.'

'Clapham isn't exactly a wilderness, is it?'

'All the same, he says I'm going to come out of it and make the tongues of the dumb sing.'

'Jesus!' Alaric was impressed. 'That's a pretty tall order.'

'And he's going to make damn sure, he says, that I get the Hartscombe seat.'

'I thought that fellow Willock was the Tory candidate.'

'He's given up after two defeats. He was a hopeless wimp anyway.'

'Oh, hopeless.' Alaric's attention had now wandered to three girls, three friends, who were laughing together and drinking Absolut vodkas at the end of the bar. One in particular held his attention – she had blonde hair cropped at the back of her neck and falling forward in a quiff, and she reminded him of a boy called Harry Barnstaple he'd fallen in love with in the Economics Fifth at school.

'So it seems,' Garth said, 'I'm bound to be selected.'

'Doesn't that depend on Uncle Gregory?' Alaric still kept his eye on the Barnstaple look-alike.

'I reckon Uncle Greg'll do anything Titmuss tells him.'

'So you'll be fighting Red Tel Flitton.' Alaric gave Terry this grandiose title although Agnes, once his most enthusiastic supporter, had long ago denied it to him. 'Didn't he scrape up a bloody great majority last time?'

'Titmuss says he knows things that will make Terry Flitton's majority melt away. Like snow in the sunshine.'

'Oh, really? What sort of things?'

Alaric seemed interested, but Garth chose that moment to abandon him. 'Sorry, little brother, there's my date.' A girl with a long fringe and a pointed nose was standing in a sudden flash of light, and Garth went towards her. Soon he was dancing in a way that was a little too young for their ages with June from the *Sentinel*. Alaric, left alone, gulped his whisky and Amaretto and, feeling uplifted but slightly blurred, approached the girls at the end of the bar. He spoke directly to the one with the close-shaven neck, saying, 'Hi, there, Harry.'

'Excuse me!' She laughed at him, showing strong white teeth. 'My name's Diane.'

'Of course it is.' Alaric favoured the direct approach. 'Why don't we dance a bit and then we might consider a fuck in the toilet?'

June had spent the afternoon in the offices of Worsfield Road Furnishings. She had flattered the Chief Executive with an interview she didn't intend to write – there was a limit, June realized, to the sexiness of traffic cones as a journalistic subject – and he was delighted to put her in the hands of the Company Secretary in charge of works records. Old files were opened, old ledgers consulted. Without much trouble staff lists were produced which showed conclusively that Flitton, R. had filled the managerial post of Manager in Charge of Human Resources over a period of fifteen years. The grey-haired secretary was puzzled. She remembered someone coming about two years ago on precisely the same quest, and the records couldn't then be found. They must have been misplaced, because here they were back again, all in order and absolutely conclusive.

'So Terry did lie about his father,' June told Garth Inwood.

'What did you say?'

'He told a lie about his father's job.'

'That's something. Are you going to go on, researching him?'

'Lord Titmuss advised me to.'

'Then you should certainly take his advice.'

'Don't worry. I intend to.'

As the music changed, June from the *Sentinel* made for the ladies' loo. She found it engaged, and neither Garth's younger brother, nor the girl who reminded him of Harry Barnstaple, were anywhere to be seen.

The Castlereagh Health Club is popular with members of both Houses. Membership costs are high but considered essential to politicians with weight problems, burning ambitions or, in most cases, both. Terry remained enviably trim, slender-waisted, broad-shouldered and was rarely ill. However, his boss the Home Secretary told him that he should 'work out', do his 'lengths' and undergo various forms of steam heat and massage if he didn't want to turn into a pale, podgy wreck of a Junior Minister like those who had pizza delivered to their offices and drank pints of lager in Annie's Bar. He and Hannah sat now, in white towelling dressing-gowns, drinking orange juice and eating vegetarian sushi, in the health-food bar with a view, through glass, of elderly Tories pounding the green water in the pool like porpoises, and a Labour peeress at Environment bounding neatly off the diving board.

'Boot camps?' Hannah Mortlock said when Terry raised the subject. 'Haven't we got a pilot scheme going in your constituency?'

'I thought we hadn't decided yet.'

'Then let's decide. The punters love the idea.'

'I've looked at the programme. There's no time in it for education.'

'The punters don't mind that.' Hannah referred to the electorate as though they were gamblers in a lottery. 'Their children don't get very much of it, so they don't see why young thugs should have it.' The Home Secretary, daughter of a fashionable surgeon, who had read history at Cambridge, liked to tease her Prisons Minister with her low view of punter intelligence.

'There's not much possibility of reform.'

'The punters aren't interested in reform. They prefer punishment.'

'It's a Tory idea. I mean, *they* started it . . .'

'And we took it over with the government. Don't you understand, Terry? The more of their ideas we take over the less they'll have to talk about. As it is they're practically speechless.' The Home Secretary crossed her legs, raised a bare foot and looked with some complacency at her high instep and unexpectedly long toes.

'Well, all right then. If you think we can afford it.'

'What do you mean?' Hannah returned her foot to the ground and covered her knees with her dressing-gown. 'Afford it?'

'I mean, of course, we're known as a high-spending Party, and money isn't any particular object.'

'Be careful, Terry!' Even pool-side and eating a vegetarian sushi, Hannah Mortlock could assume the icy stare of an outraged abbess in some strict, medieval order of nuns. 'The punters didn't elect us to spend their money.'

'I'm not entirely sure how much it costs to keep a boy for a week in a boot camp. Are you?'

'Of course I don't know. That's for you to find out.'

'I don't *think* it's as much as the Dorchester. But one of those more modest Kensington hotels . . .'

'Find out!' Hannah, still unsmiling, rapped out the words of command.

'Of course. That's my job. I'll go into the figures. It may take a little while.'

'Go into them fully. There's no particular hurry.' Hannah slid back the towelling to consult her watch. 'Time for my massage.'

Terry watched her go. When he entered the pool he felt he had, at last, done something that Agnes might be proud of.

'You're so powerful!'

Kate said it, and it wasn't a joke. She gave no hint of irony and in no way intended to deflate her husband's quiet belief that his purposes, and the greater good, could be achieved. He had told her that he meant to prevent his government declaring martial law on young offenders.

'I think Hannah'll take my advice in the end.'

It was Friday, and they were having an early night. Terry was in bed, and Kate stood naked, her image repeated in a long mirror. She pulled on a long white T-shirt, on the front of which was written 'Leave the Earth Cleaner than You Found It' over a picture of a green tree. Then she got into bed beside him. 'Didn't we have plans,' she said, 'to move to Hartscombe?'

He remembered his election promise to live in the constituency, and remembered also that Hartscombe was Agnes's territory. When he went down to his surgery he would be free to see her on evenings when Kate was safely in Tufnell Park.

'It's easier to stay here now I'm in the government. Late-night sittings and all that. We can always stay with Penry again if we have to.'

'It's just that you promised them.'

'And I will. When the time's right. I'll keep all my promises.'

Then the phone rang, and he turned away. Later he said, 'It's that journalist. June from the *Hartscombe Sentinel*. She wants to do a profile of me in depth. She sounds rather bright.'

'Is the *Sentinel* terribly important?'

'She thinks she can sell it to a national daily. She says there's a lot of interest, in the new government, and I'm typical of a generation of bright young ministers.' He yawned.

'A tired bright young minister.'

'A bit. It's been exhausting. Dealing with Hannah.' He turned on his side, away from her. Planning his return to Agnes, he thought it would be unsuitable for him and his wife to make love.

# Chapter Twenty-Five

'In a way the story begins with your husband's unfortunate death.'

'Unfortunate? Is that what you call it?'

'A tragedy. I don't suppose you've quite got over it.'

'Oh, you'd be surprised how I can get over things. Take a short run, gather up my skirts and jump right over them. I've got quite a talent for it.'

Two women were having lunch in the Swan's Nest hotel; Linda Millichip, spread vastly over one side of the table, wearing an orange satin trouser suit with a ruffled blouse in the same colour, so that she looked like a sizeable frilled sofa, and June Wilbraham, in jeans and a tweed jacket. 'Would you ladies care for any liqueurs?' the waiter asked, as though it was a mere formality, expecting the answer 'no', which was what June gave it.

'Of course we'd like some liqueurs.' Linda Millichip had no doubts on the subject. 'Cointreau, please. And leave the bottle on the table, where I can see it. And a decent-sized glass. Not a thimble.'

'I mean, if it hadn't been for that terrible accident we shouldn't have had the by-election when Terry Flitton made his name.'

'Made his name, did he? I thought he had it already. Flitton. Rather a silly one.' Linda's huge shoulders heaved; she had succeeded in amusing herself.

'I mean,' June did her best to keep the conversation serious,

'Peter Millichip had kept this seat Conservative for so long. Were you surprised when Hartscombe went over to Labour?'

'My dear. When you've been married to a politician for any length of time, nothing surprises you.'

'Do you think it was all the fault of Tim Willock? Do you think he wasn't a worthy successor?'

'He was a wanker.' Linda had taken the Cointreau bottle from the waiter and was glugging it into what was apparently a tumbler. 'And worthy successor to my husband. Let us say, the Wankers' Party lost the election.'

'So' – June had never seen the word 'wanker' used in the *Sentinel*, nor did she believe it would get past the editor of a national broadsheet – 'I can quote you as saying that it was the weakness of the candidate who succeeded your husband that lost the Tories the election?'

'After all we did to help him.'

'After all you did to help Willock?'

'Help the wankers.'

'You put in a great deal of work, didn't you, Mrs Millichip, in the constituency?'

'We got everything put straight for him. We went to an immense amount of trouble.' Here Linda Millichip spoke slowly and carefully, but however carefully she spoke the words emerged somewhat slurred. 'To see that everything was . . . tidied up.'

'Tidied up?' June felt a little tremor of excitement such as her father Pud Wilbraham had felt when he got a sniff of a story. 'What do you mean exactly?'

'I mean things in the constituency were looking extremely good. No nasty messes around, let me put it that way. Absolutely nothing to be ashamed of, thanks to our work.'

'You mean, you and your husband's?'

'Well, no.' Linda was smiling thoughtfully as she poured out more of the golden liquid. 'I don't think Peter was in much of a position to help us. Not at that time. But the Chairman was invaluable.'

'Sir Gregory Inwood?'

'Yes, of course. Such an enormously able man. And the young lad.'

'Who exactly?' June wasn't taking notes, unwilling to alarm her source, but she was unlikely to forget the answer.

'A boy really. From that sort of juvenile prison. He was on youth experience. We gave him, I think . . .' – Linda refreshed herself once more – 'Plenty of experience to remember.'

'Did he have a name?'

'Skippy, was it? Or Slippy? Something of that nature.'

'And what did you say this Slippy, or Skippy, did?'

'I didn't say.' Linda Millichip raised her index finger, on which a huge ring glistened, and trembled it in front of her mouth. 'I said my lips are sealed. No more questions about politics. Tell me about you. Do you have a boyfriend? And does he prefer you to death? I'm sure he does! So have a little drinkie and tell me all about it.' She poured a slug of the sweet and sticky liquid into June's glass and no more information could be got out of her that day.

'It's a heron!'

It was very early morning, and the river round Hartscombe lock was shadowed in mist. The weir announced its presence only by a muted roar. Above the mist, as in a Chinese painting and looking as though they were floating on a grey tide and not rooted to the earth, the lock-keeper's house, the trees on the other side of the river, the top of the old boat-house which had become Rambo's and, far away, the tower of Hartscombe church, were all clearly visible. The heron was also bright, standing on a mooring post, very upright, its neck pulled in and its head sunk between hunched shoulders, peering down into the water, looking in vain for a fish or a frog, or at least a beetle to swoop at and stab with its pickaxe of a yellow bill.

Terry looked at it and said, 'It's all going well, as far as the boot camp's concerned.'

'My father used to show me herons dancing. He called it the foreplay of the birds. They go lolloping along the bank, beating their great wings, imagining it's sexy.'

'I think I've got Hannah where I want her.'

'Hannah?'

'The Home Secretary.'

'Oh, of course. And where do you want her?'

'Where we both want her. Forgetting boot camps.'

'Oh, that. Look! He's flying.'

The distant clock on the church tower had started to strike a laborious seven o'clock. The disturbed heron's head shot up, its neck distended, its wings unfolded, but it launched itself slowly, trundling into the air like an overloaded aeroplane, and then climbed strongly.

Terry said, 'I frightened her with the Treasury. I think she'll fall for it.'

'You mean, you've solved the problem on strict monetarist principles? Very clever of you.'

'I thought so.'

'But we've got more important things to think about.'

'Have we?'

'Well, for instance, we saw a heron flying. And the river at sunrise. That'll be here, whatever the government.'

'You don't like it much, do you?'

'The river?'

'No. The government.' He was beginning to get the message.

'It's not all that bad, I suppose. Just like all the other governments we've ever had.'

'Give us time.'

'You mean, in about three years you might utter the word "Socialism"?' She looked at him. 'You won't, will you?'

'Talking about Socialism isn't exactly the way to get things done.'

'How do you know? You never tried. Anyway, it's much too nice a morning to be talking about politics.' She was standing in front of him, her hands were cool, stroking the back of his neck. He looked round nervously, afraid of dawn joggers and early fishermen.

Kate was away on a management course, calculated to improve her prospects and raise her salary at S.C.R.A.P. He had driven down after midnight, and Agnes was up with a cigarette and a glass of wine, waiting for him, he thought, anxiously. She took his hand and led him straight upstairs. Having dismissed his character and conduct, she seemed anxious to forgive, indeed cherish, every other part of him. She made love tirelessly, inventively, and he thought he had never had such long, unwearied pleasure or felt so thoroughly grown up.

When it was over they couldn't sleep; they got up at dawn and went for a walk by the river, to where the heron was patiently waiting for a catch. But now she was kissing him dangerously, and the mist cleared so he could see the long narrow walkway across the weir and the foaming water under it. He began to feel, as he recovered his senses, that once again, he wasn't being taken seriously.

'Slippy? There only ever was one Slippy. Inmate of the name of Johnson.'

'A boy?'

'An inmate, yes. A young offender. And unhygienic.'

'Was he?'

'It was a job to get him under a shower. An inmate with a rooted objection to water. You understand that everything you write has to be cleared with the prison service?'

'Every word, I promise you.' June didn't intend to write anything, but, having learnt that being interviewed struck everyone as only slightly less exciting than appearing on television, she had found that the key to Governor Clifford's office at Skurfield Y.O.I. was to offer to include him among the neighbourhood's famous names and promise, with her fingers crossed, to write about him in depth.

So she sat, with her tape recorder at the ready, in the room which had once, in Paul Fogarty's time, been decorated by the boys' strange and dreamlike paintings featuring girls, cars and wild animals, their curious statues and dashing collages. Now the walls were covered with lists, schedules, charts of admissions and prison service directives. Governor, promoted from Senior Prison Officer, Clifford sat at a tidy desk with no photographs of wife or children and only a parched mother-in-law's-tongue plant for company.

'This is strictly not for the record.' Clifford leant forward, about to indulge himself with something he'd been waiting to say for a long time. 'But the young offender Johnson was one of my predecessor's major disasters, if one may speak quite frankly and off the record, of course.'

'But off the record,' June did her best to reassure him, 'what sort of disaster exactly?'

'My predecessor allowed a performance' – Clifford used the word with distaste, as though it meant something uneasily poised between a strip show and an orgy – 'in which some of the inmates dressed up as females. He couldn't see the obvious danger in it, although I did my best to strike a warning note. In the end it happened, as I had no doubt it would. Slippy slipped out, you might say, in female attire.'

'Did he go for good?'

'His father's known to the police as a safe-cracker. Other family members have been inside.' Clifford gave a tremendously con-temptuous sniff. 'No doubt they helped him go underground somewhere. He'll be caught up with in the end.'

'While he was here did he ever go out, on work experience?'

'My predecessor was very keen on that.' Clifford gave another sniff of disapproval.

'Do you know if he ever went to work for Mrs Millichip, the former M.P.'s wife?'

'I can't say exactly. I know Lord Titmuss gave him some work to do, and Sir Gregory Inwood. They had him out for gardening jobs, as far as my memory serves me. He was easy enough to get on with, if you didn't notice the hygienic side of things.'

'Did he only do gardening? Outside the prison, I mean. He did nothing else?'

'I think he dusted Lord Titmuss's books. Why do you ask?'

'I just wanted to get an idea of life here.'

'Life as it *was* here. We haven't had a single escape since I took over the tiller.'

'There's a rumour it's going to be run by the army.'

'Hopeless!' Clifford was emphatic. 'That'd be absolutely hopeless. The army'd know absolutely nothing about the regulations.'

'While they march to turn my right, they present me their flank.' This was Napoleon's inspiring proclamation on the eve of Austerlitz, and Sir Gregory Inwood was doing his best to re-create the battle with the limited number of soldiers he had available on the table in his study. 'This girlfriend of yours. She's a journalist?'

'An investigative journalist.'

'That's the worst sort of journalist. And she's told you about a conversation with Linda Millichip?'

'She told me *all* about a conversation with Linda Millichip,' Garth assured him.

'Linda Millichip is a menace to humanity. I can well understand Peter finding death a preferable alternative.'

'She told June about you and Slippy Johnson.'

'Was she drunk?'

'Partly, I believe. She said something about you and Slippy "tidying up" after Peter Millichip died. June didn't entirely understand what she was talking about.'

'The French burned their straw bivouacs as a salute to Napoleon. The Germans and the Russians thought it was a sign of retreat. There's nothing more helpful than the misunderstandings of the enemy. Is June any the wiser now?'

'I don't think so. But she saw the Governor of the Skurfield Y.O.I. I think she found out Slippy's name, and so on.'

'Soult turned to relieve the pressure on Davout after the allied attack before dawn.' Sir Gregory moved the lead soldier chosen to act the part of Marshal Soult. 'But is she going to go on stirring up trouble?'

'I don't know. She's very ambitious.'

'But cares for you, for some reason?'

'I don't think she'd like to ruin my chances.'

'Then you must make sure her affection for you is stronger than her ambition.'

'I can try.'

'Please. Succeed. I could ask her editor to give her some less risky assignment. The advance of the 4th allied column was delayed by Liechtenstein's cavalry marching in the opposite direction.' A number of soldiers moved obediently. 'So we've got to worry about Linda and the boy Slippy. Does your investigative journalist have any idea where he is, by the way?'

'No. The chap at Skurfield had no idea either.'

'That's a pity.'

'I'll tell you who might help.' Garth looked inspired, as though he'd just discovered D.N.A. or written a sonnet. 'My delinquent young brother.'

'Alaric?'

'Yes.'

'Why Alaric?'

'He acted Slippy's best friend.'

'Who?'

'They were Rosalind and Celia in *As You Like It*.'

Sir Gregory thought this over but made no immediate comment. Instead he said, 'In the allied retreat the French artillery broke the ice on Satschan pond. A good many horses and riders fell into the water.' The memory of this seemed to cause him considerable amusement.

# Chapter Twenty-Six

Time had gained Kate friends among the younger wives she had been talking to at Linda Millichip's cocktail party when, unknown to her, her husband and Agnes had met again and taken up almost where they had left off, with only a few illusions shattered. She and her friends telephoned each other fairly often and, when one of them was about to be remarried, after four extremely irritating years with a local solicitor who came, she never tired of telling her friends, 'while taking off his socks', she had rung Kate to invite her to her hen party in the Magic Magnolia, 'and the wedding the next day, of course, if you could bear it'. Terry had a late-night sitting, so she was glad enough to drive down to Hartscombe and wondered, as she pushed open the glass doors and was met with loud greetings from the girls' table and the strong smell of monosodium glutamate, if she should tell them all, in complete confidence of course, about her adventures on the personnel management course in Surrey.

They all wore their names on badges during the course, which took place in a plastic hotel situated between a huge rural Tesco's and a vast green-field branch of Marks & Spencer, so he didn't have to tell her that his name was Craig Begsby. When he made a beeline for her in the lunch-break and set his vegetarian platter down beside hers as though it were a towel reserving the best seat round the swimming pool, he told her that he worked for a firm of charity consultants and was particularly interested in the study of interacting personal relations and the psychological effects of success values in the market-place. He was tall, with red hair, surprisingly delicate features and an unexpected grin after the most serious pronouncements.

They soon discovered they had much in common. They enjoyed the same books (having both been brought up on the Hobbits), films and music, although Kate quite liked Oasis and Craig was deeply into John Tavener and Górecki. They were both concerned with the condition of the North Pole (melting) and disapproving of those who kept pets (animal slavery), although Craig was the one who felt most strongly on this subject. He told her he had no faith in marriage, and she told him that her husband had needed a formal tie 'to reassure him because of childhood insecurity'. She also told him that her husband Terry was not only a Labour M.P. but a Junior Minister in the new government, at which Craig gave a long, low whistle and said, in an awed tone, 'Fantastic!'

'He's worked hard for it,' Kate said. 'It's what he's always wanted.'

'It's just the greatest event of my lifetime.' Craig was breathless with enthusiasm. 'And he's one of the leaders!'

'Well, he's a *Junior* Minister.'

'When we got rid of them. Election night! My God, what an event! At last something'll be done about the ice-cap. That's the first thing I thought of. The water-level rising. We've got a chance now. The world's got a chance of survival.'

'Actually Terry's in Prisons.'

'Well, of course. That's important too. Your husband!' Craig still sounded incredulous and overawed. 'In the government!'

'Of course, it means I don't see so much of him.'

'I suppose not.'

'The Home Secretary's pretty demanding.'

'So it's difficult for him. To make a full commitment?'

'To his work?'

'No. I mean to you.'

'He gets home when he can,' was all that Kate would say.

There was no further talk about Terry at that time. Craig and Kate decided that the week's speakers were, on the whole, poor communicators, and they were amazed that there was no course on women's needs in the workplace, or the special dress requirements of ethnic minorities. In the evenings they took part in discussion groups and both attended classes of Yoga as a Corporate Relaxant. Before retiring for the night they would sit on a bench in the hotel garden, the sky lit up by the orange glow of urban sprawl and share a pungent cigarette, because their hatred of smoking stopped short of a modest indulgence in cannabis resin. They discovered that they were not only the same age but were both in the same month, under the sign of Sagittarius, the Archer. During the week she spent in Craig's company, when he rang to wake her up in time for the next seminar, or made sure she had the full information pack, or worked out with her in the gym, she felt at ease with him and a relief from the respect she felt she owed the older and more successful Terry. But then, she told herself, she loved Terry, and the question of her loving Craig had never arisen.

Not until the last night, that is. She was packing to leave the next day when he knocked on the door. She opened it to find him wearing a hotel dressing-gown. He came into the room in a determined manner and said, 'I've been thinking over what you said about your husband.'

'About him being Minister with Responsibility for Prisons?'

'About him not meeting all your needs and being fully supportive.'

'Did I say that?'

'You said, "He's not fully committed to the marriage."'

'He's busy.'

'Be honest with yourself, Kate. Ask yourself the questions. Where does that leave you?'

'Well, I'm busy too.'

'Too busy to assess the situation fully?'

'What situation?'

'Terry's "elsewhere" quality. His lack of focus on the relationship.'

'I hadn't really thought about that.'

'You mean, you're asking for space? You need time for the decision-making process? I can understand that. But have you ever faced the true facts, Kate?'

'What true facts?'

'You may have married Terry because you wanted a father figure.'

'That's nonsense! Terry couldn't be my father. He couldn't have had me when he was eleven.'

'It's been known.' Craig became deadly serious. 'I just want you to know, when you fully assess the situation, that I'm prepared to make a full commitment.' At this he opened his dressing-gown and displayed a prominent, indeed formidable, erection.

Kate observed it in silence. The she said, 'I've got to get on with my packing.'

Craig girded up his dressing-gown, said, 'Goodnight, then,' and left her. No mention was made of this encounter the next day. After an early discussion group on the relationship of the work ethic to the guilt complex, they gave each other a brief, almost formal goodbye kiss in the car park and hadn't seen each other since.

So, when she sat down with the hen party and raised her chopsticks to the seaweed and battered prawns, she was contemplating telling the story of the full commitment when she heard a voice from behind her, no doubt the voice of Jilly Bloxham, whom she had seen sitting with Betty Wellover from the stables, saying, 'It's Agnes. I'm terribly worried about her.'

There was some sort of murmur from the horse coper and then Jilly's voice, clear as a bell to Kate's ears, said, 'My dear, he's a young man. Much younger. Married too. At her age! It's bound to end in disaster. I told Agnes. One thing you can be sure of, I told her. The young always win in the end.'

It was only for a brief, impossible moment that Kate thought they might be talking about Terry, but she rejected the idea almost as soon as she'd had it. She ate her seaweed and listened to a story about the new headmistress of a local primary school and the man who looked after the boilers. She never said a word about the frank and fearless approach of Craig Begsby.

June Wilbraham could take a hint, and Garth Inwood could give one with all the delicacy of Napoleon's cavalry charging the Russians at Austerlitz. Accordingly, it became clear to her that any story published on the subject of Peter Millichip's demise and the work done by Garth's uncle, Linda Millichip or Slippy Johnson to smooth the transition to Willock's candidacy would be against the political interest of her boyfriend and, indeed, the Party Chairman. June saw herself, in the fullness of time, as the local M.P.'s gracious wife, opening the village fêtes (worse than death) at which she had been used to photographing and chronicling the names of the winners of the Straightest Leek Contest or the Best Tractor-Driver's Lunch.

She wouldn't, of course, publish anything which might embarrass the Inwoods. Her caution in this respect was increased when she discovered that Linda Millichip had decided to live abroad and the white, treeless spread, including the famous swimming pool, was up for sale. However, she had some time ago asked her father, as an old crime-reporter, to see if he could find any trace of Slippy Johnson, expert lock-picker and son of a well-known villain.

Pud was proud of his daughter and anxious to help in her career. He kept an attic full of cardboard boxes which contained his old press cuttings, and something about the name Johnson and safes reminded him of a case, a long case, a case with a number of defendants which he had covered for the *Planet* because one of them had killed a security guard, something which the older professionals on the job alleged successfully they had never intended to happen. The killer was young, inexperienced and entirely, so one of his fellow accused had said in evidence, doolally, and although only employed as a look-out man, he panicked and bonked this security guard on the head with a cosh no one knew he was carrying. The safe-breakers had been lucky to get away with five years for a burglary without violence, and Pud, eating baked beans on toast and drinking Guinness in front of the television, a lonely bachelor since June's mother's death, tried to remember the name of the case.

He had been watching 'Brookside', and the name jogged his memory. Brookfield? Brooklands? Brook Green? Then he remembered and climbed to the attic where his boxes of cuttings were in alphabetical order and rediscovered all he'd written about the Snaresbrook Supermarket Slaughter. The story of the month-long trial was written for the *Planet* with, he was not afraid to tell himself, enormous punch, skill and a relentless sense of drama. He was then reminded that the expert in charge of the safe was always referred to as 'Peters' Johnson and the pub where the deal was struck and the job planned had been the Jolly Roger on Tooting Broadway.

Pud's route to Tooting led him past Wandsworth Prison, where so many of the subjects he wrote about, even after he became Mr Tittle-Tattle, had ended up. The Jolly Roger had changed considerably over the last fifteen years. It would no longer be possible to plan a decent robbery there because the conspirators could never, over the blare of heavy rock, the squeaks of Space Invaders and the clatter of fruit machines, hear each other speak. He'd downed a half of Guinness and asked the twenty-year-old barman with a glittering waistcoat if he ever had Peters Johnson in there now, a question which received a blank stare and a quick shake of spiked hair before the boy moved away to help a gaggle of girls on an office outing. Pud was about to leave when a large, bald man smoking a cigar and drinking a very small brandy said, 'Peters don't come in here since it's been modernized. Most nights he gets in the Queen of Sheba, round Nutwell Street.'

The Queen of Sheba was unexpectedly small, old-fashioned, shabbily furnished and deathly quiet. A small, restless man in his fifties was perched like a nervous bird on a bar stool, turning the pages of the *Evening Standard* backwards and forwards as though in the hope of finding some small piece of comforting news. He looked up when a faded card with the legend 'Percival Wilbraham, the *Daily Planet*' was plonked down on the Londoners' Diary. 'Peters,' a voice said, 'I always liked the way you walked from the murder charge in the Snaresbrook Supermarket job. Can I, as an old crime-reporter, have the honour of buying you a drink?'

Both men seemed in need of company, and their meeting was friendly. They had smiled at each other over crowded courtrooms, or when brief statements were made after a successful appeal, and Pud behaved like a drama critic, meeting for the first time a star whom he had always admired from afar. After three or four more drinks and a good half-hour Pud said he'd come with a message for young Slippy.

Peters took a gulp of Newcastle Brown and said, 'You're not asking me to grass on Slippy?'

'God forbid! It's for his own good, Peters. An important journalist, writes only for class papers, just wants a brief interview. She'd be willing to pay for it.'

'He's had bad luck, that boy. His mother took it into her head to live with Mad Mike Manfred while I was away. Mad Mike did something terrible to him and got twelve years for it. But my Slippy don't forget easily.'

'I'm sorry.'

'That's the reason, if you wanted to know, why it's uncomfortable for Slip to have water on his body.'

'It's nothing about that,' Pud assured him. 'This particular classy journalist will talk to him clean, or talk to him dirty. I do assure you it won't make a scrap of difference.'

'You don't want to know where he kips down, like, at present?'

'That's not necessary. This journalist will just fix an interview at the place of your son's choice.'

Peters thought it over, spread his long fingers on the bar and tapped it gently, as though in search of a safe to open. 'What's the subject exactly?'

'Young people in trouble.'

'Slip won't want to tell what he's doing. Or about his time in the nick neither. And he won't divulge his present address.'

'She just wants to know something about how he helped someone out.'

'Helped who out?'

'Some woman. Her husband was an M.P. He helped out after her old man died.'

'I'll ask the boy. What he's prepared to divulge.'

'You do that, Peters. And let me fill you up.' They stayed together for a while, and a sum of money changed hands. Pud owed his daughter a birthday present and thought he could buy her nothing more precious than information. Peters thanked him and said, 'My boy must be popular. There was someone else asking for him.'

'Oh, really. Who?'

'I don't know. Some lad he was in the nick with seemingly. He said would I mention the name "Rosalind" to Slippy. That puzzled me because it was certainly a young bloke speaking.'

'Well, I'd better be getting along.' Pud drained his glass. His journalist's curiosity was, however, not quite satisfied. 'By the way. What did you say Mad Mike did to your lad?'

'The crazy bastard.' Peters had grown more confidential as the drinks filled his small, restless body. 'When Slippy was just five Mike says he hates the little bugger for taking too much of my wife's attention. He only puts him in a sack and drops him in the river round Erith! He drove him all that way on purpose. Bit of luck some chap see it happen and fished the boy out. That's when Mike got his life sentence. Attempted murder. And why my boy don't care to wash much ever since. Thanks for the drinks. I'll let you know our Slippy's decision.'

# Chapter Twenty-Seven

One of the most obvious changes brought about by the Labour victory in Hartscombe was that the Barbarians' dinner was now a black-tie affair.

Bishop Roger was the leader of the movement for change. He had felt guilty, although it was by no means his fault, because Terry had been embarrassed and overdressed at his first dinner; so, with the old-fashioned courtesy with which Queen Victoria is said to have drunk the water in her finger-bowl when the Siamese ambassador did so, the Barbarians followed suit. The men were in dinner jackets, asserting their individuality with coloured velvet dicky-bows or ornate waistcoats, and their good ladies came in long dresses, the best jewellery, and cashmere shawls if they were old and chilly.

Kate had drawn the line at the dinner, saying that Terry having twice won the seat, she no longer felt bound to put up with old farts who ignored her and got her name wrong. He told her that it was his duty to go, however much he hated it, and in order that he would be able to anaesthetize the occasion by drinking, he'd stay with Penry rather than drive home. When he told Kate this she gave him a look he thought he had never seen on her face before, doubtful, enquiring and far short of approval. He worried about it for a moment but then put it down to her natural dislike of well-heeled countryfolk in the full soup-and-fish.

Garth Inwood was there with his girlfriend June, who, popping out of a skin-tight black frock, was extremely popular with the penguins. Sir Gregory was also there and introduced him to Terry. 'My sister Angela's son. They live at Nunn's Courtny, you know. He's the chap who's hoping to fight you at the next election.'

'I wish you luck.' Terry shook Garth's hand and was glad to talk to June of the *Sentinel*. She said she'd be calling on him soon to do the interview he'd promised, and he assured her that she could do it in any depth she liked and that he was looking forward to it keenly. He gave June his home telephone number as Titmuss loomed up between them and, striking Terry on the shoulder, said, 'Congratulations, lad! Prisons may be the bottom rung, but at least you're on the end of the ladder and it's not so completely humiliating as being Minister for the Arts. Come on. Let me buy you a drink. Or are you driving home?'

'No, I'm staying the night,' and Terry added, 'with my agent.'

'Are you indeed?' Titmuss was in an unusually jovial mood. 'How very sensible!'


'Might I have a word?' Kenny Iremonger took the seat next to Terry which Betty Wellover had just vacated after dinner. 'I had the pleasure of interviewing you on the old "Breakfast Egg", if you remember?'

'Of course I do.' Terry had much of the evening still to enjoy and was in a pleasant and forgiving mood.

'I was a big fish in a very small puddle on Radio Worsfield,' Kenny had to admit. 'Now I've been head-hunted by the B.B.C. and I'm on the box.'

'Congratulations.'

'The thing is,' Kenny leant forward as though to discuss some closely kept secret, 'I've been asked to do a programme called 'Confrontations'. Well-known people from both parties in discussion, and our hope is,' Kenny grinned cheerfully, 'that the sparks will fly! Now, as you're one of the rising stars of the Labour Party . . .'

'Oh, I don't know about that.' Terry, who privately found nothing inaccurate about this description, did his best to sound modest.

'The powers that be would very much like you to be in the first programme. We go out live, which is rather exciting. We'll try and find you some worthy Tory opponent, although of course they're a bit thin on the ground just at the moment. Can I tell my masters you'll think it over?'

'Oh, I'll do it.' Terry had no doubts. 'You may tell the B.B.C. I'll certainly do it.' With a prime interview set up and a chance to shine on television, Terry felt elated. He was stepping, he felt, up Titmuss's ladder and would soon be leaving Prisons, not to say Arts, far below.

'Well, that's enormously generous,' Kenny told him. 'They'll be thrilled. And I'll fix an early date.'

With so much publicity under his belt Terry thought the dinner had little left to offer. He said good-night to Bishop Roger, 'in the chair' for that Barbarians' evening, and made for the door, where he was delayed by a familiar rasping voice. 'Going so early?'

'I'm afraid so. Lots of work to do in the morning.'

'Yes, of course. The cares of government! How glad I am to have escaped them. Is there a crisis, then, in Prisons?'

'There's always a crisis in Prisons.'

'Oh, yes. I suppose so. Well, off you go then. And get a good night's sleep.'

So Terry left and drove, through the empty streets of Hartscombe, not to Penry's house but to the one that had once been a doctor's surgery, with its windows looking out on to the dark river. He was in too high a mood to notice the ex-government Rover which followed him across the bridge and parked tactfully round a corner as Terry was let into Agnes's house.

Later Lord Titmuss stood beside his housekeeper Mrs Ragg as, at his request, she made a telephone call to London.

*

It was just before dawn. The dicky-bow and the pleated shirt, the black shiny lapelled jacket and patent-leather shoes, bought now and not hired, were tumbled in an armchair with Agnes's jeans, her shirt, sweater and white knickers. She lay on the bed, on her side, her folded hand under her cheek, her eyes open and smiling. Terry, apparently less contented, sat upright beside her. Their lovemaking had been satisfactory, as usual, and had lived up to his imaginings during the long tedium of the Barbarians' dinner. But there was something else he thought was due to him, something he was no longer prepared to forgo now he had been offered fame to go with his success as a Junior Minister.

'You don't,' he said in a voice of quiet accusation, 'take me seriously at all. Do you?'

'Anyone who can make love like that,' Agnes said sleepily, as though the question were in itself a bit of a joke, 'has to be taken extremely seriously.'

'Even lovemaking from a shit.'

'Particularly lovemaking from a shit.'

'You think I've failed in politics.'

'I think you shouldn't worry your pretty head about that.'

At this Terry shot out of bed as though bitten, in the comfort of its sheets, by some small vicious animal. He was naked, but making his way rapidly towards his clothes. 'My God!' he said, 'you're patronizing!'

'I'm sorry.' She sat up, searching for a cigarette. 'I'm just loving you for what you are.'

'What I am!' He was on one leg, pulling on boxer shorts. From then on he spoke with passion while getting dressed. 'I'm someone who set out to get a job and I'm doing it to the best of my ability. Trying to make things a little less bad for our people. Doing the things you care about. But you don't *do* anything, do you? Only talk. What do you think you are?'

He was surprised by his anger, which once allowed to trickle, rapidly became a flood. It was fed by her constant smile, her sitting up, bare-breasted, lighting a cigarette, waving out the match as though nothing serious was happening at all.

'I don't know,' she said. 'I really don't know what I am at all. I often wonder. Do you think you can tell me?'

'I can try.' He maintained his stream of eloquence while pulling on his socks. 'You want the best of every possible world. You want to congratulate yourself on being a Socialist. An unselfish friend of the poor. And the oppressed. And the bloody skint. You want to stand up for workers' rights without being a worker at all. And you're all for high taxes while you don't have to pay them. So you can feel proud of your unselfish, noble, Socialist fight at the barricades, just so long as there aren't any barricades to fight at.' He had the frilled shirt on now and was pressing in the black studs. 'You want all the excitement and noble feeling of being a left-wing heroine without having to get yourself elected and get into power and actually do anything. And above all, my darling' – now he was climbing into his trousers – 'you want to patronize those of us who have to compromise and manœuvre and even perhaps lie a little to get to where we *can* change things, can make them better. And then you want to lie back on the pillows and light another fag and call us corrupt shits for not carrying out the high-minded, glorious, unworkable ideals you find so bloody comforting!'

'Is that what I am?' She seemed to be considering what he said carefully.

'Don't you think so?'

'I think,' she told him, 'that's probably the best political speech you ever made.'

'Patronizing!' he almost shouted. 'You're patronizing me again!'

'No, I wasn't. That time I was telling you the truth.'

'The truth. Yes. But you'll never realize it. You'll condescend to fuck me and then lie back and blame me for not being Keir Hardie or Nye Bevan or any of the other heroes who you don't have to meet or go to bed with.' He was moving towards the door.

'Where're you going?' She tried to keep the panic out of her voice.

'I'm going home. To change and bath. Then I'm going to work. To try and make this a better country. You wouldn't get your hands dirty doing that, would you? You'd rather read about it in the books you keep on your second-hand shelf. You can dream yourself into Utopia! Well, I'm not in Utopia. I'm in the Home Office trying to cope with drugs and violence and noisy neighbours. And I can tell you, it's bloody hard work!'

'Terry . . .', she said, but the door had closed behind him and he had gone. She stubbed out her cigarette and sat, her hands on her thighs, staring disconsolately into what had suddenly become an empty future.

Terry's anger kept him going until he reached London and then evaporated. He had said what he'd wanted to say, and that was over. Agnes would think about it. She'd said it was the best speech he'd ever made, and he felt proud of it. Perhaps she'd learn from it. She'd come to respect the work he was doing, encourage him, appreciate him. Life would go on, perhaps even better than before.

When he got out of the car he was surprised to see lights on in his flat. He climbed the stairs and was about to put the key in the door when it opened and Kate, in her long, tree-decorated T-shirt, stood in front of him. He smiled engagingly and said, 'Hullo, darling.'

'Where have you been?' She didn't smile.

'I told you. The dinner and then I slept at Penry's house.'

'You didn't.'

'I told you . . .'

'I rang Penry. You weren't there. Someone telephoned to tell me who you went home with.'

'Someone?'

'You're not answering questions in Parliament now so you needn't lie. You slept with Agnes, didn't you?'

The neat pattern he had hoped to contrive for his life was broken. The kaleidoscope had been shaken again, and the pieces were in chaos.

# Chapter Twenty-Eight

'She's old. How could you?'

'She's fifty.'

'Like having sex with your mother!'

'That's impossible.'

'Not at all impossible. She'd have been seventeen. How could you do it? It's disgusting!'

They were in the kitchen. He said he was going to make tea, and he hoped that, after a rough passage, normal life would be resumed as soon as possible. Kate stood in her T-shirt, glowing with youth as he brought out the teapot and mugs, a cornered man in a dinner-jacket. She asked him again, 'Don't you see how disgusting it is?'

'Not really.'

'Why did you do it? Why?'

Since she had accused him of being a lying politician he decided to try the attractions of honesty. Looking puzzled, as he poured tea he said, 'I don't know. Quite honestly I can't understand it. She was different.'

'Was?'

'Well, of course, it's over now.'

'Because I found out?'

'Because we quarrelled.'

'What?'

'She and I quarrelled.'

'You never quarrelled with me!' She said it as an accusation, but it was true, they never had.

'No.'

'So I wasn't important enough? I wasn't a grand passion? I didn't even matter enough to quarrel with?'

'It's not that.' He drank tea. 'But you've got to admit, Kate, we get on well.'

'Until I find out about you fucking an old woman. Having a passionate, interesting affair. With quarrels. Go on, then. Tell me. What did you quarrel about?'

'Politics.'

'I knew it! That air of quiet superiority. She's a Conservative at heart.'

'No. She's a Socialist at heart.'

'Is that what you quarrelled about?'

'Partly.'

'Oh? What was the other part then? Did she want you to leave me? What does she want? A nice safe marriage, for her twilight years?'

'Kate. We weren't talking about you.'

'Oh, of course not! I forgot! I'm not really important enough for the grown-ups to quarrel about, am I?'

'She just couldn't understand the way I had to do my job. She wants the world changed tomorrow. She's intolerably patronizing.'

'Oh, poor you! Poor Terry. Patronized by Mum. So he comes running home to Kate.'

'I'll always want to come home to Kate.' Terry looked at her and meant it.

'I'm not sure I'll be here for you to come home to.'

'Kate!' He moved towards her, put out a hand to touch her, and she turned away.

'If I could only understand why you'd ever do such a thing. If you could tell me *why*.'

'I told you, she was different.'

'You mean old?'

'All right. She came from a different generation. I mean, she's unexpected, strange, a bit mad sometimes.'

'Makes jokes in bed?'

'Well, yes,' Terry had to admit. 'That too.'

'Hilarious!'

'Not necessarily very good jokes. But jokes all the same.'

'And a bit dotty, you say?'

'Sometimes.'

'No wonder you find her irresistibly attractive.' Kate enjoyed a rare moment of irony.

'No longer.'

'What?'

'I told you. It's all over.'

'Not for me it isn't. For me it's just begun. I've only just found out.'

'Kate. I'm sorry.'

It was no use. She looked at him as though he were a stranger, an alien being whom she could no longer pretend to understand. 'What you did,' she said, 'it's not normal. You'd better change out of those silly clothes and get off to work.'

'And you?'

'Me? I'll have to try and think about it. Won't I?' Still looking young and beautiful she went back to bed and Terry sat alone for a long while nursing his mug of tea. Then he had a shower and changed back into the regulation blue suit and long striped tie of a Junior Minister.

When he got to the Home Office Kenny Iremonger called from the B.B.C. He would be on 'Confrontations' next week. A Conservative opponent had been chosen, but it was Kenny's policy to keep names a secret from the other participants and press until the actual night. 'That way it's spontaneous, and I'm sure you'll spark each other off wonderfully. We'll just meet for half an hour in Hospitality to talk it through. I'll fax through the details to your office. Your programme will attract a lot of attention. Help make you a public figure, if you're not one already.'

A public figure. How much did that compensate, Terry wondered, for being a private figure lost to two women? He thought about it and decided that it did. A bit.

June and her boyfriend Garth Inwood were walking by the river, his lurcher bounding ahead and barking ferociously at the ducks. It was a Sunday afternoon with the leaves turning, blue sky and scudding clouds, and June hung on to Garth's arm with all the pride of possession. Pud had rung her that morning, full of apologies. Sadly Peters Johnson had told him that his son had no wish to divulge his present address and, in any event, had no memory at all of having helped tidy up after Mr Millichip's death. Pud was sorry he couldn't help his ambitious daughter, but she had comforted him and told him that the story was dead as far as she was concerned. As dead, in fact, as the late M.P. She told her dad to start writing his memoirs, something he had been threatening to do for the last twenty-five years, and as she hugged Garth's arm he offered her another story.

'Human interest,' he told her. 'And you've got a chance of getting in before anyone else.'

'Is it political?'

'In a way. It'll be quite useful to us in the long run.'

'Who put you on to it?' June was always interested in sources.

'As a matter of fact, "he" did.' They were crossing the narrow walkway over the weir. There were white railings, and underneath the planks the water, tinged with yellow, roared and bubbled towards the green depths. They had to walk closely together, and he had his arm round her.

'He?' she asked, unnecessarily, because she knew that when he used the word with such respectful emphasis he could only mean Lord Titmuss.

Later June telephoned Kate, who was alone in Tufnell Park. She told her she was writing a piece in depth about Terry and would love to talk to her, off the record of course, about her husband's brilliant career. Could they meet soon, as it was all rather urgent, and she suggested lunch at the Caprice. There was a long silence during which June wondered if Mrs Flitton had left the telephone, but then her voice returned, strangely hard and determined, saying, 'Yes. I'll do it.'

June put the phone down, triumphant. Her expenses would not, in the normal course of events, stretch to the Caprice, but extra funding, for this special occasion, was coming from her boyfriend Garth.

# Chapter Twenty-Nine

Terry got out of a taxi in front of Broadcasting House feeling as Slippy Johnson once felt when let out of custody for a day's gardening. At home Kate hardly spoke; she had moved into the spare bedroom and behaved, consistently, as though he weren't there at all. But he was more totally, constantly aware of her than he had ever been. Before she had found him out she had been a reliable asset, a comfort always and a beauty regularly available, which he had become so used to that he could forget her for long stretches of time. But now she was always at work when he hoped against hope that she might, when he got home, be there in a forgiving mood. When they met she seemed to look through him, refused to answer his questions, went out and never told him where she was going or when she'd be back. It was as though, because of the inexplicable thing he had done, he had become invisible. It made no difference if he got in early and tried to talk to her, or left for the Home Office at dawn and stayed in the House until after midnight. It was unreasonable, he knew, and unjust, that falling in love with Agnes, however briefly, should have caused him to vanish off the face of the earth so far as his wife was concerned. So he looked forward to this evening, when he could disclose a glowing future to the nation and flicker into a million homes, as a welcome holiday and blessed relief.

He gave his name in at reception, and after a telephone call and a long wait a small, bright-eyed girl in jeans arrived and said, 'I'm

Sarah and I've come to take you to 'Confrontations'.' In the lift she said, 'Did you have far to come?' and, 'You ever been on telly before?' When he said, 'Not on the B.B.C.,' she smiled enigmatically, and no more was said until she led him into Hospitality, a bleak and colourless room with a plastic-covered settee, a low table on which uneaten sandwiches curled and a drinks cabinet before which Kenny Iremonger was crouching, unlocking the supply of courtesy beer and wine. 'Thank God you're here.' Kenny rose to his full height. 'What will you have to drink? Oh, and by the way, I want you to meet your opponent.'

The tall, balding man in the corner of the room had been engaging a puzzled sound engineer in a one-sided conversation on the subject of European Monetary Union. Lord Titmuss turned and greeted Terry like a long-lost friend.

'My dear chap! I'm so glad. No one from the Party Opposite I'd rather talk to. I'd recommend the beer. The white wine tastes like tepid lighter-fuel.' At which he grabbed Terry's arm above the elbow and steered him to the plastic sofa where they could sit side by side.

'Perhaps we could just go through the *shape* of your conversation. I've got a few subjects to suggest.' Kenny Iremonger came up like an ingratiating waiter telling them about that night's specials.

'You can trust us,' Titmuss told him. 'We're old friends. We'll find plenty to talk about.'

'Then if I could just ask you to go to Make-Up.'

'You could certainly ask, but I've got no intention of lying back in a barber's chair while some overenthusiastic girl in a plastic overall paints me bright orange. It'd bring me out in a rash. And if I know my old friend Terry Flitton, who has the bloom of youth about him anyway, I would say he's equally allergic to cosmetics.'

'You don't want to come to Make-Up, Mr Flitton?' Kenny sounded deeply disappointed.

'No, he doesn't. Now why don't you leave us alone until you've got your cameras ready?' And Titmuss turned to Terry as though they were alone in the room together. 'Tell me honestly, Terry. What do you think of the Opposition?'

'Quite honestly' – Terry tried to sound judicial – 'I don't think they're terribly effective.'

'Not effective?' Titmuss's laughter was like the clatter of ice cubes in an empty glass. 'If they got together as one man they'd have trouble blowing the seeds off a dandelion! You remember the games we used to play when we were children. He loves me . . . He loves me not . . . He loves me . . . Well, so far as the British public is concerned, it loves them not.'

'Lord Titmuss. Mr Flitton.' Sarah had been sent over by a defeated Kenny to tell them it was time for them to go into the studio. 'Take no notice,' Titmuss again gripped Terry's arm, this time to prevent him rising, 'they'll be fiddling with their damned gadgets for hours yet.'

There was, indeed, a great deal of fiddling with gadgets as Titmuss and Terry sat under merciless light in a set which looked like the corner of an airport lounge and Kenny listened anxiously to the instructions in his ear-piece. Terry, watching their images on a monitor, thought Titmuss looked as composed and comfortable as if he were reclining on his sofa in Rapstone Manor, whereas he looked like the nervous applicant for a job he didn't expect to get. He took ten deep breaths, sat back in his seat and did his best to smile. A girl came up and powdered his forehead. He noticed she didn't dare to approach Titmuss. Someone shouted, 'We're running!', a clock on the monitor ticked backwards from ten. Then there was music, the title 'Confrontations' over caricatures of politicians as boxers fighting each other, and then Kenny, beaming with simulated cheeriness, filled the screen, saying, 'Welcome to "Confrontations", the programme in which politicians are encouraged to go a few gruelling rounds with a challenger. Tonight we have, in the red corner, Terry Flitton, the rising young Junior Minister who grabbed the headlines when he won a safe Tory seat and who is tipped for stardom in the present government. And in the blue corner, none other than the voice of the Monetarist Right, the unforgettable, unforgotten, Lord Titmuss of Skurfield!'

After the introduction the studio audience, seated in serried ranks and eager to co-operate, applauded loudly in obedience to the raised hand of the floor manager, who made a cutting gesture to still the clapping as Kenny turned to Titmuss. 'I believe you took the unusual step for a Tory of endorsing Terry Flitton's campaign. Why was that exactly?'

'Well, you see, Kenny . . .' Titmuss's usual manner with television inquisitors was amused contempt. Now he twinkled, in what seemed to Terry an alarmingly friendly fashion. ' . . . I was convinced that my Party needed a time in Opposition to find its heart again. After a period of what I can only describe as betrayal. And this young man was bright enough to allow me to run his campaign for him.'

Whether or not Kenny Iremonger knew what was coming, he managed a look of amazement. 'That's an extraordinary suggestion. Terry Flitton, was Lord Titmuss running your campaign, when you won Hartscombe?'

'Of course not!' Terry's outrage was genuine. 'I was running my own campaign on behalf of the Labour Party.'

'Come off it, Terry.' Titmuss was smiling broadly. 'I know memories are short in politics, but as my staff well remember, you were round at my house constantly for advice, which I was delighted to give you.'

What was going on? Terry had a terrible suspicion that Mrs Ragg was about to be called as a witness. Kenny said, 'What sort of advice do you say you gave the Labour candidate, Lord Titmuss?'

'Basically I advised him to behave like a Tory, which he was only too willing to do.'

Laughter from the surrounding darkness was the first hint that the audience was enjoying the performance.

'I certainly don't remember taking any advice to behave like a

Tory.' Terry did his best to look as amused as the audience. 'That's a perfectly ridiculous suggestion!'

'Politics is often, ridiculous,' Titmuss went on, 'and very rarely sublime. Perhaps young Mr Flitton recalls making a speech containing a lot of soft, do-gooding rubbish about murderous young yobs just being the product of our unfair society. Didn't you say they deserved nothing less than a holiday in the Caribbean at the tax-payers' expense?'

Again the audience laughed with pleasure, drowning Terry's angry denial of ever having mentioned holidays in the Caribbean.

'You know, Kenny,' the audience fell silent, anxious not to miss more of the Titmuss one-liners, 'I advised him to drop the rubbish about society and come out for teaching the little louts a lesson they wouldn't forget. Of course he took my advice.'

'Tough on crime. Tough on the causes of crime.' Terry repeated the mantra.

'You might remember, Terry' – Titmuss leant back in his chair and contentedly sipped water – 'You even warned the voters about the sexual tendencies of a particular do-gooding prison governor.'

'Was that on your advice?' Kenny asked.

'I took the view that the voters had a right to know. Yes. So I instructed Terry accordingly. As I say, he jumped to it.'

But now the audience was silent, apparently as surprised as Terry looked. After allowing a dramatic pause Kenny turned slowly to him and asked, 'Is there any truth in the suggestion that you were simply carrying out the instructions of an ex-Conservative Cabinet Minister?'

'Of course not!' Terry was trying to sound light-hearted and unconcerned. 'Lord Titmuss is a constituent and a man of immense political experience. Naturally I was interested in getting his views. But I certainly came to my own decisions. Without any outside influence whatsoever.'

'Your own decisions?' Titmuss was now gently teasing. 'On the hunting issue, for instance?'

Terry was silent, dreading the laughter which he suspected was coming.

'What was your position on hunting exactly?' Kenny asked.

'His position was,' Titmuss was delighted to answer the question for Terry, 'hanging on to his horse's mane for dear life, as I understand it. He'd gone out for a quiet little trot and got involved in the hunt before he could help it. His horse ran away with him before he could even shout "Tally-ho!"'

The audience's laughter started then, slowly at first but gathering power, like the horse Balaclava.

'You remember, Terry' – Titmuss's shoulders were shaking in his heroic effort to suppress laughter, which added considerably to the audience's amusement – 'You were going to tell the truth about that? But when I told you it would make you sound a proper Charlie you wisely changed your tune. You said you'd gone hunting deliberately. To inspect the evidence. So you could take a detached view of blood sports. From the top of a runaway horse . . .'

Even Kenny was laughing now. He recovered as soon as he could and said, 'Well, Mr Flitton. What've you got to say about that?'

'D'ye ken Terry Flitton. With his coat so pink!' Titmuss uttered the call loudly to the ceiling, as Terry could think of nothing better than, 'It's a gross exaggeration.'

'Are you really saying,' Kenny went on to ask, 'you advised Terry Flitton throughout his campaign?'

'Oh, I admit sometimes he got off the lead. He went off on little expeditions of his own. Usually ill advised. Like the silly business of trying to pretend his father was one of the workers, when he was really a perfectly respectable middle manager.'

'It's quite untrue. My dad was always treated as shop-floor. Not third floor.'

'The records at his workplace are perfectly clear. I happen to have brought them with me in case there was an argument.' Titmuss pulled from an inside pocket the documents Terry had seen once before, fluttering in his hand. 'It's under the general heading

"Management Personnel". "Rodney Flitton, Manager in Charge of Human Resources". Oh, and by the way, I brought your note. "I have decided to denounce P.F." That's Paul Fogarty. The prison governor. Such a good pupil, Terry Flitton. He consulted me all the time.'

Titmuss, it seemed, kept everything, even the note Terry had put through his door on the night of *As You Like It*. He saw only one way out. He stood up. 'I'm sorry,' he said. 'I thought I was asked here for a serious political discussion. Not for a series of comic anecdotes about a distant by-election. I think I shall go now.'

And Terry went, out of the studio and down the maze of corridors until he found the reception and pushed his way out of the glass doors into the cool night air, and nobody stopped him.

'You seem to have lost your guest.' Titmuss was amused.

'He'll be back.' Kenny was confident. 'But just until he comes, Lord Titmuss, what's your view of the present government?'

'Conservatism and water.' The laughter was over, the rasp had returned to the Titmuss voice. 'A pretty innocuous tipple. But we're brewing a new spirit in the Tory Party. There are young men coming up who can lead us back to what Britain was. Exciting, adventurous, and where the brave risk-takers are rewarded.'

'And your view of Terry Flitton who, as I understand you to be saying, was really your creation?'

'A footnote. In the history of the Labour Party. There because of me.'

But footnote or not, Terry never came back.

At the moment when Terry was being asked this question a Ford Grenada car, stolen from a resident's parking place outside a solicitor's house in Clapham, was driven over the bridge at Hartscombe. It contained six youths who might, as in a school reunion party, all be called O.B.S.Y.O.I.s, or Old Boys of the Skurfield Youth Offenders' Institution. They were all, in varying degrees, drunk. Four of them had taken part in the attack on Lady Inwood in front of the supermarket, and though wearing the faces of Donald Duck, Popeye, Elvis and Madonna for the purposes of that enterprise, they were now revealed, less glamorously, as Dane, Robbo, Winston and George. The driver was Alaric Inwood, one time Rosalind, now in command of a special mission which he had taken some trouble to organize. He drove carefully, having no wish to attract the attention of the police. Sitting next to him, already a little dizzy from gulps of rum and tins of lager passed round in the car, was Slippy Johnson, taken from his safe house in South London, where he was growing increasingly bored, and tempted by a night out with old mates and a bit of clubbing where, Alaric had told him, the girls were all panting to be taken into the toilet.

They turned left over the bridge and along a road which turned into a track beside the river. The lights from Rambo's sparkled on the dark water, and they could hear the thud of the music. Inside the noise was deafening, the lights flashing dazzled him, the girls' faces came near to Slippy, laughing, shaking back their hair, their skin white and the lipstick almost black, smelling of powder and perfume, and passed him by. Alaric had a hand on his shoulder, and his mate, his friend, his Rosalind, said, 'Good this, isn't it?' And Slippy replied, 'Yes. Real good!' and, drinking the Godfather Alaric handed him, started to laugh wildly and for no reason at all. 'Quiet, Slippy. You wait quietly. I'll find you a girl.' Alaric vanished into the shadows and didn't come back for a while. The others approached him from time to time, some with girls clutching their waists, to hand him further Godfathers. 'Compliments of Al, you jammy bastard!' It seemed to him that, as time went on, the lights grew brighter and the music louder and then, quite suddenly, both stopped, and they were out on the moonlit tow-path, all the old Skurfield boys in a huddle with a smaller number of girls one of whom took his arm, and he looked down into a solemn, pale face and a bright bell of well-washed hair. 'That's Carol,' Alaric was shouting. 'Chat to her, Slip, and she'll be yours for free.' Slippy smiled but could think of nothing to say as the whole group straggled towards Hartscombe lock.

The sound of the weir seemed to Slippy as deafening as Rambo's music. They all stopped, looking across the shallow steps over which the water foamed and flashed, phosphorescent as the clouds blew past and a half-moon appeared. It was Winston who first jumped on to the rail of the slender walkway and, with his arms stretched out like a tightrope walker, treading delicately, sure-footed in white trainers, all the way to the lock and the opposite bank. This performance was repeated by George, Robbo and Dane and was greeted with loud cheers from Alaric and the girls. And then Slippy heard threatening voices. 'Go on, Slippy. You can do it, Slip. It's good, mate. Good as a space walk.' And then, most threatening of all, 'Slippy won't do it! He's scared of water! Scared! Scared! Scared of water! Don't wash! Don't shower! Can't walk! Can't swim!' Slippy heard the voices rising above the sound of the weir. Carol's face was looking up at him, laughing. 'You're not really scared, are you?'

'No, of course he's not!' Alaric answered for him. 'Old Slip's not scared of anything, are you Slippy?'

And then Slippy felt Alaric's hand take his gently, other hands were on his arms, and he felt himself hoisted up, as though he were flying, and his feet landed on the white rail over the walkway.

He took three unsteady steps forward, and then the hands left him. Suspended in space, he heard feet running on the boards of the walkway, shadows vanishing towards the opposite bank of the river. He tried to hurry to join them, dizzily, from where he stood. And then he trod on air and fell, hard against the stone shelf where the force of the water pushed him, rolled him, a drunken boy, and dropped him in the deep green water, where he stayed and sank, all his secrets with him.

# Chapter Thirty

'It's over,' Agnes said. 'It was always over.'

'We had a great week,' Jilly Bloxham said. 'Business is booming. What do you mean, it was always over? Last time we talked it was going great guns.'

'Like a man fathering a child when he's very old. He's not going to see very much of it. That's decided at the moment of birth.'

'You've finished it?'

'No. I told you. It was finished already. But he got angry with me. So he went.'

'Angry with you?'

'Yes. To tell the truth, rather splendidly angry.'

'Because you smoke too much? Drink too much? Because he thought you had your eye on someone else?'

'None of that. He told me I believed in . . . what I believe in, just to make myself feel good and self-sacrificing and noble, and I was quite safe because I wouldn't have to do anything about it.'

'Well, that's true, isn't it?' Jilly, going through the till receipts, said it casually. 'We all know that.'

'Do you?' For once, in a long time, Agnes was laughing. 'It came as quite a shock to me. When he pointed it out.'

'So he started the quarrel?'

'No. No, I suppose I started it.'

'That night?'

'Long before. When we got back together. I told him he was a shit because of the terrible thing he said about Paul. But a shit I quite liked fucking.'

'He must have loved that!'

'Well, no. He didn't much. But that last night. The night he was angry and left me. He didn't seem much of a shit then at all.'

'You think he told you the truth?'

'Part of the truth, perhaps. Perhaps we're both right, or neither of us. Anyway, let's go and have a drink in the Boatman.'

'Will he be there?'

'I shouldn't think so. I shouldn't think he'll ever see me there again.'

'Have you got money, or do I rob the till?'

'No, I've got money.' Agnes laughed again. 'Money's about all I have got.'

So she went out of the shop, and a flash of light made her shut her eyes, and so she appeared frowning and confused in the newspaper.

From the time she saw Kate come into the restaurant, consult the girl at the desk and then walk through the tables, her head high, her jaw set, looking neither to the right or left, like some beautiful young, starry-eyed revolutionary marching to the barricades, June Wilbraham knew that she would get a piece which would end her allegiance to the *Hartscombe Sentinel* and land her safely on a centre spread in the *Daily Meteor*.

When Kate sat and the waiter asked about a drink she said, 'Mineral water. Still not sparkling.' June hoped she was determined to keep sober enough to tell all.

'Mrs Flitton. Kate, if I may. I'm June. Please don't feel you have to talk about it. I'm not putting any pressure on you, I want you to understand that. I'm not one of those journalists who want to squeeze things out of people and ask awkward questions. If you don't want to discuss it, O.K., we'll talk about your wardrobe and what you're planning for the holidays. But if you want to, and it's entirely up to you, you can be sure I'll write the piece in the most sensitive way. I know you've been having the usual problems of a politician's wife.'

'Not the usual problems,' Kate said. 'She's an old woman.'

'That *is* unusual.'

'I think it's sick.'

'You say your husband is suffering from a sort of illness?'

'I think that's the kindest way of putting it.'

'And you want to be kind?'

'Not particularly.'

June Wilbraham breathed a sigh of relief. The prospects for the interview were excellent, so she got the ordering out of the way and switched on her tape recorder. 'You don't mind this? It makes some people nervous,' she said to Kate as the red light glowed.

'I don't mind at all.'

'I understand we're talking about Agnes Simcox.'

'Yes. We're talking about her.'

'Had you met her? I mean, were you all friends?'

'I met her once. We had supper with her. She patronized me. I suppose, at her age, she thought of me as a child. Oh, and when she was at the next table in a Chinese restaurant and she puffed smoke in my face. I was with my husband and I'm sure she did it quite deliberately.'

'After that they met secretly?'

'Secretly, yes. When he was pretending to go down to his surgery. The days when he was meant to be helping his constituents with their income support and their rehousing and their child benefit and long-delayed operations, he was helping a well-heeled Champagne Socialist unhook her Wonderbra.'

'Does she wear one of those?'

'I shouldn't be surprised.'

'And is she well off?'

'I think her father left her money. I heard about that. Her father was a local doctor, which doesn't mean she's healthy. Smokes like a furnace.'

'And drinks champagne?'

'Drinks anything she can get hold of, I should imagine.'

'And she's a Labour supporter?'

'Well, she talks about it a lot. Terry said she keeps a row of Socialist books in her shop. You know the sort of woman. Adores the working classes but doesn't want any of them coming to supper.'

'What do you think Terry saw in her?'

'God knows. Perhaps he thought she was somehow a cut above him. More sophisticated. Worldly. Terry's quite a simple soul really. Perhaps he thought she was like one of those old bats that used to go bicycling with the Fabian Society. He always spoke about her with a kind of awe, as though she were an ancient monument. Which she is, of course.'

'But was he smitten?'

'Apparently. He'd do anything she wanted, so it seems. She even got him up on a horse! I don't know who he thought he was. Squire Flitton. Lord of the bloody manor. The horse ran away with him, bang in the middle of a bunch of blood-sports enthusiasts murdering a fox. He'd probably have put on a top hat and a silly red coat if she'd asked him.'

June looked at the subject of her interview, her head on one side like a sympathetic nurse. 'You're very hurt?'

'Not so much hurt as disgusted.'

'Could you forgive him?'

They were silent then, as the waiter changed the plates. Then Kate said, 'I might have forgiven him. If it was some girl from the office, someone we both knew. Someone of my age, or his own even. But she's old! It's not acceptable behaviour. Not in this day and age.'

'Does he want you back?'

'He says he's finished with her. I don't see that makes any

difference. By the way, when you write about this you needn't do it sensitively. Don't bother to be sensitive at all.'

As Kate stabbed at her food, June thought that she had never seen anyone so angry. She was not much older than Kate but she thought she saw in her the fury of a child. A confident child who had done well and grown up to be beautifully at ease in a world she had inherited, confident in herself, only to meet some horrible and mysterious betrayal which she couldn't understand and could only avenge through the little tape recorder that glowed beside her empty wine glass.

'A photographer's coming after lunch. I hope you don't mind?' June asked gently.

'No. I don't mind.' And then, 'Have you photographed her?'

'Yes, but don't worry. She's coming out of her shop, frowning and certainly not looking her best.'

Terry's world had gone silent. Only a few days ago, it seemed, it was full of noise, people calling out to him, greeting him, telling him he looked well, asking his advice or giving him theirs, asking him to consult his diary. It had been full of meetings, committees, focus groups, deputations, prisons to visit and, often late at night, discussions with Kate about the unexpected bombshells and booby traps of government. But when he got back from 'Confrontations' and Lord Titmuss, Kate was asleep in another room.

The next morning Kate was gone without a note, without a message, without a sound, and when he rang S.C.R.A.P. she 'wasn't at her desk' or was 'out of the office' or 'in a meeting', and she never rang him back. In the Home Office it was as though he had ceased to exist. People avoided his eye and hurried past him in corridors. His secretary looked at him, he thought, with pity, and was more than usually attentive, as though his condition was incurable. Hannah didn't speak to him, never sent for him, and a message, delivered by way of his secretary, asked him not to attend his usual committees. His appearance on 'Confrontations' was widely reported and, with considerable amusement in such head-lines as LABOUR MINISTER WAS PUPPET ON TORY STRING and I KEPT LABOUR PRISONS MINISTER IN CUSTODY! LORD TITMUSS'S STARTLING REVELATION. So far as the government was concerned, the result was to ignore him.

But it wasn't long after the confrontation that Terry, arriving early at work, saw that his secretary had helpfully put on his desk that morning's *Meteor*. The faces of Agnes and himself were peering over the masthead. 'M.P.'S OBSESSIVE LOVE FOR AN OLDER WOMAN. SEE CENTRESPREAD'. He opened the paper to find June Wilbraham's interview and a full-length picture of Kate, tri-umphantly beautiful, when the phone on his desk rang. 'Have you got a moment to drop in and see me, Terry?' Hannah Mortlock, at least, sounded quietly amused. 'If you're not too busy hitting the headlines?' He closed the paper and never read the interview.

'Well, I must be quite a bit older than you, Terry. Do you fancy me?' The Home Secretary was wearing a scarlet suit with a huge, black, winking and glittering pectoral cross. She was fresh from a dawn encounter with her hairdresser and seemed in excellent spirits.

'Of course I do, Hannah.' Terry tried the resort of flippancy. 'With a passion.'

His answer had the unexpected result of wiping the smile off Hannah Mortlock's face. She locked her hands together and leant forward with the pained look of a judge about to force herself, with no particular pleasure, to pass a stiff deterrent sentence. 'Sex,' she said, 'is a matter of absolutely no interest to us.'

'Oh.' Terry felt he'd adopted entirely the wrong approach. 'I'm very sorry.'

'We don't give a damn,' the judge went on, 'if you're doing it with a trainee nun who's in the process of changing her sex. If you can live with that, we can.'

'Thank you,' was what Terry felt he ought to say.

'All we demand is loyalty. Not a vow of chastity. Not fidelity to your partner. But loyalty to your Party and to the Prime Minister. That, Terry, is the bottom line.'

'Understood,' Terry assured her. 'I don't think my loyalty's ever been in question.'

'The word loyalty, Terry, does not include putting your entire political campaign in the hands of an elderly Tory dinosaur who made Mrs Thatcher look like Rosa Luxemburg.'

'That story was greatly exaggerated.'

'If you hadn't put your foot right in it, there wouldn't have been a story to start with.'

'I was anxious to win the seat for Labour.'

'Are you sure who you were winning it for?'

'Anyway, I won it.'

'Oh, congratulations! Brilliantly done! What've you achieved? Nothing much more than an entertaining half-hour on television.'

'I've worked hard, here.'

'Junior Ministers can work all the hours that God gave, Terry, and no one will notice the difference. I've got one more job for you, and this should put your name in the papers.'

'What's that?' Terry wondered if he saw a glimmer of hope.

'Write a letter to the P.M. "I have anxiously considered my position and have come to the conclusion that the admissions I had to make during a recent television programme have seriously embarrassed the Party. I have therefore thought it right to offer you my resignation. I have enjoyed my work at the Home Office enormously and will, of course, give you my enthusiastic and loyal support from the back benches."'

There was silence. It was broken when Terry said, 'You said you weren't interested in sex?'

'Of course we're not.'

'Then why not sack me after the television programme? Why wait until Kate's interview?'

'You can put that down as a question in Parliament. I doubt if anyone would be interested.'

Terry thought this over, and then he asked, 'Have I any choice?'

'None whatever.'

'Then of course I'll do it.'

'Only one thing you need in politics, Terry.' The judge, sentence having been passed, allowed herself a smile. 'Not charm, or good looks, you've got them both. Not oratory, no one can do that nowadays. Not political judgement. Most questions the government faces decide themselves or get forgotten. No. There's only one thing you need the fairies to bring to your christening. Luck. Long-lasting and perpetual luck. And yours ran out quite quickly, didn't it?'

Terry stood and started to leave without answering that question. But Hannah spoke again before he reached the door.

'Oh, by the way, you were quite right about the boot camps. They're far too expensive. £31,000 a year for each little bugger. Almost as expensive as an M.P. So we'll forget it. There now, you see. You've achieved something.'

Something, perhaps, but nothing more. Terry went to clear his desk.

# Chapter Thirty-One

As a bright winter gave way to a grey and sodden spring, with snowdrops and a few early daffodils in sheltered gardens trying to put a brave face on it, Agnes decided to clear away all traces of her past. She emptied the cupboard under the stairs, dispatching packets of bandages, trusses, a pair of crutches, blood-pressure gauges and a Zimmer frame to the Worsfield hospital. She stuffed packets, bottles, plastic cards of pills, tablets and samples of capsules claiming to cure all kinds of complaints and fend off death, all now past their sell-by dates, into black bags, and she fed them to the dustbins. When the cupboard was empty and swept out she made a bonfire at the bottom of the garden and burnt letters from the men who had loved her. Terry had always telephoned, never written to her, so in his case there was nothing to burn.

The river had swollen in the rain, and boats on each side of Hartscombe bridge bumped against the side, almost at pavement level. As the sky cleared a little a couple strolled, where Terry and Agnes had walked as lovers, to Hartscombe lock, and crossed the weir. Garth had given his companion lunch at the Swan's Nest to celebrate his formal adoption as the Conservative candidate for the constituency.

'I've been thinking,' he said, encouraged by a bottle of Pauillac and a couple of brandies, 'about the common currency.'

'This,' Lord Titmuss said, stopping to look down at the water, 'is where it happened, isn't it?'

'Most businessmen seem to've come round to the idea.'

'Bit of a mystery, wasn't it?'

'Mike Fishburn of Worsfield Road Furnishings says it would make sales to the continent easier.'

'A boy who'd escaped from Skurfield Y.O.I. takes the trouble to come all the way back to where he might be recognized to drown himself in the weir.'

'And our European partners are already printing the E.C.U.'

'He seems to have jumped, unless someone pushed him. Of course, there was a good deal of alcohol in his stomach.'

'After all, we use our credit cards all over Europe.'

'Someone, if I remember, thought they'd seen him at that drug supermarket, Rambo's disco. But they were conveniently vague on the subject.'

'And we can't be left out, can we, in the struggle for market share?'

'Suppose he'd got drunk and come up here with someone who pushed him. Now who would want to do that to a more or less harmless juvenile delinquent?'

'There is an argument that we ought to be in there, stopping the continentals spending all the lolly on lunch in Brussels.'

'Unless, of course, he had some inconvenient knowledge.' The rain had stopped, and Lord Titmuss was watching a heron settle on a post and stare down into the water.

'Leslie' – Garth the candidate called his patron, friend and mentor 'Leslie' now – 'I've been thinking about the Common Market.'

Lord Titmuss turned, his mouth half-smiling, his eyes cold, towards his new protégé. He spoke, slowly and deliberately, as though determined to make it perfectly clear that his companion's thoughts were no longer his own. 'If you've been thinking about that,' he said, 'I'd strongly advise you not to. And I promise you to stop thinking about the untimely end of Slippy Johnson. So I don't think there's anything more to be said on either subject, do you? We'd better turn back. Mrs Ragg will have my tea ready.'

So they left the weir, and the heron, seeing the shadow of a lone fish, swooped, pickaxe beak first, into the water.


There was room enough, and to spare, on the green benches of the House of Commons when the last stages of a debate, neither sexy nor sensational, on water-metering had been reached. The Deputy Speaker called, 'Terry Flitton!', and the Member for Hartscombe and Worsfield South got to his feet and started a speech, unexpectedly passionate on the subject, making it clear that he took roughly the same attitude to water-metering as Savonarola did to group sex. Few were in the Chamber when he started to speak from the back benches, and even fewer stayed until his peroration. They missed a passage such as the Deputy Speaker had never expected to hear from the Labour benches again.

'What else, we may well ask, is now to be up for grabs? What happened to our birthright, the ownership of the water that falls from our skies, and the air we breathe? Is the air to be metered, privatized, sold off on the Stock Exchange, supervised by Off-Breath, which is reluctantly persuaded to allow special terms for asthmatics? Are we to have to pay, by the minute, for glimpses of the landscape, for walking on a beach or swimming in the sea? How much an hour for the sunshine which raises the plants in cottage gardens, or the wind that dries the washing on the line? ('Use the launderette!' was the cry of a Conservative before he left for a late dinner.) What are the principles behind the unprincipled theft of public assets?

'Shouldn't we, Mr Deputy Speaker, go back to the beliefs which set us off on the long, bumpy road to government? I think of a shelf of books. No doubt we can remember their titles, although the books are old and dusty now. But what if we took them down again? *The Ragged-Trousered Philanthropist, Religion and the Rise of*

*Capitalism*, *The Road to Wigan Pier*, *The Making of the English Working Class*, *News from Nowhere*, *The Soul of Man under Socialism*. We might learn a great deal about the hopes and values which give a meaning to the chaotic and often disappointing business we call living. You can dismiss all of these books as hopeless dreaming, a search for Utopia. All I can say, Mr Deputy Speaker, is that no map is of much interest that hasn't got Utopia on it!'

So Terry sat down, after speaking to someone he no longer saw and who wasn't there to listen to him. Later, in the bar, he met a solid figure in a blue suit, well-polished shoes and a long tie, who bought him a drink.

'Count yourself lucky,' Des Nabbs said, handing Terry his half of Guinness. 'You can indulge yourself now, and no one's going to worry. Of course, they're not going to take much interest either. You don't see too many ragged trousers around here, do you? By the way, Terry. I've never said thank you. I owe you a great debt of gratitude.'

'Why, exactly?'

'You must know. If it hadn't been for you I'd never have got Home Office Minister in Charge of Prisons. There now. Drink up. You've achieved something!'


'It's unbelievable! There's still 70 per cent of householders failing to separate their rubbish.' Craig Begsby sat in S.C.R.A.P.'s Chief Executive's office and looked at Kate, his beautiful Head of Public Relations, partner, live-in companion and significant other.

And she, looking suitably concerned, said, 'We'll make it our spring campaign.'

'You bet your beautiful life! Can you imagine, Kate? Bottles, tins, non-recyclable items, and paper! Even paper! The world's forests, all bunged together in the same wheelie bin! Do they want to murder the environment?'

'I suppose they don't think.'

'We've got to make them.'

'A cover drawing, perhaps, of a forest being carted away in wheelie bins?'

'That's great, darling! A great idea.'

When the head of S.C.R.A.P. had told Terry that they were looking for a younger man, he'd left gracefully. Craig had been head-hunted from his well-paid charity job and was still young enough to make the Board think they were moving with the times. He got up now, led Kate to a corner of the office and kissed her.

'I saw it in the *Guardian*,' he said. 'Your husband made a speech in Parliament last night. It was all about Socialism!'

'That's odd, for Terry.' Kate was puzzled. 'I wonder what's come over him?'

'Who knows? It sounded very old-fashioned.' Craig's hand went to his zip, a move which Kate noticed.

'Not now, darling,' she smiled. 'Save it till later.'

So they returned to an emotional discussion of rubbish.


Lord Titmuss stood at his library window and looked out at dripping trees just coming into leaf. He was no longer a Minister of the Crown, or the Prime Minister's closest supporter; yet he was still Lord of the Manor of Skurfield and ruler of the small kingdom of Hartscombe and Worsfield South. There he had imposed his will, organized victory and defeat and planned the long campaign which would restore the constituency to the true faith. In that restricted neighbourhood he was monarch of all he surveyed. He smiled when he thought how well things had gone and would surely go in the future. And then, in the cold damp of a late spring, he began to shiver.

None too soon Mrs Ragg came into the room, sat him down and wrapped him, as she often did now, in a tartan rug. 'I'll light a fire in here,' she promised, 'and bring you your hot drink. Someone has to look after you.' She left the room, walking delicately, and Titmuss was left alone, still shivering, looking, not for the first time, towards a conclusion that even he would find it difficult to outmanœuvre.

'They never mentioned them. Not in the particulars of the house when we bought it.'

'Let me get this clear. The house is . . .?'

'Number 10 Marmaduke Road.'

'In Hartscombe?'

'That's in Hartscombe. Yes.'

'And who didn't they mention, Mr Sibthorpe?'

'Not the ghosts. They didn't mention them.'

'You're troubled by ghosts?' Terry looked at the small, anxious man in the anorak, who sat clutching the *Daily Telegraph* as though it were a holy relic guarding him against the devil.

'I'll say we're troubled. The noises in the night. Deafening! And the sound of laughter.'

'Gurgling?' Terry asked.

'Gurgling unpleasantly.'

'It could be the central heating?'

'I very much doubt the central heating would bring the hair straight up on Daphne and cause her to arch her back!'

'Daphne is . . .?'

'Our old cat, that has lived in peace with us for years. Also I very much doubt if the central heating would cause our budgie to drop dead in his cage on All-Hallows E'en. We've had the vicar in.'

'Oh, yes. What does the vicar say?'

'He says he's never known a case like it.'

'I would advise a reliable plumber.'

'Plumbers are helpless, Mr Flitton. Against the forces of darkness. Will you kindly write to see if we can be rehoused? We can't risk another Hallowe'en. Not where we're living.'

'I'll write to the Housing Authority.' To Terry it seemed the quickest way of ending the conversation. 'Of course I'll write.'

So that was it, Terry thought, as he came to the end of his

surgery. That was his political career. A story of ghosts and drop-dead budgies.

He was reluctant to go back to London, where there was little to tempt him. Instead he drove into the country. There were patches of blue sky as he got nearer to Hanging Wood. He heard the roar and clatter of lorries and the whine of circular saws.

He walked across dead leaves, stepping high to avoid brambles, and he heard, far away in the shadows of the wood, the crash of a falling tree. He came to a clearing he remembered, a place he would never forget, but there was a gap, an emptiness; something of the greatest importance was missing. Where was Tom Nowt's hut? And then he saw it: some wooden walls laid flat on the ground, rotting floor-planks stacked up and the hopelessly wounded sofa standing alone, with no protection, under the sky.

And he also saw, in a rare shaft of sunshine, at the top of a bank covered with leaves and fallen branches, Agnes, who had also come to look. She saw him and raised her arm. It could have been a gesture of greeting or farewell. But then she turned away.